Tom Zola

Panzers Push for Victory

GLOBAL CONFLICT

Tom Zola, a former sergeant in the German Army, is a military fiction writer, famous for his intense battle descriptions and realistic action scenes. In 2014, the first book of his PANZERS series was released in German, setting up an alternate history scenario in which a different German Reich tries to turn around the fortunes of war at the pinnacle of the Second World War. Zola doesn't beat around the bush; his stories involve brutal fighting, inhuman ideologies, and a military machine that overruns Europe and the whole world without mercy. He has developed a breathtaking yet shocking alternate timeline that has finally been translated into English.

Zola, born in 1988, is married and lives with his wife and two kids in Duisburg, Germany.

Berlin, German Reich, May 28th, 1943

It was a stormy, rainy Friday night that snuffed out all thoughts of summer. Thick drops pelted the capital of the German Reich, which had been battered by the bombing, while a cool breeze blew through the streets and alleys. In the distance, the engines of English bomber units roared. Hundreds of airplanes swept across the south of Charlottenburg, dropping their deadly loads. The local anti-air guns barked everywhere. Projectiles soared into the sky, glowing. Isolated German fighter planes threw themselves protectively between Berlin and the enemy bomber formations. However, they had been doomed from the moment they ascended into the sky to attack the enemy.

The detonations echoed with a deep roar as far as Bellevue Palace, where Field Marshal Erwin von Witzleben, the Reich Chancellor of the German Reich, continued the government's work despite the bombing raids. Only the Berlin district Tiergarten and the palace itself being bombed directly could have prompted von Witzleben to leave the imposing three-winged complex and get himself to safety.

The Chancellor sat in his office, a wood-paneled room that had enough space to fit an entire football team. Situation map after situation map, depicting the situation in France, Italy, on the Eastern Front, and in the Pacific were pinned on map stands. The Chancellor's gaze wandered over the mock terrain spread out in front of him. For a fraction of a second, he was struck by all that had happened in about seven months of his tenure.

Hitler had left him quite a sticky situation.

In the first quarter of 1943, Field Marshal von Manstein, to whom von Witzleben had transferred all authority of the Eastern Front, achieved some surprising successes despite the spring mud period in the sectors of the Army Groups Center and North. The divisions operating in their areas of responsibility had been gradually revitalized by former SS men, who had been freed up following the dissolution of numerous concentration camps and the logistics these entailed. In addition, the troops of the Army Group South, like the battle-tested 24th Panzer Division, who were available because von Manstein had permitted them to conduct tactical withdrawals in certain sectors, had also taken part in von Manstein's operations in the first quarter. By the end of February, the troops of the Commander-in-Chief East had worked their way up to Tula. However, fearing that they would be too worn out, von Manstein ordered them to stop. As March drew to a close, he came to the conclusion that the Wehrmacht was no longer prepared for an offensive this year. The Chancellor, however, had succeeded in convincing him to carry through with the controversial Operation Zitadelle, which ended with a small tactical success. The subsequent counter-offensives of the Russians, however, not only overran the German formations from Orel to Stalino but also reversed almost all the German successes achieved at the beginning of the year. Thousands of villages changed hands for the umpteenth time.

The roar of the bombardments in the distance invaded von Witzleben's mind, ripping his thoughts to pieces and leaving him frantically scrambling for some semblance of order. The thundering and crashing of the bombs were a gruesome yet monotonously familiar background noise for the Chancellor. Even though every bomb that fell on a German city fueled impotent rage within him, there was nothing left for him to do besides sitting idly by as it continued. The Luftwaffe, emaciated by four years of war and constrained by a shortage of personnel and materials, only had a few fighters to oppose the Allied bombing raids. So these days, Allied aircrafts flew through German airspace as they liked. Von Witzleben had had countless conversations with Erhard Milch, the Commander-in-Chief of the German air forces, but they had always come to the same sobering conclusion: the Reich was nearly powerless in the face of terror-bombing. The enemy called it "strategic bombing" because they aimed at annihilating Germany's economic abilities to produce and transport weapons and other materiel for the theaters of military operations, but for the Germans, and especially for the civilian population, it was the incarnation of their darkest dreams. These days, one could witness 1000-year-old German cities fall into ruins within hours – the devastation the Germans had unleashed upon other nations finally had followed them home.

On an intimate, personal level, Chancellor von Witzleben experienced first-hand the suffering created in Berlin by the bombing terror: Women who dragged dead children from ruins. Boys and girls who lacked legs or arms, or whose faces were burned beyond recognition. Once, his whole body had begun shaking uncontrollably when his aide had driven him through Schoenefeld, shortly after the district had become the victim of a major attack. What the enemy did to the cities – to the people – of Germany left the Reich Chancellor speechless and stunned. But von Witzleben also was well-aware of the deep contradiction of his feelings: he was the Chancellor of the German Reich, and held sole leadership over his nation according to the laws created by his people. A single word and a single document alone would it cost him, and the bombardments would be ended within days. But he did not give this word, nor did he draw up this document, for von Witzleben was convinced that these sacrifices of the German people were the only way to save the Reich into the future – for the unconditional surrender demanded by the united front of Germany's enemies would mean the end of the German nation. The Reich Chancellor could not accept this, so the war had to go on.

He was also aware of the other side of the coin: Germany had started this war, during which the German and British Air Forces had begun to attack each other's cities. Moreover, the bombing of the civilian population was a cruel but legitimate means, in von Witzleben's eyes, to bring the enemy to his knees. The wars of the 20th century were more total and cruel than anything ever before due to the advanced industrialization, and therefore they had to be fought in the same way and on all conceivable levels.

German bombing raids against English cities were not occurring at present, but not because the Chancellor was too good-natured for such methods. Even von Witzleben would again command attacks against enemy cities if the Luftwaffe were able to do so. And should these miraculous rockets, whose inaccuracy made it difficult to engage military targets, be ready for action next year, von Witzleben would not hesitate to let them rain down on enemy cities. Then English women and children would die at his command. It was a hard time, the Reich Chancellor knew that. The wars of the 20th century did not allow uninvolved people anymore. Either you were for one side – or you were against it. Von Witzleben didn't have to like this order and these rules, but he was realistic enough to see that they existed; that the cruel game that mankind had christened "war" worked that way.

But, as he well knew, the German Reich was currently on the receiving end of aerial warfare. There was nothing the Chancellor could have done about it. So von Witzleben continued to work, while elsewhere in Berlin bombs rained from the sky, buildings collapsed, and people died. Work was von Witzleben's nostrum. The old Chancellor, who had hardly slept a night since he seized power, had deep rings under his eyes. Work determined his life. He coordinated politics, the economy, and the military. He traveled around to the hot spots and the most important armament factories. He spoke with the leading industrialists of the Reich, the Porsches and the Krupps; he spoke with the field marshals and generals;

he spoke with his ministers and the members of the Reichstag, even if they actually had nothing to report. Beck even wanted to eliminate the elective component of the state, but von Witzleben finally decided against it, although he was certainly not a democrat either. But the Reich Chancellor was of the opinion that Germans should not be expected to tolerate too many changes at once, and so the farce of the Reichstag continued in the German Reich for the time being.

Altogether, all this led to von Witzleben having countless conversations every day; he coordinated, he directed, he supervised the government; he made decisions. Above all, he had to correct Hitler's innumerable mistakes. The economy, for example, was no longer allowed to continue to act as if everything was going smoothly. Germany could not afford to produce luxury goods anymore. Everything had to be focused on fighting the war.

And there was now a pressing matter of economic and military importance to be resolved. Two men stood at the Reich Chancellor's table, on which they had unloaded a whole heap of documents and workbooks. They argued loudly about the future course of action. The two squabblers were Albert Speer, Reich Minister for Production and Armament, and Field Marshal Heinz Guderian, Chief of the Waffenamt, the German Army Weapons Agency. Both had the task of co-operating on all matters of armament and maximizing the production of war-critical materiel. Both were disputatious figures within the government.

Von Witzleben looked up with tired eyes and sighed at the two men, who like roosters puffed themselves up and punctuated their arguments with dramatic gestures, each trying to dominate the dispute.

"The development phases for all projects have been underway for a long time – some of them have already been completed. With some models, we are close to series maturity. What you are demanding is an unparalleled waste, and singularly mad!" Speer spat towards his opponent, before continuing somewhat more calmly: "Heinz, nobody understands more about tanks than you, but also consider one thing: nobody understands more about the organization of the industry than I do. So believe me when I tell you that the costs of abandoning such far-advanced projects is not acceptable."

Von Witzleben sighed again. As one of Hitler's closest confidants, Speer had been a hard sell for some members of the new government. In the end, however, two arguments were put forward which had allowed his appointment: On the one hand, after the death of the Führer, one could not simply pretend that Nazi rule had never existed, even if some would like to.

But also, the German Reich was dependent on stability in war days like these, and this could only be achieved if all the incumbents were brought on board the new regime, including all the Nazis and party friends. Speer was therefore a good candidate for a government post because, as a former minister under Hitler, he symbolized a certain continuity between the two governments but at the same time was not too fanatical a National Socialist. His professional

10

accomplishment had always been more important to him than ideology.

On the other hand, however, Speer was also simply damn good in his field: As a long-time participant in the armament industry of the Reich, he knew all the important eggheads and managers in the industry, kept a corresponding address book, and also had unmatched organizational talent. Nobody else was able to use resources as well and efficiently as he could.

He also utilized forced laborers and prisoners of war, but that was a course supported by the von Witzleben government. And that was exactly what the Chancellor appreciated about Speer: he was – if it was absolutely necessary – an unscrupulous man, and was thus in no way inferior to the old NS important figures. Even though most of the Nazis had been disposed of, in some areas one simply needed a pit bull in these desperate times – and this pit bull could be a sharp blade in a fight. The war finally had to be waged to the extreme.

Without the use of "involuntary resources," the required armaments could not have been produced to this extent at all, and even now the German Reich could not keep up with either the Soviet Union's or the USA's production – and both were Germany's war opponents!

The situation was therefore extremely dangerous, and so the question of whether or not it was reprehensible to use prisoners of war and other involuntary workers in the armaments industry, in contravention of international law, quickly became superfluous. At the moment, Germany simply could not afford to be one of the good guys.

As von Witzleben reflected on all this, both of the brawlers in front of him stared at each other with an evil eye. Guderian inhaled loudly while the anger flooded his face. If von Witzleben were not so unspeakably tired, he would be amused by the ruffled fur of the Panzers man. But the Chancellor's work of the last few months and also his trip to Russia, from which he had only returned the previous day, had left him bone-weary.

Guderian was also a contentious man in the circle of the government. Although many people held his open resistance to crazy orders in Hitler's day in high esteem, they also feared his unpredictability, his technical expertise, and his urge for self-aggrandizement. As driven and capable a military and tank expert as he was, the man was often exhausting to work with.

"Albert," Guderian began, and at 6'3" with the flashing Knight's Cross on his collar, he towered threateningly in front of the minister, "these things you want to build are a joke. They're not tanks, they're static fortresses. You're a hundred years late with that."

"I expressly resent you defaming the years of work of the best engineers in our country! The new tanks will move very well - and not only that, they will smash the enemy!"

Guderian forced a laugh at Speer's statement, then his face was distorted when he raved. "This shows that you are an architect at heart, and not a soldier. With all due respect, Albert, let me tell you, these devices are unfit. You get me? That's not just my opinion! Erwin Rommel, von Manstein, yes, any officer with military brains in his head, they'll all tell you the same thing."

Von Witzleben nearly daydreamed. Yes, the discussion taking place here was important and serious, but he simply could not follow it any longer. In the end, he would listen to the military arguments and follow his instinct, which was by now headed in a clear direction. Meanwhile, his gaze wandered across all the folders of documents and sketches lying on his desk. "Tiger II" was written on one cover page. He wrinkled his nose.

Tiger II ... that reeks of the Führer, and lo and behold, as soon as *he* came to his mind, Speer spoke about him. "The Führer himself commissioned these projects. He had the foresight, years ago, to realize what we would need these days!"

Now von Witzleben had to grin. That was really the wrong argument to use, if you wanted to impress one Heinz Guderian – and Speer should have known better, too. Guderian immediately spat symbolically and mocked him: "I don't give a damn what Adolf ordered ..."

Speer was visibly offended by this, and immediately riposted. "Our inspired leader made Germany strong again, so have a modicum of respect! He swept away the French and the English, and made it possible for us to accomplish what nobody could do in 1914. He did ... "

So many different emotions flashed over Guderian's face that von Witzleben could no longer sort them all out.

"Albert!" he roared with a threatening index finger. "Don't give me the GröFaZ again. If you claim one more time that our Adolf won any battles, I see myself forced to punch you in the face!"

Old warhorse, von Witzleben thought, *but he's right!* Speer, however, now made a face as if the love of his life had tossed him into the trash.

"You've been sitting in front of the *Volksempfänger* for too long," Guderian continued. "Jawohl, of course the Führer rode a white horse at the head of our divisions – in 1940 – and led our panzers straight into Paris!" He imitated Goebbels' voice while spreading his arms gloatingly. Speer shook his head.

"I'll give it to you straight, Albert, and please let an old panzers man tell you what he knows: These things are junk." Guderian now lifted up a whole armful of folders, and took one after the other from it: "Tiger II?" He laughed uproariously. "I beg you! We can talk about that in ten years, when the Tiger I finally works!" And zap, the file landed on the floor. "Panzer Maus? And it even comes in two different versions from two different corporations? I hope you'll also build a tractor that can haul the monster up to within combat range of the enemy tanks! Or should we just lay rails in front of enemy positions?" The Panzer Maus folder also landed on the ground.

"VK4502-P? So Porsche is tinkering with multiple mechanical failures in one design? Beautiful!" The next folder landed on the ground. "And here, this Leopard! Too slow for a reconnaissance vehicle, too weak for a tank! Besides, we're just getting started producing the 234. Why the hell is its successor being developed, without us having gathered any front experience with the 234 model?" Another folder went down. "Then this whole E-series! What is the purpose of this? Either they are super heavy monster tanks, so you need ten trucks in order for them to move at all, or they should already be the successors of models that have just reached maturity phase." A few more folders landed on the floor.

"My aim is to standardize production processes, and utilize as many common components as possible," Speer said in a thin voice.

"And what is this, please?" Guderian held the last two folders directly under Speer's nose. "P-series"?

Speer wanted to defend himself, but Guderian did not give him the opportunity, he just barreled on: "Panzer Ratte? A land cruiser? What's all this nonsense about? 69 meters in length and 1,000 tons in weight? What's that?"

"I had the P-series discontinued earlier this year. I have enclosed the development folders only for the sake of completeness."

"You don't understand what I'm getting at: Whoever designs such tanks ..." Guderian formed quotation marks in the air with his fingers while pronouncing the word tank, "... even considering such a concept is completely insane and proofs that its developers don't know a damn thing about fighting a war. What are you supposed to do with monsters like that? I mean, aren't your highly-acclaimed engineers aware that the enemy ... well ... has planes?" The last question was snapped out angrily, and now Guderian loomed intimidatingly over Speer with a grim expression. He seemed at a loss for words, he was so overwhelmed by the stupidity of the design flaws. Again, von Witzleben had to laugh to himself. Speer was actually an ingenious man who knew how to out-maneuver opponents and strengthen his own position of power. But in the face of panzer man Guderian, the "Fast Heinz," Hitler's architect seemed like a heap of misery. Now the folders of the P projects also landed on the wooden planks.

"I think it's sad," Speer began in a very meek manner, "that you don't appreciate at all the great achievements of the engineers at Daimler-Benz, Porsche, and Krupp. The Tiger II, for example, is a magnificent combat vehicle – against which not a single word has been spoke n."

Guderian took a step towards Speer and responded with a sorrowful note: "Albert, please, for the last time: all these projects are due to Adolf's megalomania and have nothing to do with reality. Whether you like it or not, we didn't win in France because of the outstanding leadership of our GröFaZ. In 1940, the French army was considered the most powerful in the world. They were better equipped, had the stronger tanks – and even more of them than we did! So why did we win? Tactics, Albert! Tactics and speed! We knew how to use our tanks as an independent, fast weapon, while the Frogs distributed their vehicles to the infantry companies, thereby paralyzing them. Speed, and thus the attainment of the moment of surprise, are the great advantages of the armored branch, and we have only won our victories because we alone understood this principle. That's the point. With all your new tank projects, we'd be making the same mistakes that drove our opponents to ruin."

"We need … "

"No, Albert! Tell me, the Panzer Maus? Yes? That Panzer Maus? How fast should it be able to go?"

Speer considered. "Porsche's or Krupp's?"

"Like... the one from Krupp."

"About ten."

"Ten what? Hectares per second?"

Speer rolled his eyes: "Ten kilometers per hour."

"Ten kilometers an hour? TEN? And as we know, the finished tank rarely achieves the promised performance! Here, look at our dear Chancellor! He's an old infantryman. Ask him, Albert, ask him how fast a soldier can move. Go on, ask him!" Then, addressing the Reich Chancellor, Guderian demanded, with a curious face like a little child: "Please, Erwin, tell him."

Guderian obviously took a mischievous pleasure in this.

"That's why these things aren't usable," he closed his speech, nodding without waiting for an answer from the Chancellor.

"The Tiger II!" Speer suddenly whispered. "Where's your difficulty with the Tiger II? It is an excellent tank with 38 kilometers per hour peak speed. And we have already ordered the first test models."

"My dear Albert. Have you ever seen a bridge in Russia? Or a road? First of all, this Tiger is still slower than our other fighting vehicles, and secondly this thing weighs 70 tons! 70!!! Should an entire transport company be driving ahead of each Tiger II to build the corresponding infrastructure? I really wonder how the

17

GröFaZ imagined it! Added to this is our acute shortage of resources. We have hardly any diesel, we have hardly any oil, we are running out of most metals. The answer can't be that we build even bigger tanks, which consume even more fuel and are even more complicated to produce. We need a powerful force that is mobile and fast! We must also increase our production output in order to approach the Russian production figures. But that won't work if we spread our capacities over 37 million paper pusher fantasies." Guderian gasped.

"Here's my solution, if we don't want to lose this war next year at the latest: Focus on our current models. The Panzer IV is an excellent vehicle. The Tiger's good. The Panther's good. The assault guns too. I'd rather put our efforts into them, eradicate all their teething troubles. Maximize armor and armament, and simplify production where possible so we can continue to increase our numbers. This has the advantage that the production facilities do not need to make any time-consuming changes. This also has the advantage that we avoid investing precious weeks for our panzer crews to train on new equipment; we just gradually re-supply them with improved versions of their well-known tin cans. In short: Panzer IV, Tiger, Panther, and assault guns as the backbone of our tank weapon. In addition, some adventurous devices in small numbers; I'm talking of the Ferdinand and so on. But do not continue to fritter away the limited capacity of our industry in developing twenty or thirty different models. Don't waste it, dear Albert!" Guderian suddenly stopped and took a deep breath, then looked at Speer with an intense expression. Reich Minister for Production and Armament just stared back and didn't know what to say. Finally he turned to the Chancellor. "Herr Reichskanzler," he began, panting. "We have currently commissioned the Tiger II. Krupp and Porsche have also made great efforts to prepare everything for the production of the Maus ... if we stop that now ... "

Speer's speech was halted by a sharp glance from von Witzleben. He then turned to Guderian, who grinned like an American film star. The Chancellor could only shake his head, lamenting the things Hitler had ordered.

"It is better to stop production now, than to sink further resources into it," von Witzleben decided in a calm voice, and it was obvious to his listeners that he chose his words carefully. "In this matter, Marshal Guderian is simply right. What we need are functioning combat vehicles without mechanical troubles, not prototypes. Therefore, the following must be our policy: Further development of existing vehicles, rather than new development projects."

Speer seemed to want to start arguing again, but then remained silent. It appeared he realized he'd lost.

"It is, of course, deeply troubling that we have invested a lot of time and money in these projects," von Witzleben continued, "and it is maddening beyond all measure that it took us so long to get things in order ... and that we have only now become aware of these things. I therefore see, Heinz, that your appointment as Chief of the Waffenamt was the right step. And I agree with you. Shelving these projects is the best solution, with one exception: We should continue the development of the Tiger II, but take our time with it; and only bring it into series production when it really *is* ready for the front. After all, the enemy won't sleep either, and will work on heavier tanks, so it's good to have something bigger than our current models up our sleeve at some point.

However, prudence must be the order of the day, and there must be no more rush production as with the Panther. And with all this attention to tanks, we can't ignore the other projects. The troops have bigger worries than new tanks.

We must continue to develop the new carbine, to name just one example. We need to get the MP 43 out to the forces as soon as possible. We must finally provide modern weapons to all the units that are still fighting with rifles from the Great War. What about the Axis technology share program efforts in this respect?"

The Axis technology share program was one of the projects von Witzleben personally brought into being. He was confident that better collaboration with Germany's allies was vital in order to survive this war.

"Unfortunately, mostly no success," Guderian said for the record. "What can I say? When it comes to rifles, our allies are at the same state of the art as we are. If we want to implement the agreed-upon improvements, we must develop a new carbine ourselves – or look again at our own existing developments."

"You are certain?" von Witzleben asked.

"Yes, I'm afraid so, even if producing an existing weapon would have been much faster than developing a new one from the scrapbook."

"We must generally accelerate the pace of licensing," pondered von Witzleben out loud. "It's unacceptable that we're still in the process of reviewing things, while the Italians are already building Panzers IV, V, and VI, to give just one example."

"But we can't rush into anything, either. Every device has to undergo extensive testing ... we have to comply with regulations," Speer interjected.

"That may be so. Nevertheless, the process must be accelerated. Put more men on the project. Come and see me if you need any further funds, or if any obstacles are placed in your way."

"Yes, thank you, I will."

"Has *something*, at least, come up so far?" the Chancellor wanted to know. Before Speer could answer, Guderian cut in: "Unfortunately, the tanks of the Japs are hardly usable. They're of outstanding design, but limited; just for the Pacific region. Light, fast vehicles for soft ground, but unsuitable for distinct fighting in the wide wastelands of soviet Russia. I think Japan is very grateful for our help in this." The tank man grinned playfully. "However, there are two very respectable Japanese amphibious combat vehicles that we are right now considering for the project. We're currently evaluating the troops' need for this type of tank. Well, what else?" Guderian shrugged his shoulders. "The Italian tanks, for example, are much worse than you hear."

"I understand. I trust you both to make the right decisions."

"Well then, dear Albert, we have a lot of work to do. Let's see what we can do to increase our production figures," said the panzers man as he grabbed Speer by the arm. He nodded again silently, but then released himself from Guderian's grip and turned once more to the Chancellor.

"I have another thing of the utmost importance, Herr Reichskanzler," he said.

"Tell me."

"It may have been a considered decision to stop and reverse the deportation of Jews to those camps, as well as to suspend that special project, but I must point out that we are drastically short of labor force, and it is already affecting our figures."

"This decision is irreversible, Herr Speer."

"Herr Kanzler, I need more workers."

"You will have the prisoners of war. You'll have our own prisoners. And right now we're starting a program to try to recruit volunteers in the occupied territories."

"That's not enough by a long shot. The Jews were also excellent and qualified workers."

"You want to go back to the decisions of the Wannsee Conference? Those are not acceptable in this war."

"I don't care who works on my projects or where they come from, but I need more people. Why, for example, are no more laborers from the eastern regions made available to me? Since the tragic death of our Führer, I have noticed very clearly how these policy changes have cut my capacities. And now – after half a year – it can also be seen very clearly in the figures."

"We will no longer deprive people of their homes, otherwise the partisan problem in the occupied territories can never be solved."

22

"Then my hands will be tied, too, and the Reich will have to make do with a reduction in production."

"Then so be it. On the other hand, we must not forget that the Hitler regime had begun to set up a huge logistics system for these camps and the so-called special project. By reversing all these measures that went beyond addressing actual criminals, we not only free the men of the interned ethnic groups to take up arms for the Reich, we also can send to the front those troops who were previously tied up in this logistics and the camps themselves – all in all, over 350,000 trained soldiers!"

Speer nodded resignedly and picked up the folders from the floor.

"Didn't our estimable General Beck want to send all the camp guards home?" Guderian asked with an impish face. Von Witzleben shook his head resolutely: "The old man is irreplaceable in his position, but sometimes he misjudges the situation in which we find ourselves. If it were up to him, the Wehrmacht would soon only be equipped with sticks, because everything else is too cruel. A pinch of realism would be very good for the *Reichspräsident*."

"Well, then, if that's all?"

Speer and Guderian said goodbye, then both left the room. Von Witzleben looked after the two with narrowed eyes. Once again he had seen up-close what a ruthless fellow this Speer could be. During the war, the Chancellor needed some such men. But if peace ever came, Speer had to go. Definitely.

23

To Frau Else Engelmann, May 26[th,] 1943
(23) Bremen
Hagenauer Str. 21

Dearest Elly,

Thank you for the splendid support package, I was in desperate need of that! As you certainly know by now, our attack against Kursk was very successful. There you go! We have taken another step on the way to the end of the war! I think the worst and longest time of the war is behind us now. At some point the Russians have to realize that this matter has to be settled at the negotiating table and not on the battlefield. At least I sincerely hope so, otherwise we have to be prepared for a long and bloody fight. Sometimes it's like fighting the Hydra – Feldmarschall von Manstein coined the saying, but he's right. You cut off one head, there come two new ones! But the Russians have lost strength after all.

So you see, you don't have to worry so much anymore. Soon everything is over, then I can come home and do not have to leave again so fast. Oh, how I miss you and little Gudrun! I pray that this year it may work out again with holidays, and it looks actually quite good. In the Kursk operation, we suffered many losses and are therefore no longer able to fight at the moment. So I'm counting on us being pulled out of the front as soon as possible. Then it's back to the rear echelon (and this time not just a few kilometers behind the front, like Stalino, where the Russians came closer every day and you had to be afraid that the training grounds would suddenly become a battlefield. This time we'll get right out of the mud zone!). Maybe we'll even get moved back out of the East? With a little luck, we will come to Germany or at least to Italy or France for our refit. But I'll get out of the fighting in any case! So don't worry,

I'll be hearing from you again soon. Give Gudrun a big kiss and say hello to everyone who knows me. I love you! I miss you.

Your Sepp

South of Mikoyanovka, Soviet Union, June 1st, 1943

Lieutenant Engelmann's 9th Company had only three Panzer IIIs left, all prominently marked with the brand-new Citadel emblem. The tank crews had built firing positions behind a sunflower field which extended to the horizon. The armoring of all three panzers was scarred with wounds earned from antitank rifles, Pak, artillery, and enemy tanks. The ruptured steel and the perforated side skirts mounted above the drive-wheels shone in the light of the setting sun. In an hour, eternal Russia would be shrouded in total darkness.

The Panzer Regiment 2 had been hit really hard in and around Kursk. In many of the battles, the enemy superiority in numbers was overcome by the fighting strength and the better training of the German soldiers – so therefore many of the units involved in the attack on the Kursk salient were still at high fighting strength. Panzer Regiment 2 actually was one exception, it lost nearly all its tanks in the operation. The greater blood-price of this battle, however, was paid by the Russians. But it could not be ignored: Every tank destroyed, every aircraft shot down, and every liter of fuel consumed hurt the Germans much more than the Soviets. This evened out the overall loss figures of the Red Army – a little. In addition, the whole Wehrmacht was on a knife edge. For a long time, there had hardly been a single formation of the German armed forces meeting its required personnel and materiel strength, therefore every loss hurt twice. At the same time, a German soldier who had served on the Eastern Front for a while couldn't help thinking that Russian tanks and soldiers kept on sprouting out of the ground like weeds.

Panzer Regiment 2 had therefore again just surpassed the actual strength of 100 tanks after days and nights of effort by the workshop companies, and the supply of materiel from the near-to-empty reserve stocks. The workshop crews, however, had not been able to save Engelmann's tank "Elfriede."

After the lieutenant and his crew had to leave behind their tank, when the Russians attempted to break out of the Kursk pocket, a Soviet tank shell had penetrated the panzer's armor, and good Elfriede was thus destroyed. So Engelmann and his crew had to get along with "Franzi," their all-new friendly Panzer III.

The lieutenant opened a red can as he looked out of his cupola into the wide, yellow sea of sunflowers. He stuck a piece of chocolate between his teeth and sighed, because he had to remember that days ago he had hoped to finally be able to leave Russia. But as so often during the war, everything went sideways. The Kampfgruppe Sieckenius, of which the Panzer Regiment 2 was part of, had positioned many of its forces in front of what was an important airstrip of the VIII Air Corps. The combat formation consisted of a mere of 320 tanks of all sorts – including one heavy tank battalion. It also commanded 64 batteries of various guns: pioneers, paramedics, and two motley regiments of infantry – composed of everything from well-equipped and excellently trained veteran

27

infantrymen to tankers who had been handed a rifle. Engelmann had had to give up his own replacement personnel for the infantry companies of the kampfgruppe.

The sun was on the right flank of the lieutenant's panzers, moving slowly towards the horizon. The sky shone blood-red – but the last drop of blood of the day had not yet been shed.

Lieutenant Engelmann's face darkened under the tension that weighed on him. The onslaught of enemy tanks, which were pushing through the sunflower field straight towards his position, was marked by the bending and disappearance of entire rows of sunflowers. A Russian tank regiment approached unstoppably. They did not yet know that they were running straight into a German defense line involving tanks, marksmen, Pak, and "Acht-Acht" guns, although a recon aircraft had fully scouted the German positions before it was shot down.

It's all your own fault when you don't equip your tanks with radios, Engelmann pondered with an evil satisfaction. But he also wondered which would be better: 200 tanks with radio communication, or 20,000 without. In addition, the Russians were anything but resistant to learning, and were slowly retrofitting their tank hosts with radio systems.

"This time I'm sure," Sergeant Münster explained. The lieutenant looked down at his driver.

"This time I'm sure," he repeated, "that we'll be dealing with a Tiger tank with red stars on it right away." Münster looked up at his comrades with an expectant face.

28

"Don't talk nonsense," Staff Sergeant Nitz hissed.

"I told you a thousand times the Soviets didn't steal that damned tin can," Engelmann threw in.

"And I think they did. Who else would steal a Tiger?"

"It wasn't stolen! The morons dumped it somewhere, and then didn't dare confess that to their company commander."

"What about partisans?" Private First Class Ludwig hazarded.

"It has not been stolen, for god's sake," Engelmann made clear once and for all. "No Red knows how to operate a thing like that."

"We'll see … " Münster murmured.

The enemy forces approached; inexorably the rows of breaking sunflowers rolled towards the Germans. Engelmann clung with both hands to the lid flaps of his cupola, while the loudspeakers of his headphones cracked silently. Nitz had put the company frequency on the lieutenant's headset, so that he could command his entire unit directly.

Then the enemy broke out of the field, and the steel storm began. German shells pelted into Soviet T-34s, which rolled out of the yellow sunflower sea everywhere. Tongues of flames danced over Russian tanks, ammunition loads detonated, turrets were blown off. But once again the enemy appeared in great numbers. The field spewed out more and more tanks, which crashed onto the plain that lay between the German line and the sunflower field. The distance between the opponents was just about 200 meters. Every hit meant death and destruction. If Engelmann was normally anxious to fight at a greater distance, he

29

had to rethink this now since he had been put into a Panzer III. Those tanks with their five-centimeter barrels could only become dangerous for a Russian T-34 and comparable combat vehicles in absolute close combat. Since the Russians in this section once more showed up with incredible masses of people and materiel, and the Kampfgruppe Sieckenius still had some of the no-longer-produced Panzer III in its inventory, the Major General in command had decided to meet the Russians behind the protection of the sunflower curtain. The muffled striking of powerful anti-aircraft guns and the lighter banging of anti-tank canons – a German gun battery was located 100 meters behind the front troops on a slight ridge – mixed with all the other noise of the war.

Engelmann dived into the shelter his panzer turret offered and quickly closed the hatch, while Russian tank shells darted over the German positions. Right in front, a T-34 raced at full speed across the battlefield.

"Tank in transverse!" the lieutenant shouted. "Fire!"

Franzi's barrel vibrated as the projectile shot out. It hit the Russian tank on the side, making it half-turn with the force of the impact. A detonation from inside finally threw the turret into the air. Rust-red flames shot out of the tank and wrapped it in smoke.

Both fronts spat fire. On a width of two kilometers, the Germans and Russians hammered at each other. Behind the T-34s, infantry troops stormed out of the field. On the German side, MG nests, which lay in position between the cannons, opened fire. The initial German fire attack had exacted high losses from the Russians, but now, as more and more Soviet soldiers and vehicles stormed the battlefield, numerous German positions and anti-tank guns were blown apart. The Russian infantry pushed forward relentlessly, while dozens of men fell in the German defensive fire. Most of them remained still once they hit the ground. Nevertheless, red infantrymen swept against German gun positions in mass waves, while the T-34s concentrated on their panzer counterparts. The battle was murderous, overlaid with a crescendo of deadly racket.

Engelmann gritted his teeth while Jahnke, his new loader, pushed the next tank shell into the gun's automated breech.

A detonation just in front of Franzi ripped the earth open and wrapped the tank in a cloak of earth and turf. Through his vision block, the lieutenant spotted a T-34 that had taken up position 150 meters in front of his tank. Engelmann looked directly into the dark muzzle of the tank's barrel.

"Half left, 150, single T-34," he screamed with a hoarse throat as Ludwig swiveled the turret and brought it to bear on the target.

"Have him!" the gunner finally yelled.

"Fire!"

In the twilight of the setting sun, the T-34 exploded right in front of Engelmann's eyes. The lieutenant wiped the sweat off his forehead. Once again the acrid stench of battlefield air was in his tank. It smelled of fire, of boiling oil, and of all sorts of body vapors.

Nitz, who listened to the frequency of the regiment via his radio, browsed his notebook of encryption codes, then raised his head and reported: "On behalf of

31

the regimental commander, we're ordered not to break out of our line! The Stukas are almost here!" The sergeant plucked his mustache nervously and turned towards the radio again. The German dive bombers approaching from the northwest should be visible from the battlefield, but Engelmann could not see them through the narrow eye slit.

Daylight is almost gone, he moaned silently.

The battle of attrition continued. The Russian and German lines were further thinned out with each volley of cannons. German machine gun crews were now killing enemy infantrymen as they broke out of the sunflower field. The Red Army soldiers took positions under heavy losses. But German infantrymen also bled: they were hit with metal fragments of shattering guns, or were directly targeted by Russian weapons.

An entire squadron of 60 Luftwaffe dive bombers surged into the battle, engines roaring. In fact, the German air force once again with great effort accomplished the feat of gaining air superiority over the numerical-advantaged *Voyenno-Vozdushnye Sily* – the Russian Air Force – in the section of Army Group South. The Soviet tankers, however, had recognized the danger from the air and let their engines howl. Some engaged reverse gear and retreated back into the field. Auto-cannon rounds chased after them, hurling sunflowers up into the air.

"Gutless Bolsheviks!" Münster shouted. Through his narrow eye slit he had only a few Russian tanks in view, all which retreated back into the sunflower field. Meanwhile, Engelmann's eyes widened.

Uncoordinated as ever, nevertheless the majority of the enemy tank forces did not retreat, but had seemingly come to a silent agreement to step on the gas, dashing into the German positions.

Exploding shells dug funnels into the ground, while most of the enemy's steely front rolled forward and finally banged into the German lines. The two armored armies interlocked, shooting from close range at each other. Fireballs covered numerous steel colossi. Others just stayed lying down while all life died inside them. The tank then froze while its crew perished miserably. In the background, the Stukas plunged down, their Jericho trumpets shrieking, but they could not strike where Russian and German fighters wrestled at bayonet range. Through their headless and courageous attack, the Russians had shaken off the German air superiority. The steel birds with the strangely-bent wings circled the sky in search of prey, which for its part tried to escape from the hustle and bustle of battle. The dive bombers hummed like irritated bumblebees.

From close range, the opponents mauled each other. The decimated Russian attackers suffered further losses, and now both Germans and Soviets were wildly uncoordinated and the battle mixed to a grey-olive confusion.

Engelmann clawed himself with all his might to his seat, which was attached to the turret wall like the gunner's place. He spat out target assignments, then Ludwig fired again and again – seven kills already claimed during this battle. Burning tanks lined the battlefield, and tankers from both sides tried to scramble free. Charred corpses were scattered all over the place. Some were crushed by tank tracks. First gaps occurred in the German frontline as more and more panzers went down the drain. Many, however, received only hits in the tracks or had their turrets jammed, and would be recoverable by the workshop companies later – assuming the Germans hung on to win this encounter. The Russians recklessly bumped into such gaps, which was the only way they could avert their downfall: They had to break through the German tank line and engage the guns behind in close combat. In any other case, within a very short time they would be dismembered by the 88-millimeter Flaks, which were mercilessly firing straight into the turmoil of tanks of both armies.

"Anna 1 to all. Take new position at those shrubs with the three destroyed Panzers IV at two o'clock. We lock that area down completely, otherwise the Russians will break through to our Pak batteries," Engelmann shouted into the microphone of his headset, trying to drown out the clamor of the battle, which penetrated the steel armor as a muffled carpet of noise. At the same time, 10th Company with its 14 remaining battle tanks broadened its defense line to also support Engelmann's 9th Company. Once again, radio communication was a great thing.

Münster accelerated, set the next gear with the shift lever, and pressed the clutch pedal, then the tank jerked off. With rattling tracks, Engelmann's company inserted itself into the gap, which had also been discovered by a group of T-34s. They immediately fired at the 9th's panzers, but the Germans were lucky. Anna 3 got its right track blown to pieces, and the rest of the shells missed their target. Both groups of tanks were racing directly towards each other, now less than 30 meters apart. Nitz had immediately reported the gap to the regiment. A clever man at the other end of the line promptly initiated countermeasures. Immediately, a wall of dirt was thrown up in front of the Russian tanks as a battery of eight-eights opened fire on them. The gun crews quickly found the right range, and the Red tanks flew apart, exploding and sending their turrets high in the air. There was nothing left of the crews but burned flesh. Engelmann's tanks rushed into the gap the next moment. When the curtain of earth dipped, there was still one T-34, which now went full-throttle directly to where Franzi held her ground. Both fired at the same time. The German shell hissed over the Russian tank, while Engelmann's tank clattered and banged as he absorbed the hit. The panzer jumped forward before the engine died. The steely walls were boiling hot from the energy of the impact, but in the end, the projectile had hit nothing vital – a miracle! The MG in the front hull had been shredded, the steel around it torn open and scorched. Nitz's radio had been destroyed, which became obvious when the sergeant screamed as he accidentally touched the glowing steel.

Münster pressed the starter, but the engine remained silent. Once again he tried to start it. And again. Nothing happened. Engelmann pressed his face against the Kinon glass of his vision block and had Ludwig swing the turret to the right. He had lost sight of the surviving T-34.

"The engine's gone," Münster roared.

"Radio down," Nitz added, breathless.

By hand-cranking, Ludwig rotated the turret to the right, where Engelmann suddenly saw the enemy tank heading straight for him. He only closed his eyes in anticipation of the collision; there was not enough time to do anything more. A huge blow shook Franzi and threw the crew inside all about. The lieutenant was tossed from his seat and crashed into the turret's steel wall before whirling against Jahnke. Engelmann moaned loudly as a violent pain shot through his left hand. He immediately held on to the injured spot, which swelled in a flash and shimmered bluish. The whole Panzer III rattled as the T-34 pushed it forward before it finally elevated Franzi by shoving itself between her and the underground. Engelmann's panzer threatened to tip over. A swift "Our Father" scampered through his spirit, even though he did not want to call upon God on the battlefield. He clung to his commander's seat with his right hand and tried to pull himself up again.

"Damned slow-poke!" Münster hissed, and he fired the starter again and again. Suddenly, Franzi's engine roared to life.

"Yes, sweetheart!" the driver gasped out. He got the clutch engaged and accelerated. The transmission made a sound like a saw blade eating into hardwood as the gears meshed. The tracks began to move, clattering. The steel groaned as the right tread went over the enemy tank's hull, while the left tread dug into the earth. Franzi lunged forward, her right side impacted back on the ground. Immediately Münster sped her up, while the T-34 was blown up in a fireball

– Engelmann's gunner had opened fire immediately after Franzi had released herself from the tank dovetailing.

Now Franzi drove clockwise in a circle until Münster threw himself into the levers and steered in the opposite direction. Apparently, the rear idler wheels had taken a blow after all. Lieutenant Engelmann pulled himself up in his seat and took his post again. He moaned briefly as he grazed the armatures with his injured hand. It hurt terribly.

"Claim it as a wound," whistled Nitz. "That'll get you your Wound Badge in gold!"

"Oh, don't be silly, Ebbe."

Engelmann pressed his face against the narrow vision block as he tried to endure the throbbing pain in his hand.

"Turn the turret back," he ordered. In the meantime, he could see nothing more than the tanks already shot to pieces. Farther back in the sunflower field, artillery fire plunged down and tore the plants apart.

"Blimey!" Engelmann spat out and held his wounded hand. He no longer had radio contact with his tanks, and with only the narrow vision block, he could forget about getting a proper overview. He bit his lower lip while the motionless, suffocating warm air surrounding them made him sweat like his body was a spring itself. His face glared from sweat, and his hair was so wet it was as if he had been bathing. His tanker helmet slipped back and forth on his head, and underneath it, his scalp itched terribly. Engelmann was still fighting with himself, but he knew who would win the duel between his inner soldier and his instinct for

37

self-preservation and duty as a family man – it was the soldier, as it so often did. Which he sometimes regretted.

With his uninjured hand, he pushed open both lids of his hatch, then – after a moment gaining enough courage – he stretched out his upper body and thus was exposed on the battlefield. In a flash, he turned around in all directions, trying to get a full picture of the situation. The most important thing first: His company was still intact, even if Anna 3 was stuck a little farther back, not able to move. Everywhere, there were isolated Russian tanks in retreat, while the battleground was littered with burning or motionless wrecks. The Russian infantry tried to disengage and move back where they had come from, but German bullets and shells chased them mercilessly and cut up what was left of the sunflower field. The Russian attack was over. Stukas roared down and pounced on the escaping enemy. Pak and Flak thundered into all Soviet movements. The German line had withstood the attack, but dozens of the combat formation's panzers were destroyed in the action, and many more German soldiers had been killed. Engelmann let himself sink back into his tank and sat down. It wasn't over yet, not by a long shot. The Russians threatened to retake Kharkov and the surrounding area with strong attack forces. Kampfgruppe Sieckenius had only fought off, with considerable losses, what had been merely a kind of vanguard.

The situation was tense and dangerous, because Ivan had hit the Wehrmacht unexpectedly and violently. After the success at Kursk, German High Command had assumed that the Soviets would be so badly burned that they would not even start their summer offensive – only to find out that General Zhukov was bold enough to insist on the planned offensive movements anyway, and thus gave the Germans a real surprise. With three attack formations, he was currently pushing into the German lines in the area from Belgorod to Kharkov, and had achieved some deep breakthroughs. The Voronezh Front and the Steppe Front had gathered their troops for this purpose. In the south, the 57th Soviet Army surged past Kharkov and then turned north, where it was about to unite with the 1st Tank Army and the 5th Guards Army, which had gotten north of Kharkov and were right now trying to turn northwest of the city. Both the 1st Tank Army and the 5th Guards Army had suffered enormous losses due to Operation Citadel. They had been augmented in a hasty ad hoc reinforcement effort from the staging area. It seemed almost as if the Soviets were simply grabbing all the units within their reach, putting them haphazardly into the armies that had started the attack, and desperately throwing them against the German lines. After all, the fact that the Russians only attacked here with a few armies, instead of with entire fronts, proved that their resources were also finite.

Finite maybe, but almost endless compared to what the Germans had.

The German troops had still not been able to stop the Russian advance, even though they once again inflicted enormous losses on their enemy. Farther north, the 7th Soviet Army together with the 5th Guards Army passed

Belgorod to the south to turn north behind the city. Here the situation was truly dangerous: the equivalent of more than four Soviet Armies remained in the pocket west of Kursk. These forces had still not surrendered and posed a serious threat. The Germans only held a narrow strip of land on the eastern edge of the pocket, from Olkhovatka via Kursk to Belgorod. The German 6th Army was there in action; it had been augmented with two reserve corps. Should the Russian 7th Army succeed in pushing into the pocket, not only would the Wehrmacht units in the Kursk area be cut off to the south, but the encircled Soviet troops would also be set free and pour out over the surrounding German formations. The catastrophe would be inevitable.

But there was also a Russian attack in the Oryol region going on. If both offensive attempts were successful, the German units in and around Kursk would suddenly be cut off. Anyone who took a closer look at the situation map realized that Zhukov did not only rely on mass. Zhukov was a brilliant tactician. He had correctly recognized the German weak points in the front, had taken advantage of the opportunity, and within days had launched a powerful, even if improvised counterattack. He risked a lot. A failure would not only bring the Russians even higher losses, it would also immobilize the Red Army for at least one year, because Zhukov had apparently thrown all reserves into the battle.

The Red Army was on the move everywhere on the Eastern Front. Even Leningrad was being fought over. There the Soviets tried with all their might to blow up the siege ring around the city, which so cruelly held the population in its clutches.

Meanwhile, Combat Formation Sieckenius had been tasked with preventing the further advance of the 7th Soviet Army in the south.

If Kharkov were to fall to the Russians, there was only one option left for von Manstein: he would then have to withdraw the Southern Army Group back behind the Dnieper, before the Russians could quickly break through to the river and encircle entire German armies.

Engelmann would do everything in his power to prevent this. The loss of Kharkov would mean the loss of the entire region. Then Belgorod, Prokhorovka, and Kursk would also have to be abandoned. In that case, all of Operation Citadel would have been in vain. So much blood and steel with which Kursk's conquest had been bought would have been counted for nothing. No! Engelmann had to think of the good men who had fallen there. Born, Laschke, many others. It shouldn't have been for nothing! If they didn't stop the Russians here, they would lose everything down to the Dnieper, and the Soviets would be much closer to home again. Such thoughts put a real sting in Engelmann's guts. He knew what the stakes were, and the Wehrmacht had put everything it got into this. Now von Manstein's backhand blow was a win; but with that kind of victory, the Soviets could only be stopped – no war could be won that way. Time worked in favor of the brute economy of Ivan, which in a single month produced as many tanks as the Germans in a year; time was clearly against the Reich. Added to this were the immense amounts of vehicles, weapons, and equipment provided by the Western Allies' Lend-Lease program, the addition of which to the Russian clout could not be overestimated.

Therefore, a thorough and savage beating had to be administered. If the Russians were bled to death in German defensive fire, Stalin might be willing to sit at the negotiating table at some point. But until that was the case, a lot of blood would have to be shed and a lot of steel would have to be scorched.

Engelmann looked around in all directions. Everywhere, the battlefield was now littered with death and destruction. Once again the Russians had suffered losses, in tanks alone, at a ratio of one to five.

It's possible, he encouraged himself. *At least if the Western powers stay still.* Engelmann sighed. Everything was on a razor's edge. He looked over to his tank with the codename Anna 2, which had taken position 30 meters from him. Its commander, Sergeant Hagen Gunthermann, opened the two flaps of his hatch and finally stuck his head out of the turret. The side skirt of his panzer was holed like a Swiss cheese. Gunthermann looked over at Engelmann and with a questioning expression, tapped against the earphones of his headset. Engelmann gestured to the sergeant that his radio had failed. He nodded in understanding.

In the background, the German forces reorganized themselves. The crew of Anna 2 had climbed out of their panzer and retightened the track, which had miraculously not been damaged. 1,000 meters farther to the east, the heavy battalion of the combat formation was on its way and apparently already formed up for further deployment. Mighty Panther and Tiger tanks took advantageous firing positions and dug in, while infantry forces advanced from the rear to secure the German tanks that had been left behind. Engelmann let himself fall back, landing clumsily in his seat. His injured hand burned and pulsated. It was thickly swollen, like a fire jellyfish. Moreover, the sweat poured down his face and soaked his uniform. The lieutenant felt the tiredness press against his eyes, snatching away the slightest desire for action from him. He looked around in his tank, into the exhausted eyes of his crew as far as he could see them. Nitz had a laceration on his forehead, but it didn't bleed much. Münster seemed to have fallen asleep with his eyes open, while Jahnke was counting the remaining main-gun rounds. Ludwig was observing the perimeter through his optics. They all seemed limp and tired. Days of fighting had consumed them. But once again, they had merely held up against a vanguard here, while the overall Russian attack continued unabated. Franzi was also very haggard. From the outside, the Panzer III looked as if it had been banged in front with a wrecking ball. One of the machine guns was broken, the radio damaged, and the steely skin cracked in a thousand places.

Suddenly, someone knocked on the commander's hatch. Engelmann heard a very dull "Herr Leutnant?" It visibly cost him to move, but then he stretched himself up and looked into the face of a lance corporal from Anna 2.

"Herr Leutnant," the man started his report. "Orders from the regiment: We bypass the sunflower field to the right and follow the ridge to take enemy forces in the flank at Hill 201.4. We're supposed to leave in 15 minutes. 10th Company takes the lead this time, we're to secure our regiment's six."

"Got it," Engelmann mumbled. "So we will still be in existence tonight?"

The lance corporal nodded.

"Thank you." The lieutenant disappeared into his tank. So things would go right on. That was probably the correct course of action, but already everyone was at their limit, longing for a break. Engelmann looked at expectant faces.

"We're moving on," he whispered. His men nodded.

Naryshkino, Soviet Union, June 1st, 1943

Russian 76-millimeter divisional gun shells struck the center of the settlement with a great din. The main street was torn up again and again – rock and dirt flew all over. Each detonation brought with it vibrations, and these vibrations shook the ruins left by the war at Naryshkino. The Germans called those 76-millimeter guns Ratsch Bumms because of the two sounds it made during firing; first one hears a jarring *raaatsch,* followed by a *boom* when the shell explodes.

Sergeant Franz Berning from Austria pressed himself against the wall underneath a shattered window and squinted his eyes half-closed. Outside the room he was hiding in, Russian artillery shells threw up dust and dirt like earthy cascades. Berning pressed his stahlhelm tighter against his skull with both hands. In the foreground, the impacts conjured up a coat of dry fog that covered the entire city center. Again and again, the Russian artillery hammered into the settlement of Naryshkino. The men of 2nd Platoon clung to the walls of the shaking buildings. Hell-hot metal fragments hissed around, clapping against the outer walls of the houses. Glowing shrapnel chirped through the air, piercing the concrete. Screams of death's distress sounded. In Naryshkino, hell itself had opened its gates and poured out the embers from burning boilers over the city. The air pressure squeezed the soldiers hiding in the ruins against the walls, like insects. Some men were close to madness. With their eyes forcefully closed, as if the lids alone could shield them from all the cruelty of the war, and their hands pressed against

45

their ears, they huddled together, enduring the gruesome game.

Berning's breathing went faster and faster. This was not the usual morning blessing from Ivan. He knew that the enemy artillery was merely preparing an attack of tanks and soldiers, and he also knew what to expect. Trembling, he forced himself to look out over the windowsill. A gigantic cloud of dust blocked his view.

The sergeant had taken up position with his squad on the ground floor of a destroyed shop. To the right of him, under the other window, Hege sat with his machine gun and Senior Lance Corporal Weiss, whom Berning had made his second fireteam leader and, as it were, served as the second gunner of the MG 42 too. The rest of the squad was scattered over the other windows, doors, and breaches in the building created by the fighting – the remaining division formations had been combined into two reinforced regiments, which was why it had been possible to have nearly all sub-units regain the required strength once more. Thus Berning had a full squad at his command again. And here they were, bearing the enemy artillery fire. Again a salvo of shells slammed into the city, but the fire fell too short to be dangerous to the Germans.

North of Kursk, even after the success of the Citadel operation, the Red Army had moved on to numerous counterattacks, which threatened to expand into a genuine offensive. The enemy advanced north and south of Oryol in two wedge-formed attack patterns, and had achieved several deep breaches through the German lines. Both attack movements together formed

– seen on a map – a slight arc, which ends both pointed south. To the south of Oryol, the 3rd, 27th, and 53rd Soviet Armies stormed past this city. Von Manstein figured that their intention was to turn south behind Oryol and free the surrounded troops in the pocket of the former Kursk salient. Just like Kharkov, this would have catastrophic consequences for the Wehrmacht in the Oryol region. Here, too, was the omnipresent danger of cutting off those weak German blocking forces on the narrow strip of land from Olkhovatka to Belgorod, which was bordered on both sides by the Russian front line, and by the Wehrmacht troops in the north.

North of Oryol, however, was the real danger threatening this section of the front: well-trained and well-equipped Red Army forces joined the attack; the 4th Guards Army, the 11th Soviet Army, and the 11th Tank Army. At first the German High Command had thought that this attack movement would also circumvent the city on its left and pass to the north, but the day before yesterday, the Russians turned sharply to the south and were now standing in front of Naryshkino, which was only 20 kilometers west of Oryol itself. Thus the encirclement of Oryol hung as a threatening sword of Damocles over the German defender's heads. Both sides knew the importance of the city: Oryol had served the Wehrmacht as a logistics center since its occupation and was generally regarded as the last foot in the door to Moscow. If the city was lost, the Russians wouldn't give it back. Then the road to Moscow would probably be blocked for the rest of the war. No rosy prospects, so Oryol had to be held at

47

all costs. While von Manstein and von Witzleben had agreed to give up Kharkov in a dire emergency, both shared the opinion that they would defend Oryol to the last drop of blood. The only bright spot were the reinforcements on the way. In about two weeks, the 15th Panzer Division would reach the Oryol theater. This division consisted of well-trained and – much more important – veteran tankers from Africa. But two weeks was a long time; the Germans had to keep this front sector of all, even if Kampfgruppe Becker – pulled together from depleted units of the original Citadel attack forces – had been continuously in battle. In the area north of Oryol, too, the Russians had, on the whole, obliterated von Manstein's successes in the first half of the year. Once again, the front line had moved a long way away from Tula.

One more time, Berning dared to look over the windowsill. A dense grey wall had built up in front of the position of his 2nd Squad. There was nothing more to see from the main road, it was so hazy thanks to the dust. More Russian shells thundered into the settlement, then the enemy stopped the artillery fire. The roar of the explosions ebbed away, but for a few more seconds, rocks and earth trickled to the ground. Then a deceptive calm crept onto the scene. One of Berning's soldiers coughed, and somewhere far away, shots were fired. The sergeant closed his eyes, listening into the dusty fog. His heart beat strongly, and sweat bathed his face. June 1st was another very hot day, but not even the sun penetrated the cover of dust and dirt that Naryshkino was now under. Suddenly Berning heard a sound that made every infantryman afraid: the squeaking of tank treads suddenly filled the air. Berning took cover under the window again and clasped his K98k carbine even tighter.

Oh no! Two words that ruled his mind.

"Russian tank!" whispered one Landser.

"T-34, two of them bastards plus infantry, 3rd Squad reports!" hissed another one.

"What is it?" Hege asked in a hoarse voice. He did not hear very well since Kursk.

"Two T-34!" Weiss nearly screamed in his ear.

Berning nodded. So they would stay here in position and wait until the enemy had passed. They really couldn't do anything against tanks. They only had rifles, a few hand grenades, and one machine gun.

Suddenly Staff Sergeant Pappendorf was standing in the house entrance with a fully packed bag. He marched purposefully towards Berning, squatting next to him. He put the bag in front of him on the floor.

"Unteroffizier Berning!" Pappendorf hissed.

"Yes, Sir?"

"Unteroffizier Berning! Now you can prove what you're made of!" Berning stared at his platoon leader with his mouth open. He opened the bag, and satchel charges – big explosive charges, of several grenades tied together – came to light.

"1st Squad made these," Pappendorf commented, grinning gloatingly, "just for you."

Berning's eyes grew wide, but Pappendorf continued unabated: "Your mission, Unteroffizier! Form a tank killer team, advance under MG cover fire towards the enemy tanks, and destroy enemy tanks on the road. Repeat!"

49

Berning screwed up his face. He could not imagine that he should go out there, armed only with satchel charges, to destroy enemy tanks that were probably accompanied by infantry. He looked at Pappendorf like a dog who didn't want to perform his trick. The senior NCO's face darkened... Pappendorf was dead serious.

"I'm supposed to form a tank killer team and destroy tanks in the street," Berning stammered.

"Herr Unterfeldwebel," Pappendorf added.

"Herr Unterfeldwebel."

"Well then, let's go!"

Hesitantly, Berning grabbed the bag, then looked up.

"Barth, Schapnick! To me!" he ordered. Pappendorf raised one eyebrow. From different rooms of the building, two young soldiers were trooping in; both not yet 20 years old, and both with little service time on their backs. They had just been transferred from the replacement battalion to the Schnelle Abteilung 253.

"Taking the two most inexperienced soldiers in the squad with you," Pappendorf remarked. "Good move, Unteroffizier, good move." The staff sergeant nodded with a mocking look. Uncertain, Berning looked up to his platoon commander, but then he pressed his lips together as anger flooded his mind.

I don't care what this Piefke is thinking! Ignoring Pappendorf's gaze, Berning turned to the summoned soldiers -- this meant that Pappendorf's behavior did not go unnoticed by Berning at all, rather he desperately tried to ignore it.

Outside, the squeaking of crawler tracks became louder, the rattling of the Russian tanks clearer.

50

Berning took another look over the windowsill. Still there was nothing to see but a wall of fog, but slowly -- very slowly – the dust vanished. Berning had to hurry.

"Notice!" he told his tank killer team. "You two take two satchel charges each. Rifles stay here! I'll go first, you'll be right on my heels. Understand?"

"Understood," the answer came out like of one throat.

"Herr Unteroffizier," Pappendorf added immediately.

"Herr Unteroffizier," the two soldiers repeated.

Can't this guy just shut the fuck up? Berning got over it. He almost said something. Almost! Then he remembered his mission.

"Follow me!" he breathed. He jumped up and climbed over the windowsill.

*

Pappendorf looked after Berning's sad tank killer team as they disappeared into the dusty mist.

"Well, in your place, I would have assigned my MG to deliver some suppressive fire," he muttered to himself and shook his head.

Hege looked at his platoon leader with an insecure expression. "Should I lay down suppressive fire, Herr Unterfeldwebel?" he finally asked, and pressed his machine gun's buttstock into his shoulder. He grinned helplessly and insecurely, with his bad teeth visible.

"Not at all," was Pappendorf's short answer. "How else is he gonna learn?"

Hege's face still had a big question mark in it. He said, "What's that, Sir?"

"How else is he going to learna!"

"He's a good turn?"

"LEARN! HE!"

"Who?"

"Berning!"

"I see ... shall I shoot or not, Sir?"

"For the Lord's sake! No!

*

Berning quickly sprinted across the street and pressed himself against the house wall on the other side. The squeaking of the tank tracks was now quite loud, so the enemy combat vehicles were close. Berning felt the road vibrate under the steel colossus. Fear and despair rose in him.

His two soldiers were each ready with a satchel charge. They looked with serious expressions into the thinning dust cape, which was still fogging the city center. Russian calls echoed out of the mist.

"Follow me," Berning spoke under his breath. "We push along the wall into the alcove in front of that post office over there. Then we'll wait, let ourselves be bypassed, and then we'll strike." His soldiers nodded, then the sergeant dashed off. Always hugging the wall, he ran along the partially-torn building facades until he reached the post office, a small building with a red brick roof. There was a slight indentation, into which a small car could fit. Berning and his two soldiers pressed their bodies against the house wall and kept quiet. The non-commissioned officer could clearly hear his breathing, which was like background music to all the other sounds. The tracks of the enemy tanks rattled like a medieval drawbridge, getting closer and closer. The road trembled and the buildings shook under the rumble. Suddenly an olive steel monster – a T-34 – broke out of the dusty curtain like a primeval ogre and clatteringly passed the post office. With his eyes wide open, Berning looked after the steel colossus as it rolled farther up the road. He'd never been this close to an enemy tank before!

"Now!" Berning whispered, and hit Schapnick against the helmet. He nodded while a "Jawohl, Herr Unteroffizier" fell from his lips, then he ran out. His right hand tore off one safety cap, and he tugged the pull cord out of the handle.

The private first class stormed the road, rushing towards the tank. Suddenly there was a gunshot. The projectile blew Schapnick's helmet away and drilled itself into his head, where it caused irreparable damage by smashing the zygomatic bone and finally burst from his face between the nose and upper lip. Schapnick's legs gave way, then his skull hit the cobblestone ground where he remained motionless. Immediately, hectic Russian cries echoed loudly in the street.

Berning pressed himself as hard as he could against the wall of the house and grabbed his rifle with all his might. Even Barth stared spellbound at the dead Schapnick.

"Scheisse!" Berning puffed out. It did not remain a secret to him that the owners of the Russian voices approached rapidly. The sergeant yanked up his rifle and aimed at the corner of the alcove, but his hands shook badly. Surely there was a whole Soviet platoon on the road! Or even a company! With the tanks, it felt like an express train was thundering past.

"Shall I try it, Sir?" Barth asked with a brave voice.

"No," Berning whispered, slowly leaning towards the corner behind which dozens of Russians might be lurking.

"We're fucked," he concluded, jittering.

Suddenly, an MG-42 stuttered from the other side of the road. Pappendorf's men had opened fire! The fog had become very light, Berning could see flashes of muzzle through the dust from the positions of his unit. Sparks of fire hurtled across the road, cracking the cobblestone and wringing brick and plaster splinters from the buildings. The Russian voices were suddenly loud and panicky. Enemy weapons returned fire. Instantly, the most forward tank stopped and pointed its main gun at the buildings in which squads from the 2nd Platoon had entrenched themselves. Berning bit his lower lip when one of the MGs of the tank began to bark. The bullets crashed into the positions of his comrades. Screams and wildly-roared orders filled the air. Then the T-34 fired its main weapon. The explosive shell penetrated the building's wall, shaking it terribly. Concrete chunks of all sizes rained onto the road.

"We must help them," Barth groaned, and grabbed his satchel charge. Again, the tank shot his main gun into the building, the left half of which collapsed completely.

Berning fought with himself. He could hear his comrades screaming desperately, while several German machine guns were still firing on the road.

54

Horrible, human screeching sounds from the Russian position suggested that they were also suffering losses.

"We have to help them, Sir," Barth insisted. Berning dug his incisors into the flesh of his lower lip - he hesitated a moment – then struck Barth on the shoulder. The private jumped up and sprinted off. Berning hurried after him. The two German soldiers ran into the street as fast as their legs could carry them. Russian fire chased after them. The cobblestone next to Berning's feet burst high. Fine splinters sprayed into his face. He held his left arm in front of his eyes and kept running. All he saw in front of him were Barth's boots pounding across the street.

Finally they reached the tank. Berning could hear the Russian orders at his back. He imagined they called: "Shoot the sergeant! Shoot the sergeant!" He believed at that moment that all the shots of this war were for him alone. His breathing had also increased to infinity. His pulse was pounding in his throat. His stahlhelm slipped back and forth on his head. But he just ran on. Nothing else controlled his body, disturbing thoughts troubled his mind no more.

Barth pulled the detonator of his satchel charge and hurled it onto the tank, right at the main gun barrel. The bundle of grenades bounced off the top of the hull, jumped up again, and came to rest exactly between the turret and the hull. Barth and Berning kept running. Bullets from both sides buzzed through the air, tearing scars into the buildings; but the two Germans on their tank destroyer mission were lucky. The moment they reached the positions of their platoon and climbed back into the building through a window, there was lightning behind them at the tank, and a loud bang echoed across the street. After that, the T-34 remained motionless. Externally it seemed unscathed, but it did not fire again or otherwise moved. The tank was destroyed, or at least its crew was.

Berning once again pressed himself against the wall under "his" window and tried to control his breathing. Once more his squad took up the firefight with the Russians, but the enemy – shocked by the destruction of the T-34 – withdrew, shooting back, and finally disappeared from the sight of 2nd Platoon. The other Soviet tanks could be heard but not seen in the slowly-disappearing mist. They seemed to retreat too.

Berning gasped and snorted as he lay underneath the window with his mouth open.

"No casualties," Weiss reported immediately. "Ammunition at 80 percent."

Berning just nodded and gestured to the senior lance corporal to pause for a moment. He first had to get his breathing back under control and choke off the emotions that flared up in him. Suddenly, however, Pappendorf stood in front of him.

"Berning!" he bellowed. The non-commissioned officer jumped up to his feet immediately and waved both arms before straightening the helmet, which sat crooked on his head.

"Yes ... Herr Unterfeldwebel?"

"1st Platoon reports three more enemy tanks. Predestined for you! Grab some more satchel charges and brace yourself for your next tank destroyer mission!"

Bern, Switzerland, June 2nd, 1943

For half an hour, Thomas Taylor and Luise Roth lay silently next to each other in bed, enjoying each other's body heat and the cool air flowing into the room through the open window. Outside, the darkness shrouded the city of Bern in a dark cloak. Luise wouldn't be going home that night. She'd stay with Thomas, like almost every night.

Since Luise's mother was dead and her father was stationed somewhere in England, she was in the unusual situation for a young woman of being able to do what she wanted with men. Nevertheless, her father would hardly like what she was currently doing in Switzerland.

Thomas knew that; they had already talked about it. He was therefore truly glad that the old patriarch was not within reach. Thomas had to grin. What would that old Tommy think about his daughter jumping into bed with a German ten times a week? There was simply no stopping her on that point – she had gotten over her initial embarrassment faster than Thomas could blink. He sighed, then he lit a cigarette. Luise just closed her eyes in his arms, but Thomas couldn't think of sleep at the moment. Too many things were rattling through his head.

What do you want me to do? That was the big question that hovered above all other thoughts. Thomas hadn't asked Luise about the invasion of Italy for days now, because he was too afraid she would get wind of his real intentions. Accordingly, poor Thomas had failed to submit his last report to the Abwehr, the Military Intelligence Service.

What do you want me to do? So many doubts, so many feelings; and also his sense of duty gnawed at him, struggling for his attention.

Thomas felt Luise's warm body clinging to his own. She was asleep – her chest rose and lowered evenly, her eyes closed and her face very peaceful.

Thomas was in love – and contrary to what he had initially thought, this feeling had neither vanished after a short time nor was he able to fight it successfully. He could not get rid of his deep affection for Luise. As a magnet attracted metal, so she attracted him with an irresistible force he could do nothing about. But what was he supposed to do? His first dilemma was that he had an official mission here, and the information he gathered could save the Reich's ass. On the other hand, he wondered what else he could get out of the British consulate's employee in the way of a tip, apart from the approximate attack date for the Allied takeover on Italy – which he had already gotten. From the outset, the hope of the Abwehr had rested on Luise's father; but, disappointingly, Taylor had learned that she had very little contact with him. And their relationship was also quite tense. So only her activity in the British consulate was left as a source, but she wasn't exactly a manager or some other important employee there.

Thomas' second dilemma was the very foundation on which his relationship with Luise rested. His name was not Aaron Stern, and neither was he a Jew, but if Luise ever learned of his true identity, he would not know what to fear more: the Swiss police, or the girl's furious rage. She could be damn temperamental. Sometimes she was really fiery – not just in bed.

Thomas seriously wondered if it might not be possible to live a life of lies and spend his days in Switzerland with Luise as Aaron Stern. But he, of course, knew that this was not possible. Activities in enemy territory always had to be of short duration, because at some point someone or something would expose him – even if it was only a stupid coincidence. No, that wasn't an option either.

Thomas sighed again. He pulled hard on his cigarette. Well, then? Do what? He had no choice but to let things go on and see what would happen. Maybe the eggheads of the Abwehr would pull him out soon. Maybe Luise would reveal some useful information after all. Only the future could tell.

So wait, and ... well ... take care of Luise. Thomas flicked the cigarette butt out the window, then eyed her naked body for a moment.

The things you do for your country!

Mikoyanovka, Soviet Union, June 4th, 1943

Engelmann had been lucky; his hand was not broken. Although the swollen wrist still throbbed painfully, he could still use his hand, could continue in his function as tank commander and company leader. Nonetheless, he had to move the book he was carrying into his healthy hand after a few seconds, as the bruise hurt too much.

The sun of the late afternoon blessed the plains of Russia with glistening light and pleasant warmth, without which it was unbearably hot that day. The Russian attack, with which the enemy had tried to advance through the Kharkov area in the direction of the encircled Soviet units only to be halted by Kampfgruppe Sieckenius, had more or less stopped for two days now. After their success south of Mikojanovka, the Germans had even been able to achieve some deep breaches into the Soviet front line. Finally, however, they were pushed back by the Russians to the Mikoyanovka airfield again.

At the moment, the Russians even stood on the well-paved road from Belgorod to Kharkov and blocked it. German supply convoys therefore had to take long detours in order to reach the front troops. The situation remained extremely dangerous for the Wehrmacht: Since yesterday, the airfield near Mikojanovka had been repeatedly under artillery fire from the enemy. Due to heroic efforts by the Luftwaffe ground personnel, bomb craters which had been blasted out of the runways were constantly patched up, and airplanes damaged by shrapnel repaired. Untiringly, the pilots took off again and again – often directly under artillery fire — as soon as their steel birds had been reloaded and fueled. Only supply shortages kept the planes on the ground from time to time.

The Russians, however, were now less than two kilometers away from the airstrip. Any further advance by the enemy would result in the Luftwaffe having to give up this base immediately. Then fighter-wing Jagdgeschwader 52, as well as dive bomber-wing Sturzkampfgeschwader 2 "Immelmann" with its more than 140 airplanes, would have to move dozens of kilometers to the west – perhaps as far back as Poltava, where there was also a large air base, because the other, closer-in airfields of the region, near Kharkov or near Belgorod, were directly threatened by the enemy as well. In any case, the approach routes to the front would be significantly extended. The airfield near Mikojanovka was therefore an important piece of the mosaic in the fight for the Kharkov region.

Apart from the exchange of artillery shells, it had remained quiet today; the Russians seemed to have taken a break. Engelmann had used the day to have his men carry out makeshift repairs to the panzers. Truly, they would actually need a tank factory to put their battered armored vehicles back into working order, but through improvisation and inventiveness, they were able to make sure that the panzers would be operational for yet another day of gruesome action. So they had done some work on the tracks and idler gears, refilled the ammunition loads and restocked supplies – if any were available - and repaired any minor damage.

Münster – a mechanical virtuoso – had been struggling with Franzi's right tread for half a day, but after he had disassembled and then remounted the track for the second time, patched some connectors and replaced a wheel, he had finally ensured that the Panzer III only pulled minimally to the right. Nitz had also been out scrounging all day and had been able to get himself a new radio – of a different design, but it worked. The new radio was now installed in the tank and wired in to the headsets of the driver, radio operator, and commander. The only thing that couldn't be replaced was the hull machine gun, which was ready for the scrap heap. It was really impossible to find a replacement gun these days. For example, the grenadier battalion of the combat formation, which provided ground security forces for the area around the airfield, did not even have a single machine gun at all. Each grenadier carried a K98k with 15 rounds of ammunition. That was it! No hand grenades, no radios, no anti-aircraft guns, no Pak. Improvisation and freeloading anything that could be fought with was the order of the day. After all, the reports from the south gave them hope: At Stalino, the Russians had proceeded as far as to the city limits, but the withdrawing German forces had delivered the enemy ferocious delaying fights in accordance with von Manstein's strategy of backhand blows, meaning they repeatedly launched counter-attacks that hit the Red troops where it really hurt. The Russians had to pay for the gain of 80 kilometers with severe losses – at the worst point, sometimes in the ratio of one to eleven. Letting the enemy come and then attack his flanks or rear echelon had proven itself after a few days of the Russian offensive: The Soviet Southern Front had bled to death on the German forces in the area, and was no longer capable of any further movement.

But in Izium, at this hour, there was still fierce fighting for the Donets River crossings going on. Both banks had changed their owners countless times since the Russian attack had begun, but the Red Army had not yet succeeded in building permanent bridgeheads across the river. In this front sector, the 10th Panzer Division and 334th Infantry Division participated in the action; the two formations represented nearly half of the former Afrika Korps, which had always been distinguished by outstanding fighting strength. However, the German defense successes stood on shaky legs. Ivan was still strong at Izium, as at Oryol and Kharkov. If a breakthrough through the German lines was successful only in one of these sectors, and the enemy managed to reach the Dnieper, then von Manstein would be forced to withdraw all of Army Group South and Army Group Center back behind that very river. To stop the Russians, German defense efforts had to be successful not only at Izium, but everywhere.

Engelmann sighed. The day was coming to an end. There was nothing left to do with his panzers. All three tanks were parked in a small forest 300 meters east of the runways, and fuel and ammunition were at 60 percent. Since the lieutenant was of the opinion that rest periods were just as important as maintenance and repair work, he had dismissed his men a few moments ago to "after-duty hours." While Münster almost collapsed in the cover hole under Franzi and ever since slept like a baby, Nitz, Ludwig, and Jahnke as well as some crew members of the other company tanks had left to pay a call on the Luftwaffe boys, who allegedly had vodka and cigarettes. At least, it was with that promise that a lieutenant of the Luftwaffe had invited the tankers to a celebration that evening. The reason for the celebration was probably the return of two Hungarian groups of pilots to the VIII Air Corps.

Engelmann felt tired to death. He was also hungry, because the evening rations had been more than poor – Company Sergeant Major Kreisel had only brought a few slices of bread and jam for each soldier.

Lieutenant Engelmann walked away from his company's area of responsibility. He trudged over the large open space that began at the end of the runways and finally reached a long stretch of forest, where he sat down in a hollow between two old pines. After days crammed into a confined space with four other men, after days of weary endeavor and cruel fighting, he wished for nothing more than to spend half an hour in solitude – half an hour without voices and without the smell of other people. In his hands, Engelmann held a blood-stained novel entitled "The World Set Free". Eduard Born had the book lying next to him when he was fatally hit. He had poured his lifeblood over it before he took his last breath. Engelmann wanted to try to get a new copy of it from Elly before Kreisel would send Born's personal items to his family. The lieutenant did not want the boy's parents and siblings to receive a bloody book from their lost son. Since Born's death, Engelmann had carried the book

64

with him, but understandably he hadn't been able to read it yet. He could also imagine many other books which he would rather deal with than such science fiction nonsense. As a confirmed lover of German literature, he was worried enough that he could hardly read during the war. On the one hand he didn't have the time, on the other hand he couldn't carry a library around with him.

Somebody really needs to invent a small device to store and retrieve a thousand books, Engelmann mused. He imagined it would be like a digital clock: It needed changeable plates, each of which could display any letter by switching coils off and on. These plates would then have to be arranged in rows next to and below each other, in order to always be able to display the corresponding book page by clever recalling of the letters and words. The lieutenant loudly puffed air out of his lungs. However, that device had not been invented yet, and all he had left at the moment was the one blood-stained book he had in his hands – because his Bible was lying somewhere with the rest of his things at the troop impedimenta. So "The World Set Free" it was, although fantasy wasn't really his genre. Engelmann was more of a classicist – he liked Fontane and Goethe, but also Bennett and Hugo.

The lieutenant pulled his pocket knife out of his pants pocket and carefully separated the book pages glued together by the blood. Finally he opened the first page. Despite the fact that everything was dipped in red, he could recognize the black letters well. He had just skimmed over the first chapter when suddenly there was a whistle in the air.

Russian artillery shells! A blink of an eye later, fountains of dirt shot up behind the aircraft hangars.

"Shit!" moaned Engelmann, and closed the book. His body – every fiber of it – resisted standing up and get moving.

It's nothing, except a little Ratsch Bumm barking! The lieutenant pulled himself together and set off at the run while the alarm sirens went off over at the Luftwaffe compound. Engelmann watched countless people as small as ants from here push the Stukas and fighters out of the hangars. He hadn't gotten halfway back yet when the first pilots started their engines, taxied onto the runway in their planes, built up speed there, and took off only 100 meters away from Engelmann, so that they flew away just above his head. They quickly gained height.

Is there something cooking after all? the lieutenant contemplated, panting. The lack of sleep and food affected his condition noticeably.

Scheisse, now the Russians attack, when it's almost bedtime, he complained in his thoughts.

Soviet fighters appeared in the airspace, entangling the German planes in dogfights. Glowing projectiles buzzed across the sky like burning threads. Suddenly a German Messerschmitt Bf-109 spewed fine smoke before she caught fire. The slender propeller machine with the thick crossbeam behind the pilot's cabin lost height, rushed towards the ground, and finally vanished in a gigantic explosion that ignited the surrounding trees. No parachute was seen. All of a sudden, a constant thunder of guns firing and shells exploding started in the distance. The new sounds of

66

war came from the south and mingled threateningly with the siren sounding at the airfield.

There's definitely something cooking! Engelmann had almost reached the forest where his company was bivouacking. Within the blink of an eye, the enemy artillery fire stopped. The last salvo dug more earth out of the ground behind the hangars. A Bf-109 had apparently rolled into a crater while taking off – some men tried to push it out of the hole. From a distance, it looked as if the ground had swallowed a wing of the fighter.

When Engelmann finally reached his panzers, he was relieved to find that Nitz and the others were already there. Once again Nitz proved to Engelmann how valuable a staff sergeant he was: all the crews were already sitting in their vehicles, and the camouflage material had been removed. The company was on stand-by for action.

The lieutenant jumped on Franzi's hull and climbed through the commander's hatch into the turret. Expectant looks greeted him.

"Situation report," Engelmann demanded from Nitz. The staff sergeant plucked his mustache and replied, "The enemy will attack up the Belgorod-Kharkov road."

"They want this airfield," Münster remarked, but Engelmann abruptly cut off his words: "Shut up, Münster. Let Papa do the talking."

"The regiment has lost all comms with the kampfgruppe. They cut the phone lines!"

"Damned partisans," Münster spat out. He had opened his hatch and looked out at the airfield.

"Shut up, for God's sake! Nitz, what are our orders?" The lieutenant pulled his headset over his head and adjusted the throat microphone.

"Burgsdorff has ordered all units to stand by. He must have sent a messenger to Sieckenius … "

" … and until then we keep still?" Engelmann finished the sentence. "And do nothing, while the Russians are on the move?" The lieutenant was upset. Then he whispered, "Burgsdorff, that damn reservist … "

"Stuck here, we are no good for anything. We should be supporting the front line!" Ludwig said, reaping Engelmann's approval, even if he did not say so.

"If we're unlucky, the Ivans will be here soon anyway," Nitz returned with a painful grimace. One could literally see his tenacious back pain.

Engelmann stretched his upper body out of the cupola and looked down the apron. The Corps' planes were still taking off with roaring engines. Suddenly, Russian Hurricane fighters, painted olive and with red stars, swept across the airfield and fired at the planes trying to get off the ground. Fountains of soil erupted. Asphalt patches so large that even Engelmann could see them were ripped open and scattered across the runway. The German anti-aircraft guns, on the other hand, remained silent, because with all the blue forces in the sky, the hazard of friendly fire was real. Before the Russian fighters pulled up and disappeared into the sky, one of them managed to hit a German Stuka that had just gained enough speed to be able to get off the ground with his last shots. The dirt fountains breezed in two long rows towards the German bird and struck sparks as the bullets battered it. The hit aircraft went into a spin and tipped over on its nose so that the propeller broke off on the ground. Then the Stuka flipped over and slammed the stern rudder and the cockpit window into the runway and stopped. Immediately a jet of flame erupted, billowing black smoke into the air.

Engelmann had witnessed the scene with a queasy feeling. He tapped his throat microphone, then leaned down into his vehicle and said, "Battle mode! Turn on the tin can and get me on the air."

"Yep, Sepp." With these words, Münster turned the ignition key while Nitz switched on the radio. Franzi, the steel monster, came to life, rumbling.

"Anna 1 to all. Prepare for battle. Stand by to proceed south."

"Anna 2," Gunthermann's voice cracked in the headphones.

"Anna 3," confirmed Klaus, commander of the third panzer. The tankers of the company had gotten used to only giving their call signs as confirmation of a radio message, since these were short and thus valuable seconds were saved in battle.

"Hans, step on it and make our way into the open. I need to get an overview."

Münster obeyed and Franzi hit the road. The tank lunged forward, left the protection of the treetops, and drove out into the open space. Engelmann held on to one lid of his hatch with his one good hand. Concentrating, he sized up the airbase's hasty scramble. The last German airplanes had just taken off and gotten into the sky. Meanwhile, the ground crews

69

were in turmoil. The lieutenant saw dozens of men running around like fruit flies in the distance. The radio crackled on; Engelmann's headset was tuned to the company frequency.

"The airfield is under fire with light arms from the west." Nitz's Leipzig dialect gave each of his words a very special intonation.

"From the west ...?" Münster wondered.

"From the west?" Engelmann asked the same question, and began to ponder: "Partisans, perhaps?" West of the airfield lay a large forest area of many hectares. Intel had already suspected partisan camps there in the past. Wehrmacht troops had therefore taken action against suspected forces in the forest, but without success.

"That's not all," Nitz shouted. "The Luftwaffe suspects that Russian airborne troops will be landing here any minute now."

"Where's here?"

"Somewhere in the area. Russian transport planes are heading straight for the airfield."

"They'd never be so stupid and jump right onto the airfield," Münster snorted.

"Silence, Hans," the lieutenant bellowed, wringing a bewildered expression out of Münster's face. Engelmann looked into the sky. The yellow star up there shone particularly brightly that afternoon, making the lieutenant squint. Minutes later, he recognized a buzzing fleet of large Soviet aircrafts in the distance. The planes were twin-piston-engined Lisunovs with a wingspan of 30 meters, and the olive color typical of the Red Army. The Americans used the same aircraft but called it a Douglas DC-3.

Immediately the German fighters, who were still in aerial combat with their Soviet counterparts, broke off and went for the crowd of Russian transport aircraft. But the Lisunovs' escort was alert and pushed the Germans away. On both sides, burning planes went down.

Engelmann meanwhile counted twenty-one Russian transport aircrafts, which gave him sweaty hands. There was a whole battalion up there! And indeed: Russian paratroopers wanted to jump into the middle of the airfield while anti-aircraft shells – the gunners no longer paid any attention to risking blue planes – burst between the Lisunovs and covered the sky with black clouds of smoke. The cargo doors of the transport aircrafts opened and tiny men jumped out. Seconds later, their parachutes drew mushrooms into the sky. They slowly sailed towards the airfield.

"Prepare to defend against enemy airborne," the lieutenant yelled into the company channel. The other tank commanders immediately confirmed.

"Ludwig, to the machine gun!"

Engelmann closed his eyes and focused on the plain and its high grass, which lay between his company and the airfield. That was hundreds of feet of level terrain. Everywhere around him Panzer III and Panzer IV awoke and rolled out of their revetments, but the enemy could not be underestimated. To take excellently-trained paratroopers with unsupported armor was no walk in the park. In addition, the air battle was still hot up in the sky. Two-seater Il-2

Shturmoviks – nicknamed "Black Death" or "Slaughterer" by the Germans – now thronged the airspace. The German fighter planes were still very busy, therefore they could probably not guarantee absolute protection of their own panzers on the ground.

The first of the enemy paratroopers landed between hangars, right in the crowd of Luftwaffe ground personnel. A gruesome brawl broke out. From Engelmann's perspective, it looked as if tiny ants were pouncing on each other. And more paratroopers landed – more and more. Every second they struck the earth, freed themselves from their silk chutes, pulled out their weapons, and entered the fight. Shots and screams echoed over to Engelmann. Only now did the lieutenant notice the Russian gliders, which descended silently through the air. They were thick-bellied and had a kind of needle on their muzzle. They were rapidly approaching the ground. Finally, they slammed down on the open field; they furrowed through the meadow for a few dozen meters before they came to a standstill. Part of the small fuselages and the long wings disappeared in the high grass and between the ferns. Engelmann figured that the gliders bring the paratroopers' heavy weapons.

"Burgsdorff says we're off the chain! Our company is to move over the open to the forest edge and take firing positions there. The others will secure the airfield." Nitz passed on the message that had just come in via radio.

So to the open field with that damned high grass! There, where the enemy could hide easily. The lieutenant thought for some seconds and then gave the marching order. Immediately the panzers of 9th Company started to move. Like primeval dinosaurs, the German tanks mowed down the grass. Engelmann had Nitz switch briefly to the other company frequencies, where he made arrangements with their COs.

"Move over to the right. We take the right flank, next to the 10th," he finally said into his throat microphone. Anna 2 and 3 confirmed and maneuvered to the right. Together with Franzi, the three panzers lined up in a row next to each other facing the forest on the other side of the battlefield. They pushed their way through the grass while the hostile paratroopers landed in front of them, lined up as if they were pearls on a necklace, and immediately disappeared into the dense ground vegetation.

"Fire on the gliders as soon as you have a clear sight on them," Engelmann ordered, then leaned over to Ludwig and nudged him.

"Slant to the left, there's a glider!" Ludwig nodded and aligned the main gun with the target, which was about 400 meters ahead of them in the high grass. Only one of the wings was sticking out of the vegetation. It was tricky to spot the enemy at all.

"HE, Siggi!"

"Jawohl, Herr Leutnant." Jahnke loaded the appropriate shell. The cannon's breech slammed shut.

"Battle mode, Siggi," Engelmann reminded.

"Yes, Herr ... Engelmann ... Herr Josef."

"Goddamned kiddos in uniform," Nitz said and grinned sourly. Then Engelmann told his driver to stop. Franzi came to a halt, groaning mechanically.

"Fire, Theo!"

Ludwig shot, but missed. A balloon of dirt and fire rose up in the air next to the target. Immediately the next shell went into the loader, and Ludwig pressed the electric trigger again. Score! A ball of flames swallowed the glider; nearby red paratroopers threw themselves to the ground. Münster picked up speed again and accelerated. In this very moment, a hard blow thundered against Franzi's armor.

Anti-Panzer rifles. This thought raced through Engelmann's mind, and he disappeared into his cupola. He quickly closed the lid flaps. With enemy paratroopers nearby, he really didn't have to be out there.

Muzzle flashes were to be seen all around the battleground. The paratroopers lurked everywhere in this goddamn grass, and could move as they liked thanks to the dense vegetation. Again an anti-tank rifle projectile banged against Engelmann's tank and scorched the steel.

"Hopefully the armor will hold!" Münster screamed in the racket.

Suddenly it got loud on the radio circuit. "Tanks from the left! 800!" Klaus yelled.

Huh? was Engelmann's first thought. He turned to the right side and blinked his eyelids in amazement.

"What's that?" blurted the lieutenant.

"Tiger! TIGER! HOSTILE TIGER!" was the only message on the radio ether. Exactly in front of 3rd

Company, which still had 38 armored vehicles, the wood cracked as a white-painted Tiger tank, on whose flanks huge red stars were emblazoned, fought its way out of the woods. With the power of 700 horses, the brute's panzer tracks ground up tree trunks and undergrowth. When the steel monster reached the edge of the forest, it stopped and immediately fired. The shell ripped up the ground at 11th Company's panzers and covered them with dirt like a bell. Instantly Engelmann saw the panzers of 11th Company stop, while those of the 10th had already turned around and gone full throttle. For a short moment, Engelmann was amused by the realization that an enemy Tiger had the same psychological effect on the Germans as a German Tiger often had on the Russians.

"AP shell!" the lieutenant yelled, and Jahnke executed the order. Münster shouted excitedly: "I knew it was stolen!"

"All right, now you can say it," bellowed Engelmann.

"Say what?"

"What you said earlier."

"What, hopefully the armor will hold?"

"Prior to that."

"Never are they that stupid, to jump right onto the airfield?"

"Prior to that."

"From the west?"

"Prior to that."

"Yep, Sepp?"

"Even prior to that."

"Damned partisans?"

"Exactly. Do you remember everything you said?"

"Every word, Lieutenant. I want to write a book about my experiences later."

"Aha."

"I think I'll call it *Lost Victories*. Somehow I have to capitalize on this shit."

"*Lost Victories*? Stupid title … "

"What about *Achtung Panzer*?"

"Way too attention-grabbing, Hans. If you come up with a reasonable title, I'll offer to proofread your book."

"Proofread? No, thanks, I'll write it myself."

"Let's get on with it," Nitz threw in, "let's do something, please. Please!"

The German tanks fired at the Tiger, but the projectiles bounced off the steely skin like tennis balls, scattered, howling, in all directions and finally painted blazing figures onto the battlefield when exploding. Again the Tiger shot, but missed one more time. Engelmann noticed that the commanders of 10th and 11th companies must have ordered their panzers to retreat. They now blundered straight into the Russian paratroopers, who had spread unnoticed over the entire plain thanks to the dense ground vegetation. Hand grenades and anti-tank rifles brought an abrupt demise to the first combat vehicles. The panzer companies had gone straight into the trap. The tanks tried to regroup and take action against the infantry. MG fire stuttered away.

Engelmann clawed himself to his seat, looking through his narrow viewing block at the edge of the forest.

"Swing to the left," he ordered Ludwig, and at the same time assisted the gunner by cranking the lever attached to the commander's side, so that the turret turned faster. The enemy Tiger shot again. The clarion punch of his 88-millimeter cannon snarled across the plain, but he missed again. The shell hit somewhere near the escaping tanks of 10th Company.

Finally Franzi's turret was aligned to the Tiger. Münster had let the tank continue the whole time at reduced speed, and now he pulled her to a stop.

"Aim right between hull and turret, Theo," Engelmann whispered, then he yelled, "Fire!"

Ludwig shot and hit the enemy tank, but the AP shell didn't scratch it at all. The Tiger swallowed the shell as if it was just being struck with a stone.

At 600 meters against that beast! What am I thinking? Engelmann blamed himself.

The Tiger now turned to his panzers. Engelmann only saw smoke blurting of the Tiger's main gun barrel, then he heard the detonation of the shell as an earth-shaking bang somewhere behind his tank. Only then did the thunder of the shot echo over his company's combat vehicles. Suddenly, however, something tugged with brute force at Franzi. It clattered terribly, as if a thousand metal pots fell rattling on a stone floor. The whole tank concussed, shaking like a bull in the arena.

Then Franzi died.

The engine gurgled, shut down, and all the electronics turned off. Inside it was pitch-dark, only through the many but narrow vison blocks did even a shard of light infiltrate. Engelmann was immediately

77

reminded of an opera hall as the lights were switched off before the show began. His injured hand trembled, but this time he had been able to hold himself on the seat.

"The Ivan's taking the bread out of our mouth," Ludwig muttered, and Jahnke nodded strongly. Münster pressed the starter several times, and eventually he hammered repeatedly on it with his fist, but nothing happened. Filthy curses left his lips.

Now, however, some other big gun started to fire – at the rest of 9th Company. Meter-high flower bouquets of dirt shot out of the ground in five-second intervals in between the company's panzers, then the tank codenamed Anna 2 received several hits in a row. The right track got completely shredded; metal parts whirled in all directions. Projectiles slammed into the panzer, cracking the armor. Glowing chunks were ripped off and hurled through the air. After one and a half minutes, the spectacle was over. Anna 2 was standing still with her track destroyed, and Anna 3 had used her smoke launchers to fog herself in and was lying in wait. The enemy Tiger's main gun banged again, but was now, however, zeroed in on the panzers of 12th Company. Its shell whistled threateningly past the German tanks and detonated far back. 12th Company had not fled, but tore into the hostile steel monster with everything it could offer. German 5-centimeter shells hit the Tiger with little effect. Engelmann held his breath. That thing was indestructible! Damned made in Germany quality!

Abruptly, that other big gun fired again. The Germans had not been able to reconnoiter its position yet. Its bombardment now impacted at 12th Company, where an explosion suddenly erupted from one of the tanks. Scalding hot metal parts were ricocheting around.

The racket breached into Engelmann's panzer as a dull background noise, wooing the tankers with ice-cold fingers. Carefully – very carefully - Engelmann stretched out upwards to the lids of his cupola. There were circular, quite narrow vision blocks, through which he could get a panoramic view of what was going on now. He saw the Tiger in front of his tank, its main gun aligned on the tanks of 12th Company. Engelmann got the impression that one track of the Tiger was already torn to pieces from all the bombardment by Panzer IIIs and IVs, but he couldn't be sure.

He also saw Soviet paratroopers emerge from the grass near the 12th and hurl grenades at the tanks. One Panzer III spotted the infantrymen and turned. It already had the Russians right in front of the barrel of its hull machine gun. But it didn't shoot, instead it accelerated and buried the startled men under its chassis weighing tons. The grinding tracks squeezed them into the ground and chopped them to fleshy mud. Since the supply situation was so dire, the Wehrmacht had issued the slogan "Rolling is better than shooting" to all tank men, and the German soldiers followed this gruesome order with grim insistence, which made meat pâté out of people.

Suddenly Engelmann spotted that enemy's big gun. He recognized, almost invisible in the high grass, the long, flattened path the glider had ploughed into the vegetation during landing. At the end of that path the engineless plane rested – completely covered by the undergrowth – but Engelmann made out something metallic and shiny, between blades of grass and fern, that flashed in the setting sun.

An AT-gun shield! went through his head. Again the Tiger shot from the woodland edge, and again it completely missed its target.

"Thank God we've stayed right in front of the Tiger's barrel," Münster joked in an attempt at gallows humor. "Apparently we're safest there." Ludwig and Jahnke grinned, but Nitz stared at his commander with a tense face. The lieutenant had long forgotten the Tiger and found a much more rewarding target for Franzi's 5-centimeter cannon.

But what good did that do? They couldn't shoot without electronics.

"Theo!" Engelmann hissed. "Nine o'clock, 250. Enemy AT-gun." Ludwig pulled himself up and looked outside, then he nodded.

"What shall we do, Sepp?" he asked dejectedly. "Franzi's dead."

Ludwig fired the coaxial machine gun instead, but the bullets burst and bounced off at the AT-gun's shield like hail. Unimpressed, the Russian gun crew kept shooting at German tanks. 12th Company took a massive beating. Even if the gunner of that captured Tiger wasn't exactly Deadeye Dick, the enemy Paratroopers and the anti-tank gun at the glider gave it hell. Six panzers had already been destroyed or severely damaged. Engelmann realized in this second that the entire battle was on a knife's edge. Back at the airfield, there was incredible turmoil. German grenadiers stormed the runways and hangars from two sides. They were about to throw the Russian paratroopers off the airbase. Tanks of Panzer Regiment 2 rattled into the middle of the chaos, giving the beleaguered Russians an additional kick in the ass. Meanwhile, half-track vehicles pushed their way towards the woods with their machine-guns blazing, then stopped at the forest edge and unloaded grenadier infantry. These stormed under covering fire into the undergrowth and busted the partisan's chops. The situation also improved among the panzer units ambushed by the paratroopers. Burgsdorff and his staff had reacted quickly and built a circular laager of the tanks – an iron defensive ring. From this position, they took the enemy infantry under crossfire and left it no chance. The Russians were swept away like grass under the strokes of a scythe.

In the air, the fight continued unabated, but now far away. At Engelmann's position, on the eastern flank of the battlefield, the Russians threatened to cement their positions. And the lieutenant was fully aware of the consequences: The airfield was again in German hands; all enemy paratroopers had been thrown back into the high grass of the plain. Russian artillery rounds then immediately fell on the runways again. The projectiles were accurately smashing the aircraft hangars and pelting the panzers of Panzer Regiment 2. Evidently, the paratroopers had artillery observers with them who were now passing target coordinates to the rear batteries.

Engelmann bit his lower lip, then he made a decision.

"Stay here and hold this position." That got him startled gazes from his crew, but Engelmann had no time for further explanations. He opened the lid of his hatch and climbed outside with a "Cover me!", then he immediately jumped off the turret and disappeared into the grass. A few meters behind him, Anna 2 lay motionless. Engelmann sprinted on, past some holes that AT-gun shells had dug. After all, the craters were small, so it couldn't be a big caliber. He pulled out his pistol, although he knew that if there were well-trained paratroopers nearby, he wouldn't stand a chance. They would kill him without hesitation.

Engelmann kept running, the high grass blocking his sight. Razor-sharp, slender green fingers tried to grab him. The racket of the fighting sounded in different mechanical and organic voices.

Only when he had reached Anna 2 did he realize that the tank hadn't just been out of action because of a shredded crawler track. It smelled of fire, and fine smoke fumes seeped from every crevice of the panzer. Gunthermann and his men must have burned to death inside.

A dull bang echoed over the plain. Again the Tiger had shot, again he had not scored a hit. But at some point the gunner would learn – or at least be lucky. Engelmann had to hurry. Even the anti-tank gun was still firing rounds at the panzers of 12th Company. Its barks continued to echo across the grassland. In the distance, a great volume of small-arms fire was reverberating.

Engelmann sneaked past the destroyed tank. About 15 meters beyond was Anna 3, where the artificial fog from the smoke launchers was slowly clearing. Apparently Klaus had recognized that the lieutenant was on his way to him, because he was keeping his panzer lying motionless.

Suddenly Engelmann's nose picked up the biting stench of burning oil – and then something else. It was a sweet, almost pleasant scent. For a moment Engelmann gave in to the smell, absorbing the aroma. That treacly odor bewitched his senses ... it was the smell of burnt flesh. This realization abruptly hit him with the force of a thousand fists. He was struck by dizziness while his legs turned to pudding. He staggered and was in danger of falling. What he saw lost its color, and his field of vision narrowed. He only saw infinite blades of grass in front of him. Only the deep cough of the Tiger's 88-millimeter cannon brought Engelmann back to reality, as if someone had poured a bucket of ice-cold water over his head. He shook himself. The smell had disappeared from his nose.

Muzzle flashes twitched over the edge of the forest not far away from Engelmann's position. First he did not notice what the enemy was shooting at, then a projectile clanged against the sizzling Anna 2. But Ludwig was on his toes. He swung Franzi's turret around to the woods and opened fire. The MG stroked the forest edge, and all enemy fire stopped. Then smoke grenades flew out of the open commander's hatch of Anna 3. Within seconds, the tank had disappeared under a white hood. Engelmann sprinted over to the artificial fog bell and climbed the hull of the panzer. At once Klaus opened the lid flaps of the

83

cupola and looked out. The continuing roar of airplanes dominated the din of battle, even as the Russian AT-guns and the Tiger were still firing. Apparently, however, even that damned gun did not have an infinite supply of ammunition, so its crew had given up continuously firing at everything and anything and was now sparingly targeting shots, causing powerful sparks to splash over the steel of German tanks and, above all, inflicting damage every time they hit a tank's track. The enemy fire was still concentrating on 12th Company, whose panzers were enduring bravely under the attacks while fighting off paratroopers, who attacked again and again out of nowhere. Even an Iron Gustav – yet another nickname for the Shturmowik – had gotten into the action, sweeping over the formation of German panzers and firing rockets at them. But the Russian steel bird, too, had had no luck.

"Herr Leutnant?" Klaus looked at Engelmann with a grim expression.

"Nine o'clock, around 300, enemy AT-gun at the glider. Kill it immediately!"

Klaus stretched his body to the extreme, but he could not see anything. "I can't see it," he yelled.

"You have to drive up! You'll recognize it if you're next to my tin can."

"Well, then, hold on, Lieutenant."

Engelmann clung to the armor side-skirt around the turret while Klaus gave the order to pull away. Following Engelmann's direction, the tank first jerked and then drove on at half speed.

"Prepare to fire!" Klaus shouted into his throat microphone. After a few seconds the At-gun position at the glider became visible, so at least it could be approximated. Engelmann's target directions helped. Klaus' gunner turned the turret accordingly, then fired. The shot shook the tank and almost threw Engelmann off, forcing him to hold on to the turret side-skirt with all his strength. A burning pain shot through his injured hand.

He gritted his teeth and concentrated on keeping his balance. The glider flew apart in front of him, and the Russian gun remained silent, its mangled body revealed by the pressure-wave-flattened grass.

Engelmann knocked appreciatively against the steel of the turret. Klaus grinned.

"Klaus, you're the whole damned pride of the 9th, now that my Franzi's gone, too."

"I thought so. I'm just glad you're still in one piece."

"Stop licking my boots!" They both granted themselves a small moment of celebration that they were still alive.

"Drive over to the commander of the 12th and see if Hauptmann Stollwerk needs your help. Looks like he could use it."

"The only prize missing is that Tiger."

Engelmann with a nod of his head indicated the sky, which was again controlled by German warplanes. The few remaining Russian aircrafts were in great distress.

Klaus saluted casually, then he disappeared into his cupola. Engelmann got back on his feet again and set off back to his tank. From the corner of his eye, he saw

85

how the Tiger suddenly swiveled its muzzle exactly to his position.

Thank you, Lord, for finally aiming at us. Then at least we're safe! The thought actually brought a pinched grin to his face. But then new muzzle smoke shot from the cannon of the Tiger. Instinctively, Engelmann threw himself to the ground, while Anna 3 behind him burst into a thousand flying pieces, buzzing around. There was nothing left of Klaus' tank but a ripped-open and now burning chassis.

With a cry strangled in his throat, Engelmann made an exclamation of horror as he pulled himself together and watched the steel behemoth at the edge of the forest through the tips of the grasses. The Tiger's armor was perforated by hits, however, it was simply no mean task to knock that beast out.

North of Oryol, Soviet Union, June 4th, 1943

The reconnaissance squadron was given a day off, after the mechanized forces of the Wehrmacht had pushed the Russians back a few kilometers farther north. The fronts were now facing each other at the hill of the one-horse-town Borilovo. Berning's unit would also move to the front in the evening hours to seal off the road to Oryol, east of Kamenka.

Currently the men of 2nd Platoon were located in a lonely kolkhoz north of Oryol. In addition to the soldiers, there were even a few civilians who had been hit hardest by the war. They were homeless, had nothing to eat, and many were injured or sick. Infant wailing filled the air above the collective farm.

"The drill for fighting side by side with a tank killer or assault gun must be familiar to all of you in theory, but in the past, I have all too often noticed that you have considerable practical knowledge gaps in this area." Staff Sergeant Pappendorf looked into the exhausted faces of his men, who had gathered in the barn of the farmhouse for unit training lessons.

The soldiers stood lined up – sitting down on the ground was not allowed by platoon leader Pappendorf. He was at daggers drawn with anything that could give a soldier some rest.

So they all stood there at ease, which meant that their feet were shoulder-width apart, their left foot slightly in front, and their arms hanging straight down.

In front on the right was poor Berning. He felt a dull pain in his coccyx and an itching one in his feet. He definitely did not want to stand any longer, because he and the men had already spent the entire morning standing while cleaning their weapons. Normally this was done sitting down – even under Pappendorf – but the staff sergeant had forbidden his men to talk. Someone had disobeyed at some point and said something, so the whole platoon had to clean weapons standing up for five hours, then take their meager rations standing up, and now also endure these lessons standing up. Meanwhile the other platoons of the company lazed around, because in them both the soldiers and the NCOs were glad to be allowed a short respite after the hard fighting of the last days. Pappendorf was the only one who had no concept of breathing space. He knew only combat, training, and drill.

"So what do you think," Pappendorf continued, striding up and down in front of his men with his arms folded behind his back. The staff sergeant's silver-colored combat aiguillette with the gold-plated shield at the shoulder, which represented the 10th time that he got that award, dangled beside the other medals on his uniform.

Pappendorf finally stopped, slowly bobbing forwards and backwards, assessing his entire platoon. All the soldiers looked spic and span. What could be cleaned and sewn was immediately cleaned and sewn. This Pappendorf had made sure yesterday evening, when the squadron had finally been moved to this collective farm after 45 hours of fierce fighting, including the exhausting pursuit of retreating Russian forces. The other platoons had gone for a lie-down and still looked like miners today. Pappendorf, however, kept order in his platoon. And he had a very pedantic understanding of order.

"So what do you think," he reiterated, "why did I schedule exactly this class for this evening?"

"Because you hate us," Lenz threw in impertinently. In Pappendorf's eyes, young Private First Class Lenz was one good soldier – and sometimes he allowed good soldiers to actually take liberties with him. The staff sergeant turned up his nose at this statement, while some of the men chuckled tiredly. Berning didn't laugh. Berning was seething.

Because you're a son of a bitch! he stormed in his mind. *Because you're the greatest man-hating slave-driver of all time*! Pure hate filled the sergeant's soul. His legs burned awfully. A deep exhaustion tried to knock him to the ground. Slowly he leaned forward and hoped to keep his flabby body a little longer at ease. His eyes almost closed, meanwhile nothing other than anger flooded his insides.

"Not at all because I hate you," Pappendorf spoke slowly, emphasizing every single syllable. "I know I'm tough. But this epic struggle of two nations makes it a necessity. If you hate me for it, believe it or not, I can understand that. But one day you'll thank me. Maybe years after this war has ended, but one day you'll thank me."

Pappendorf looked at his soldiers with little sympathy, and now he continued undiminished: "Well, why am I teaching you this? Who can tell me that?"

"Because our kampfgruppe has two Sturmgeschütz battalions, and therefore it may happen that we have to

89

fight together with them," emerged from PFC Lenz, quick like a shot.

"Exactly! Marder 2, Panzerjäger 1, and Ferdinand are steely comrades, whom you may meet in the coming days on the battlefield – especially since one tank killer unit is currently at Kamenka, in readiness to move forward." Pappendorf nodded contentedly. "As the great Field Marshal Rommel always likes to say, there is nothing better for the soldier than good education. Following this slogan, I'll be with you for the next two and a half hours… "

Oh, no, Berning thought. He had to resist an urge to just fall over.

"...to discuss the theoretical basics of joint operations with a tank killer, and to check your willingness to learn outside at the sandbox, where we will go through different situations. I expect the highest concentration from everyone, because hardly anything is more dangerous than fighting in the immediate vicinity of a tracked vehicle without knowing how to behave. And believe me, comrades, the Wehrmacht can't afford to lose men because they got under the treads or clogged the barrel of a tank killer. Always remember the principle: Even a small limb can trigger an early detonation of an explosive round.

If you survive any such stupidity – and I can only advise you not to survive it – the tank killer commander will kick you in the balls… "

Pappendorf turned his head to the left, then to the right, and pressed his lips together into a narrow line.

"…and then I'll breathe down your neck so bad that you'll wish the shell's blast had blown your skulls off."

Pappendorf let these words work on the men for a moment, while Berning's eyelids became heavier and heavier. A fatiguing tiredness settled on the room and pressed against the soldiers from above like a cover made of concrete, but nobody dared to move.

Berning went over and over in his mind that Pappendorf always had to pronounce such idiotic threats, and he tried to frighten away his tiredness, *None of us intends to stuff scrap metal into our own tanks in battle!*

"I will also teach you how a tank killer or assault gun engages the enemy in battle, how they set up hillside positions, how they conduct a surprise fire, how they ... BERNING!"

Pappendorf shouting his name scared the hell out of him. The pictures in his head evaporated, and the image of a quivering cardboard village materialized before his eyes.

"What were you thinking loitering in my formation like a crooked Slav grandma? Attention!" Pappendorf spat out his words. Moist speckles showered the men in the front row.

"Jawohl, Herr Unterfeldwebel!" Berning moaned and pushed his back straight, but Pappendorf still didn't seem satisfied. With a threatening look and loud steps, he approached the sergeant until their two nose-tips were only a centimeter apart.

"Unteroffizier, I said attention!"

Berning didn't know what Pappendorf wanted. He was shifting around his body.

"Come on, Berning. Come on or I forget myself... "

"Herr ... Herr Unterfeldwebel, I'm standing at... "

"No, Comrade Lace-up! You aren't," screamed Pappendorf as he spit in Berning's face. The sergeant reflexively closed his eyes, as if his platoon leader were about to beat him at any moment.

"H.Dv. 130/2a, first chapter, page eight. The left foot is slightly placed in the forward position!"

"Yes, Sir." Berning immediately took a tiny step forward with his left foot. To Pappendorf, such little things were sometimes enough to get punished with an extra watch shift. Once the staff sergeant even gave one poor landser one week of arrest, after he had caught him three times with an "improper" uniform. Pappendorf was one dangerous fellow.

"I expect my NCOs to know the rules!" he hissed. Berning – embarrassed on the outside – burned inside with a true firestorm of rage.

There are 10,000 regulations in the Wehrmacht, you gorilla! How can one expect to know them all? he raved inwardly, but nevertheless had to admit that Pappendorf – although he certainly did not know everything – had always been able to quote the document corresponding to a situation.

"Gee, Berning!" rustled Pappendorf at the end of his tirade. Once again, the platoon leader had humiliated him in front of all his comrades. The staff sergeant then continued with his lecture. For three quarters of an hour he recited about the interaction of tank killers and infantrymen, explained to his men how to communicate with the tank men, how to assign targets to them by tracer bullets, and how to fight disembarked enemy soldiers out with the machine gun.

Berning attended the class with an exhaustion that threatened to collapse him; but also with a hatred that made him tremble.

At some point the large wooden door to the barn opened, and Lieutenant Balduin, commanding officer of the squadron, entered. His most prominent distinguishing feature was a very clearly receding chin. Balduin had joined the squadron straight from the replacement depot. Despite his lack of combat experience, he had shown himself to be a useful commander in the battles of the last few days.

Pappendorf interrupted his speech in the middle of a word and yelled: "Achtung!" Immediately he and his soldiers stood still. Then he duly reported to the officer.

"Unterfeldwebel Pappendorf, step forward," the lieutenant said with a pleased undertone.

"Jawohl, Herr Leutnant." Pappendorf took a step forward and stood directly opposite Balduin with his lips pressed against each other and his chest thrust out.

"Herr Unterfeldwebel," Balduin began, "since you took over the platoon, you have led it in exemplary fashion. In the struggle for Naryshkino, the 2nd Platoon under your leadership destroyed four enemy tanks. I'm promoting you to master sergeant."

Balduin smiled broadly and shook Pappendorf's hand.

"Give me your service book, will ya? I'll directly register the promotion."

Pappendorf did as he was told. None of those present noticed at that moment that one German non-commissioned officer with Austrian origin was standing in the front row, threatening to burst with rage – his fingers quaking and his thoughts already reaching for his rifle.

Mikoyanovka, Soviet Union, June 4th, 1943

The captured Tiger's last hour had come when the sun set. While the Russian airborne attack had been repelled and the Red Army had lost an entire battalion of valuable paratroopers, the surviving partisans had fled back into the forest. Only the tankers of that damned Tiger had not yet recognized their unfortunate sitrep, and continued to sprinkle the grassland plain with explosive rounds. This way they tried to scare the Germans off, since both tracks of their Tiger were torn to pieces. Their tank could move no more. And it should run out of ammunition any moment now.

The German panzers had withdrawn behind the airfield and thus outside the range of the Tiger, because the order had been given not to destroy the hijacked tank, but to recapture it as intact as possible, since every single combat vehicle was valuable to a German army that was on its last legs.

Now the still-furious steely predator menacing the airstrip was crept up on from two sides by German panzergrenadiers. Like ants overpowering a huge beetle, they finally jumped on the hull of the Tiger. The turret of the tank began to beat angrily at the soldiers, and to shake like a dog's tail. The Tiger's MG barked, but the infantrymen stayed out of its effective range. Muzzles of submachine guns were inserted into all openings, triggers were pressed. The salvos resounded through the inside of the tank with a clanging sound. The Tiger didn't move no more. The Red Army had lost this battle – but with the help of a bold airborne assault and the support of partisans, it had inflicted considerable losses on the German armored forces in the area without using a single tank. 29 combat vehicles of Panzer Regiment 2 were destroyed or left in need of repair on the plain, and another seven wreckages of former panzers were located directly on the runways of the airfield. The regiment had finally been whittled down to a battalion - and 9th Company had ceased to exist.

Engelmann and his men, however, still existed. Meanwhile, Burgsdorff, the commander of Panzer Regiment 2, had summoned the battalion commanders and all company leaders to a location west of the airfield that was in between two tree-covered ground waves. The remaining operable panzers of the regiment collected themselves at the same time in the light forest that could be found behind those ground waves. Tall but thin birches rose up there and offered the German tanks at least a minimum of protection through their lush canopy of leaves. White bark, as wrinkled as the skin of a 100-year-old, peeled from the trunks. The thin trees were, in an emergency, no obstacle for a tank. In addition, the birch trees stood far enough apart so that the entire regiment could easily hide in the forest.

Engelmann and his crew squatted on the back hull of a Panzer IV of 10th Company, and were thus transported away from the battlefield and to the regiment's assembly point. The tank men of the regiment left their dead behind for the time being, because von Burgsdorff had called for haste. They, or other German forces, would later take care of the fallen.

The Panzer IV came to a halt, rattling, in front of one ground wave. Engelmann and his men jumped off, while the lieutenant called a word of thanks to the tank commander. Once he set off in search of the other officers between the ground waves, his crew remained in place – what else could they do? The regiment had finally run out of panzers to operate for them.

Lieutenant Engelmann spotted one of the other officers, just disappearing behind the crest of the ground wave, and followed him. As he did, he heard metal clanging on metal and the surging of aircraft engines echoing from the airfield at his back. He paid his comrades from the Luftwaffe respect in spirit, for the fact that they had endured so long directly at the front. But now they were hectically preparing for relocation, because if the enemy could somehow manage to break through here, the planes of two squadrons would fall into his hands. That would be a disaster. The last hours had delivered evidence enough that this threat was real.

Lieutenant Engelmann managed to find his regimental commander standing in a group of senior officers. Von Burgsdorff was a skinny man in his late 50s, sporting a Hitler memorial mustache on his upper lip, otherwise distinguished only by his extremely high forehead. A round pair of nickel-frame glasses were enthroned on his nose. In Engelmann's eyes, von Burgsdorff was a bungler – a lawyer whose military training and combat experience came from the last war – no comparison to his predecessor Sieckenius, who had climbed the career ladder based on his great performance in the battle for the Kursk salient. He was now the commander of the whole combat formation.

When the last officers arrived, von Burgsdorff immediately began his briefing. Right at the beginning, he pointed out that they had no time to lose. The regiment had to intervene instantly. Engelmann wrinkled his nose while listening to the words of his regimental commander. The situation was difficult: enemy breakthroughs in several front sectors. Belgorod was on the brink of being lost, and with it the whole southern connection to the troops near Kursk. Enemy airborne landings blocked the Belgorod-Stalino railway line. Further west, a Russian armored attack formation had swept over the German lines, and had been stopped only at Nikolskoye – a mere 20 kilometers from the center of Belgorod. German positions were being contested by the Soviet forces on both sides of the Donets.

Engelmann shook his head. Kampfgruppe Sieckenius, which had been stuffed into holes everywhere in the front line as a emergency reserve, did not have enough quick reaction forces to be able to help everywhere. At the same time, he was horrified to discover that the Russians had done their homework. The enemy's paratroopers had been deployed specifically against German railway lines, connecting roads, airstrips, command posts, and telecommunication outposts before Russian main forces troops assaulted the front lines. Thus the Russians found the Germans in many places confused and weakened and unable to resupply and reorganize, and had therefore achieved all these small breakthroughs. It was the same old story: The Wehrmacht, which in 1939/1940 had put the world's most powerful armies in their place by conducting joint operations of infantry, artillery, the Luftwaffe and independently operating tank forces, taught its enemies the lessons of modern warfare with every battle. Neither the Western powers nor the Russians were so ossified as to be unable to adapt and evolve. In 1940, the Wehrmacht had fought against British formations that still used tanks exclusively as support weapons for the infantry, slowing them down and lessening their unique firepower. Now the Germans would no longer be lucky enough to meet such idiocies from the enemy. That was the way it was with the Soviets. Just when Engelmann, after countless encounters with the enemy, had again come to the conclusion that Ivan was merely taking everything in man and material that he could get hold of and threw it into battle, the Russians surprised him with such insights of warfare as the airborne assault in advance of an conventional attack. Now, however, it was necessary to find an appropriate response to the latest Russian attack moves – and Major General Sieckenius believed that he had found it in an advance against Nikolskoye. There the enemy stood closest to Belgorod, and there a Russian breakthrough was the greatest threat, because at this hour only two decimated companies with machine guns and two captured Russian AT-guns defended the whole city. By some miracle and the clever use of weapons, the defenders had been able to convince the Russians that there was a whole regiment or more entrenched there. But Ivan could not be led around by the nose indefinitely. So Panzer Regiment 2 had to march to the sound of the guns.

Von Burgsdorff ended his assessment with the sober statement that 9th Company no longer existed, but that the regiment structure would nevertheless be maintained.

At last one good idea from you, Engelmann commented to himself, while the officers were drifting apart with lead-gray faces.

It was clear to Engelmann that he was actually out of the game for the time being. Then, suddenly, a shiver came over him as a completely different idea came to his mind: he had already had to hand over four of his tankers and all of his replacement men; that was when the Kampfgruppe Sieckenius had been build overnight, and the order was given that anyone who could not be accommodated in a tank would be temporarily integrated into the infantry, because every single company fighting in the sector of Army Group Center badly needed men to fill up their ranks. The poor devils from Engelmann's unit were now wandering around with all the dogfaces, a rifle in their hands and nothing more than a wet foxhole to sleep, live, and fight in.

At first the lieutenant had assumed that he would be attached to the impedimenta – a truly horrible fate for a soldier and officer like Engelmann, who did not want to see his men in battle while he himself sat in the viewing stand. But now it occurred to him that an even

100

worse fate could come to pass for his crew and for him; that of improvised infantrymen.

"Josef?" The somber voice of the 12th's commander ripped Engelmann away from his thoughts. The lieutenant shook himself briefly, then he looked around and saw a big captain trudge up to him. Engelmann shook hands with his comrade. They exchanged serious looks.

"I'm sorry about your men," whispered Captain Arno Stollwerk, a man with grey-blue eyes and a rugged visage who originated from the outskirts of Gdańsk. The sigils of the disbanded Waffen SS flashed on his collar. Stollwerk had never made a secret of where he came from – and since he was a good soldier and officer, his superiors let him carry on with this improper uniform.

"Yes." Engelmann could only nod.

"Do you still have your crew?"

"Yeah, we got lucky. Not a scratch." Engelmann smiled weakly.

"Well, as luck would have it, I have a panzer for you – a III. No scratches, either."

Engelmann gaped at Stollwerk, eyes opened wide.

"Just follow me. My boys took the tin can with them to the assembly point."

Engelmann nodded and could not suppress his joy. He straightaway felt ebullient.

"But you should take a few minutes and clean the inside," the captain finally added with a sharp voice. "Those forsaken Bolsheviks have made a godawful mess in that tank; I can tell you."

101

Meanwhile night had arrived, throwing its dark cloak over the land. The regiment advanced in column formation at the paved main road to Belgorod, and from there the German panzers now took the road to Nikolskoye. On their way to Belgorod, they had come across Russian forces at one point blocking the road. A vanguard of the enemy had apparently slipped through the German lines and positioned itself in wait directly in front of the gates of Belgorod. But the regiment was needed more urgently in Nikolskoye, which was why the watchword was given to step on the gas, break through, and push on to the regiment's destination.

The breakthrough had been accomplished. Now the panzers of the regiment were on the road to the south, and a few kilometers before them – wrapped in complete darkness – opened up to Nikolskoye, a small village with only a few hundred inhabitants, of whom most had escaped the war by fleeing. Its strategic importance lay in the bridge over the River Toplinka, a narrow tributary of the Donets, because to the west of the Toplinka's source the area was marshy and therefore not passable at all. Of course, the river could also be crossed without a bridge, but that would take time due to the steep embankments in many places, especially to get vehicles and tanks across. And around Nikolskoye itself, the ground was swampy and difficult to traverse, so that in this front section all ways over the river went through this battle-tossed town, where every house had already been barraged to ruins.

The long column of tanks and vehicles moved down the road with only blackout lights switched on and at half speed, so that it was difficult to navigate either by eye or ear. Covered little lamps pointed downward, illuminating tiny segments of the road ahead, and the little pools of light moved evenly towards the south. In the area just ahead of the regiment's advance, lightning flashed as gunfire and the rattle of small arms slowly swelled to a new concert of death. The last remaining officer in Nikolskoye, a captain named Droste, asked the staff of Kampfgruppe Sieckenius almost every minute when the reinforcements would arrive. The Reds were already probing his positions again, and had belatedly realized that there were only a handful of Germans left manning the defenses.

"Not so much gas, Hans," Engelmann warned when his driver let the tank get too close to the panzer ahead again. Münster made an annoyed sound, but obeyed.

With set faces, Engelmann and his crew remained in their new Panzer III and endured its rumbling and rattling. The tankers were overtired and exhausted. The fatigue was close to shutting their eyes. Münster stared apathetically through his narrow eye slit into the darkness outside, where he could barely recognize the tank driving in front of him as a blunt outline in the twilight of the camouflage lighting.

Within the column, they rolled along with 12th Company, which Engelmann now graced with his own expertise. In their new tank, it stank with the horrible sour smell of corpses – the bodies of the dead crew had fermented in the evening sun for an hour. Due to the lack of time and the dwindling light, Engelmann and his men had not been able to completely remove all the blood – the interior of the vehicle had virtually been awash in the red ink of life. They had only wiped it once with two blankets, which weren't particularly absorbent. The armatures, levers, and chairs in the tank were still sticky. Engelmann thanked the Lord that it was now too dark to see where he had reached again. In the dim glow of the interior lighting, he, however, sensed the dried blood sticking to his hands, and he was delighted that no one had been burned in this tank. Not only because it had to be a cruel death, but also because Engelmann, strangely enough, had a feeling that he couldn't stand the smell anymore since experiencing it when his former loader Eduard Born had been hit during the Russian outbreak attempt in the pocket of Kursk.

"That's disgusting!" Ludwig kept moaning and shaking. He had sat down directly in a pool of blood that they had completely overlooked while cleaning. Now his trousers were wet and clotted, as the blood dried slowly. A wet pair of trousers would certainly not have bothered anyone considering the level of heat in the panzer. But the knowledge of what was really stuck on their uniforms and hands tugged at the nerves of the men in a way that hunger or cold could not.

Ludwig licked his chapped lips. Engelmann looked over at him. In the darkness, a pale pair of eyes glanced out from Ludwig's dirt-crusted face, an expression full of fatigue and listlessness. The facial expressions of the others were not much different.

"I am thirsty to death," Ludwig whispered. "And I could puke if I think too hard about what we're sitting in here."

"Thirsty? Goddamn right," Münster responded and rubbed his face. "But *I'll* puke if I have another sip of that salty tea we've had for days." Ludwig nodded heftily, and Jahnke also signaled approval.

Engelmann felt the same way, but as a military leader, he was not allowed to participate in the moaning of his men. Instead, he said, "Stay on your toes a little longer. Only this village left, then they will let us get some rest ... they have to."

"Hopefully, Sepp." Ludwig's voice was thin.

"What kind of water would I take!" Münster hissed. "Just ordinary water! I mean, it doesn't even have to be beer. Water would be enough for me!"

Then they all went quiet with their own thoughts circling in their minds. Engelmann thought of home. Finally, when the lingering smell of corpses and the stench of oil had settled in Engelmann's nose like a tick and he was overcome by the feeling that a noose of stinging fog was strangling him, he suddenly pushed his body upwards and threw the hatch lids open on both sides. He stretched his upper body out of the tank and felt the relief as the fresh night air flowed into his lungs.

After minutes of silence, Münster spoke again: "And something decent to eat. That would be fine." He got approval from the others. "I mean, really something real. The brass can start to gorge on those shabby meat pies themselves!"

"Wait and see. Once the big battles are over, we'll be better taken care of." Engelmann's answer was half-hearted and unconvincing. He almost didn't believe it himself. He too was aware that the soldier's life was an existence full of privation, but as the war continued, everything became more and more difficult. Hot meals were now a rarity, dry bread and shoddy side dishes the rule. The National Socialists had always talked about the Germans as the master race. Well, if Engelmann looked at it that way, he had found out that at present, about twelve million German men were living anything but a master-race existence. But such thoughts he quickly wiped away. The situation was what it was. He couldn't help it. He could only make the best of it.

"No!" was Münster's response to Engelmann's attempt to keep hope alive. "I've been doing this shit for three years now. And for three years, they've been saying, 'Wait a minute, it's gonna get better.' I'm 26 now. How much longer do I have to wait? I spend my best years waiting for better times! I'm really starting to get mad at our highly-praised brass, especially the new one since our Führer has died, when I see all this!" Anger had boiled over in Münster and now gushed out with every syllable the sergeant spoke. While his hands continued to rest on the steering levers, he now shook his head vigorously and distorted his face. "They all can fuck off," he grumbled. Afterwards the tankers went silent again and resigned themselves to the rattling of the tank engine, while the whole panzer vibrated to the movement of the tracks. Engelmann wrinkled his forehead. Small things like the poor

106

supply – the lack of fuel, ammunition, and everything else – meant daily new deprivations and burdens for the German soldiers, which certainly did not make the war more bearable for them. Engelmann's soul also was increasingly burdened by the difficult overall situation, but now for the first time he had experienced how quickly morale could deteriorate – how dangerous it was to deprive the German soldier of any basis for hope in his life, draining it away with a thousand tiny pinpricks. But he couldn't change that either. There he was, a lieutenant, a mediocrity in this huge army. And so they drove, mute, along the road. They slowly rumbled toward the lightning created by humans fighting against humans, and the thunder generated by apparatuses they had invented solely for the purpose of killing their own kind. The radio stayed soundless. Silence on the airwaves was ordered, so no Russian listening post could pick up what was moving towards Nikolskoye.

After about three minutes, Münster broke the hush again: "Franzi is kicking up some vibration I don't like at all."

Engelmann listened, "Something bad?"

"I can't say, Sepp. It's only that I can feel the levers vibrating oddly. Maybe the steering is fucked? But Franzi's still running."

Engelmann just nodded, while Jahnke mumbled, "Franzi's dead, man."

"Then make a suggestion for a new name. You can go right out and paint it on the gun." Münster grinned diabolically, but Jahnke pondered immediately.

"How about Elfriede?" he threw around.

New rage seized Münster. "No! Shut the fuck up! I don't care what this screwed tin can's called," he ranted. "We call her Franzi II. That's it." After a few seconds, Münster looked up mischievously, blinking at the lieutenant: "Unless Herr Leutnant has something against it?"

"It's all right." Franzi II it was.

Nikolskoye, Soviet Union, June 4th, 1943

"Ivan's coming again," moaned Private Emil Walther resignedly when he heard a Russian call from afar echoing over the plain. He looked over the projectile-eaten windowsill into the verge, which was shrouded in complete darkness.

"Now they're finally going to bash us up," whispered his comrade, Private First Class Remigius "Remme" Tillmann, his pale face visible under his stahlhelm despite the darkness.

"Shut up, you two whiners!" Sergeant Hans-Joachim "Ha-Jo" Brinkmann intervened verbally. "You two crybabies are nothing to write home about!" His strong dialect revealed that he came from the depths of Bavaria.

"But ..." Walther began, to be immediately stalled by Brinkmann: "No buts! Our tanks are coming. They're gonna make Ivan leg it. Until then, we have to hold out."

At that moment the Russian Ratsch Bumms tossed another salvo into the city center of Nikolskoye. The buildings shook under the impacts, but they did not bring any further losses to Anti-tank Battalion 355. It had already been badly affected by the fighting of the last few days. Again and again the enemy's artillery fire cascaded into the village, without the Russians having really understood where the German positions were. The defenders of Nikolskoye still believed they were fooling the enemy about their true strength.

Walther, Tillmann, and Brinkmann squatted in an arbor riddled with bullet holes at the southern end of the village and listened into the night, but no further noises could be heard. Only the chirping of insects and the cracking of branches in the wind broke the silence of the scenery.

Suddenly there were a lot of dark figures in the distance, rushing over the plain with long leaps.

"There!" Brinkmann growled. "The Russians are coming. Take your positions, men!"

Behind each of the four southeast-facing windows, and thus covering enemy territory, were loaded machine guns and carbines. In addition, an improvised breach in the wall led directly into a trench, which was about 80 meters long and ran along the edge of the village. Tillmann reached under one of the windows and pulled out a machine gun, while at the same time Walther disappeared into the trench. There, also, several loaded weapons waited to be employed. After the heavy fighting of the past few days, the battalion had lost dozens of men. For once, however, there was no shortage of weapons or ammunition.

"Let's show the Russians that there's a whole battalion here!" Brinkmann hissed, and grinned. "Surprise fire on flare gun shot." The sergeant reached for the signal pistol and looked over the windowsill. Several men with rifles in their hands ran across the meadow, sidestepping.

Brinkmann fired the flare gun. With a puff, the projectile left the barrel of the weapon and marched into the firmament, where it turned into a brightly shining star that made the front area of the arbor shine like it was under a spotlight. Immediately the barking of the MGs of Walther and Tillmann began. Fine, glowing lines darted into the foreground, where tracer bullets painted bright spots into the meadow. One of the Soviet soldiers collapsed and began howling. His comrades retreated while shooting wildly.

Brinkmann, Tillmann, and Walther changed weapons almost every second, and thus fired bursts of MG 34, MG 42, and a Russian PPSh, as well as single-fire with carbines. Walther paced up and down the whole trench to simulate fire from different positions.

After a few seconds, the light ball in the sky went out and the cloak of darkness covered the land once more. The Russian who had been hit held his stomach and screamed loudly, while his legs were kicking violently, as if to fend off an attacker. Russian words rang through the night, but the rest of the enemy attackers was no longer visible.

Brinkmann grinned, satisfied, while Walther fell back into the arbor. Snorting, he let himself sink to the floor next to the wall. Brinkmann looked over the windowsill again and saw the fiercely squirming man. His bowl-like helmet, typical of the Red Army, was glaring in the moonlight. It was cruel, but often it was better to wound the enemy than to kill. This had nothing to do with humanity, but was due to the fact that a dead soldier was dead, while a roaring, wounded man was able to demoralize his comrades and immediately tied down half a squad during his rescue. In addition, most soldiers simply did not leave their fellow behind, so Brinkmann and his men only had to wait and see.

The three German soldiers had grabbed K98k carbines in order to be able to fire targeted shots. They looked spellbound into the verge, where the Russian wounded one wriggled like a horse with broken legs. In a wavering voice, he screamed for help. One didn't have to speak Russian to understand the meaning of his desperate shouts.

"I want to see clean belly shots, men," Brinkmann said. His yellow teeth flashed in the darkness. "Always the liver or kidneys. Then the Ivans' definitely done for – but not right away." Walther and Tillmann nodded, their faces grim.

Suddenly, a Russian Maxim machine gun started chattering mechanically. The projectiles randomly scattered into the village. The three German defenders ducked away under their windowsills, but then immediately peered back into the verge. The shrill screeching of the wounded Russian, whose thread of life Atropos had already in between her scissor's blades, still penetrated through the enemy cover fire to the ears of the Germans.

"Yes, Kameraden! There, I tell you!" the sergeant rejoiced. "Ivan can be relied upon! They're about to send in some poor devil."

"The Russians never leave one behind," Tillmann remarked without any irony.

The Soviet attempt to recover the wounded man began at the exact moment the Maxim machine gun fell silent. Two Red Army soldiers raced in bounds over the plain and finally reached the wounded. He moaned and held his stomach while his legs twitched. Brinkmann told his soldiers, by hand signal, to wait for the right moment. Tense, he held his hand in the air and narrowed his eyes to slits, while one of the

112

Russians shifted his submachine gun to his back and then lifted the screamer by the shoulders. The other one crouched next to him, nervously looking around. The enemies were seen only as shadows in the darkness, but shimmered brightly enough in the moonlight, so that no further flare light was necessary.

When the bearer had just settled the wounded man on his shoulders and he continued yowling, Brinkmann let his hand down. One shot each, from the rifles of his two compatriots. Walther caught the bearer in the thigh. The Russian howled and collapsed under the weight of the wounded man, who buried his comrade under himself, still bellowing. Tillmann's bullet slammed into the chest of the squatting Red Army soldier, shattered his solar plexus, and cut the nerve channels that curled around the spine. Immediately the man collapsed, as if he were imploding. He lay there screaming and did not yet know that he would never be able to move his limbs again.

"Sacrament!" said an amazed Brinkmann, "a true medal shot!"

Three screaming Russians were now lying on the verge, and just at this moment the Maxim began to stutter again.

The projectiles sprayed far into Nikolskoye. After only a few seconds the enemy stopped firing, then the background noise again became the screeching of the agonized Russians and their cries for help. In complete desperation, the men croaked. Quantities of blood shot out of ruptured arteries, flowing into their bodies and uniforms. Probably they knew that they would bleed to death, but still did not want to admit their fate, and reared up in a cacophony of lamentation against it.

"Morons!" Brinkmann literally spat out. "Always falling for the same trick."

Walther joked, "That's what you get if you mess with the German Reich," while the Russians on the meadow were struggling to die.

"Didn't the Ivans somehow ... had no choice?" Tillmann remarked. He could not tear his gaze away from the events before him. The screaming of the Russians was soul-shattering.

"Ha, no choice? It's their own fault if they were born in Russia, I'm just saying," Brinkmann said. His words were almost completely drowned out by the horrifying cries of the wounded.

The Red Army soldier with the thigh hit, a stocky man, fought his way out from under the man with the bullet in his stomach. Moaning with exertion, weakened by the already high blood loss and trembling with pain, he heaved himself up and finally managed to kneel on all fours. He lifted his head, as if he wanted to fight against his death sentence, as if he wanted to shout from full lungs: "I am still alive! The Grim Reaper hasn't taken me yet!"

"Iron him over, Emil, will ya?" Brinkmann said while looking on at the spectacle of the fighting Russian. Walther immediately brought his K98k over the windowsill into position and looked over the iron sights at his target. He pulled the trigger. The projectile slammed out of the barrel with a loud rumble, while the carbine drove hard into the shoulder of the PFC. Brightly, the tracer round whipped like a glowing

114

string through the night and zipped past the Russian just next to the skull. He looked around phlegmatically, but because of his high blood loss, he didn't seem to fully understand what was happening around him.

"You blind ox!" Brinkmann raged in a whisper, and ordered Walther to try again. The PFC immediately reloaded his gun and took another shot at the Russian. This one went home and threw the Red Army soldier's helmet off his head with a loud clang. The upper body twitched, reared up once more, then the victim fell over on his back. Blood, shimmering bizarrely in the moonlight, poured over his face like a thousand-legged octopus.

Again, the Maxim went off, and this time the impacts were right next to the arbor. Bullets clapped against the outer walls.

The three Germans took cover before the last Russian burst of fire echoed over the plain.

"Watch out, the next ones will show up soon, I can tell you that. It's going to go on all night now," Brinkmann roared. He nodded triumphantly. And he would be right:

The next ones appeared, but the noise accompanying them made the German soldiers freeze and pale. Tank tracks were squeaking across the meadow ...

Brinkmann ducked away under the windowsill and grasped his weapon tighter, then he pulled a big question mark with his face as he pondered. Walther and Tillmann also disappeared from the windows and took cover.

"*Dawai*! *Dawai*!" Russian shouts rang out over the outer area. "Come on!"

The shiny metal of a T-34 appeared out of the darkness behind the wounded Russians. Infantrymen surrounded their wounded comrades, and the tank rolled directly towards the arbor. A machine gun DP, mounted in the tank's hull, began to speak, stroking the facade of the arbor. At 600 rounds per minute, the Germans had projectiles flying all around their ears. The fire tore the window frames apart, and bullets dug themselves into the walls where they shattered the wood paneling. The Germans threw their hands protectively over their heads, endured the fire, and hoped to be spared.

"Remme, give me the knocker," Brinkmann yelled during a break in the firing from the tank. The crawler tracks of the T-34 continued working their way inexorably towards the German position.

"That thing is gonna squash us like bugs!" Walther screamed at him until Brinkmann realized that silhouettes of Russian infantrymen were advancing behind the tank. Immediately some of the Soviets took care of the wounded.

Meanwhile Tillmann had sprinted to the window next to the breach to the trench, where along with some pistols, hand grenades, and ammunition, a Faustpatrone ordnance device was lying – a narrow wand one meter long, with a warhead at the tip. Tillmann rushed over to Brinkmann, who immediately took the anti-tank weapon from the hand of the PFC.

"Cover me with the machine guns!" the sergeant yelled. Immediately the two grenadiers seized a MG each and pulled the triggers. Muzzles flashed, illuminating the arbor. Tracer bullets raced through the night, bounced off the tank's steely skin, or lost themselves in the distance. The T-34 engine stopped rattling. Only 50 meters lay between it and the arbor. Slowly it aimed its main gun at the Germans, while fire from Russian small arms struck the walls and drilled holes in them.

Brinkmann jumped up. He roughly aimed the Faustpatrone at the tank – this weapon did not have a sight for exact aiming. Brinkmann pulled the trigger. Smoke and hell-hot steam chased from the rear part of the anti-tank weapon and heated up the whole room within a blink of an eye. The warhead, on the other side, darted at the tank and hit the steel colossus to the right of the main gun on the turret. But the charge slid from the sloped armor of the T-34, whirled into the ground, and ignited there in a fluorescent explosion. Flame tongues licked at the Russian tank but could not harm it. Instead, it opened fire and spat an explosive shell into the arbor with a loud roar. The three Germans threw themselves flat on the ground while the building around them was torn apart. Rock chunks and splinters of wood shot through the air, burying the soldiers under them. Dust and the stench of cordite ate into their lungs and choked them, making them cough violently. Panting and struggling to breathe, the men wormed their way out of the rubble. Their hands and faces were bloody and dusty, their uniforms torn and dirty.

"Retreat to the Biber line!" Brinkmann screamed and pulled his pistol out of the holster. Walther was still reaching for a K98k, but Tillmann couldn't find a weapon and just stormed off under the fire of the Russians. The two grenadiers followed Brinkmann, who jumped into the trench, then out of it, and headed for the next ditch, 150 meters behind it, running around the village. From there he intended to get to the main road, which he only had to follow for 100 meters before they would reach said Biber line. There, two soldiers waited behind a Russian Ratsch Bumm to welcome enemy troops who tried to enter the town. There was also an MG nest in a window on the first floor of a pub. Unfortunately, the Ratsch Bumm had only six rounds left, while the AT-gun on the other side of the village – also a captured weapon – still had 40 rounds to distribute among attackers. Since the cannons were of different calibers, however, ammunition supplies could not been balanced.

Captain Droste had had to disperse his sparse personnel over all of Nikolskoye, because the Russians were looking for weak points in the defense everywhere. The German officer had installed four defense perimeters around the village – called Iltis where Brinkmann's fire team was, then Biber, Hummer, and Tiger. Tiger was located directly at the bridge over the Toplinka River, which was why this last-resort perimeter had to be defended at all costs. Droste hoped that this tiered defense would wear the Russians out to such an extent that the enemy had already bled to death by the time they reached the Tiger perimeter.

Brinkmann's field of view narrowed as he plunged through the darkness. He heard his soldiers snorting behind him. Russian bullets filled the air, but the darkness protected the German soldiers. The crawler tracks of the T-34 started up again, then the tank turned slowly and rumbled towards the road. Russian cries became loud, the enemy infantry unleashed. Brinkmann could almost feel the breath of the enemy in his back.

In the glow of moonlight, he had no chance to distinguish the second trench from the ground and finally tumbled into it. A stabbing pain shot through his right ankle, but he ground his teeth together and only moaned loudly. At that moment, Russian artillery shells whistled over his head and descended into the heart of Nikolskoye with a loud roar. Walther jumped next to him into the ditch, and they ducked together.

"Where's Remme?" the sergeant gasped. He nearly couldn't breathe.

"I don't know," Walther panted.

Brinkmann glanced with a racing pulse into the night, when suddenly the contour of a typical Wehrmacht stahlhelm appeared out of the night.

Tillmann's facial skin shimmered like a light blob through the darkness. The private first class dashed towards the ditch, heading to his comrades. Suddenly a bullet pierced through his abdomen. Tillmann fell to the ground, hit it with his helmet, and dug his fingers into the dirt.

"Scheisse ... " groaned Brinkmann. He wanted to jump out and pull his comrade into the protective trench, but something held him back. Russian Mosin Nagat rifles and PPSh submachine guns were still rattling everywhere.

A German infantryman with his K98k, which had five rounds and had to be bolt-fed each fresh cartridge, usually was no comparison against the concentrated firepower of the Soviet soldiers with their semi-automatic and fully automatic weapons.

So Brinkmann and Walther merely took cover in the ditch, pressed themselves against the earth wall, while at that moment Tillmann began to cry in terrible pain. Walther pushed his teeth together, and Brinkmann bit his right hand. The desire to help his comrade fought against his fear of Russian bullets.

"Ahhhhhhhhhhhh!" Tillman's nerve-wracking cry resounded over the battlefield. His screams mixed in with the racket of weapons. Tillmann sniveled; he coughed and his breathing bubbled.

Brinkmann couldn't bear to hear his fellow soldier like that. He first tasted the iron tang of blood in his mouth, only then did he feel the pain in his hand. His teeth let go of the lacerated flesh.

Carefully, the sergeant looked over the edge of the trench. The Russian fire had almost completely died out, with only a little combat noise still sounding in the distance. Ivan had challenged Droste's Iltis perimeter, everywhere, for a full hour.

Tillmann was lying only 20 meters from the salvation the trench offered. He roared and gasped for air as he held his abdomen and wound like a doomed man hanging from the gallows. And Tillmann was a doomed man, because belly shots were rarely recovered from.

"Give him his coup de grâce already!" Brinkmann pleaded aloud. The Russians who hid somewhere in the darkness remained silent. There was also nothing more to be heard from the tank. Brinkmann felt the pistol in his hand. He himself could never shoot a comrade ... a friend.

Brinkmann let himself sink back into the trench and pressed his helmet into the earth wall behind him. Cool lumps of damp sand and topsoil rolled into his sweaty collar, giving him a pleasant feeling in his back for a moment. But Tillmann's screams tore at his spirit.

"Ha-Jo!" the private first class cried all of a sudden for Brinkmann. "Ha-Jo! Emil! Please ... please." He coughed and gargled and begged for help. He screamed for his comrades, then for his mother and father. He screamed as only someone with a piece of metal digging through his intestines could scream.

"We won't leave Remme behind," Brinkmann clarified. Walther nodded decisively and grabbed his rifle.

"Then come on!" The two soldiers jumped out of the trench and stormed towards the screaming Tillmann. Brinkmann felt his pulse hammer its way up his throat, how the throbbing beat louder and louder in his ears and finally louder than all the sounds of his vicinity. His field of vision narrowed to a tunnel. Suddenly Tillmann appeared in front of him as a dark grey mass that lay struggling on the black ground. Immediately the sergeant holstered his pistol and crouched down next to the wounded man. Walther also stopped, lifted his rifle, and checked the area around them. He couldn't detect any enemy movement, but in the darkness the Russians could have been 30 meters away and Walther wouldn't have seen them.

121

"Ha-Jo!" Tillmann groaned at the sight of his sergeant. Joy and fear sounded in his voice at the same time. Tears had flooded his face. The sergeant grabbed the hands of the grenadier, hands that were freezing cold.

"Remme, boy," he whispered.

"Ha-Jo," Tillmann whimpered.

"We'll take you back, then you'll see a doctor."

Tillmann just nodded and twitched, but the sergeant had already grabbed his body and lifted it over his shoulders, groaning.

"Fucking mess," Walther muttered.

Suddenly shots slammed into them from the edge of the forest. Walther was hit immediately and collapsed in an exclamation of pain. Brinkmann felt the bullets penetrate Tillmann's body. Suddenly the human on his shoulder fell silent and went slack. A blink of an eye later, he sensed a biting pain in his loins that robbed him of all strength. Brinkmann collapsed under Tillmann's body. He felt it get all warm around his abdomen. He tried to lift his legs, but they didn't move. He was trapped under his dead comrade. Brinkmann heard Walther's soft lament before Russian yelling drowned everything out. Men approached out of the darkness, and the engine of the T-34 came back to life. It howled and roared before setting the squeaky crawler tracks in motion.

*

The majority of the regiment bypassed the village of Nikolskoye on the left, where the combat formation's

122

pioneers would soon begin to build a floating bridge across the river. This way the Germans could cross the water under cover of night and could then immediately fall on the Russian flank. 12th Company, however, had received orders to enter the village directly and to secure it. Von Burgsdorff had already met Captain Droste, and a sitrep was announced via radio com: The enemy had reached the main road on the outskirts of Nikolskoye, and had clawed its way through the German defense perimeters into the settlement. In many other places, by nightfall the Ivans had occupied individual buildings and pushed the Germans back into the interior of Nikolskoye. Just moments ago a German gun on the main road had foiled a Russian attack and destroyed a T-34. But now there were only two shells left for the cannon. It wouldn't be able to repel another attack. Therefore von Burgsdorff decided to deploy 12th Company on the main road to seize it to the end of the village. From there, the panzers could also quickly be dispatched to any point in the town as a quick reaction force.

In a long column, the German tanks rolled through the night and crossed the narrow bridge over the Toplinka River into Nikolskoye. The buildings to the right and left of the street disappeared into the gloom. Engelmann didn't like it at all, having to drive through urban areas in the deepest night. A fast-acting and clever tank killer team could be a real danger to the German panzers here.

"This is Wels." That was the codename of Captain Stollwerk. "To the right of the B 12-19, there is a large B 24-12, where the company will assemble and wait in

123

readiness for deployment," the captain's voice cracked from the speakers of Engelmann's headset. The lieutenant had had Nitz switch him to company frequency. Stollwerk obscured site designators and other important terms by the use of codes from the radio notebook, which was changed regularly.

Engelmann climbed back into the turret and looked at Nitz, who had been listening, with expectant eyes. A slight twitch around the sergeant's mouth told the lieutenant that he had already deciphered the codes.

"B 12-19 denotes a church, B 24-12 the cemetery," Nitz explained.

"Thank you, Ebbe."

"Bär follows me down the B 02-01 to the front of our comrade's positions, called Biber perimeter. I'm assessing the situation, radio silence until then."

"Main Street," Nitz commented, without looking into the notebook. Engelmann nodded with clenched teeth. It worked for him. In front of Franzi II, the first panzers passed the church and turned right just beyond it. Suddenly, Russian artillery shells whistled over 12th Company. They went down on the other side of the Toplinka River at the edge of Nikolskoye, and the dull detonations reverberated for a long time. Engelmann keyed his throat microphone and began to speak: "Wels! Anna here. Request permission to follow you in Bär's place."

Münster looked up and moaned.

"You're not satisfied until the Ivans shoot up every single tin can our asses ever sat in."

"Shut up, Hans!" Engelmann demanded. Nitz, too, gave Münster a bitter look, while Ludwig and Jahnke remained silent. Shaking his head, Münster turned to his levers.

"Permission granted," Captain Stollwerk's voice was heard over the airwaves. "I'll take B 02-01 with Anna in order to reach Biber."

One by one the other commanders confirmed as it crackled in the speakers. Engelmann pressed his back against the uncomfortable commander's seat. He rubbed his eyes, as if that would dispel his tiredness. Finally he looked up, pulled his tanker's cap off, and turned his attention to Münster.

"Listen, gearbox clown," he snarled at his driver.

"Just leave me alone," Münster responded and clutched so that Franzi II lost speed. On the road, the panzers of the company temporarily dammed up as one after the other turned into the cemetery. The tank treads leveled God's acre with mindless violence.

"If you want to get your EK 1, find another driver. I'm still young, I don't want to die in this shithole."

The lieutenant grimaced. For saying that, he could make life really difficult for the sergeant, but Engelmann trusted that an intelligent conversation could dispel any tension better than draconian punishments.

"Listen to me," he said to Münster. "If you think I'm a medal-grubber, you really don't know your commander well, I can tell you that. I just want to take the reins myself rather than be demoted to a recipient of orders. That's why I want to be at the point of the spear, want to come up with my own impression of the whole situation, want to make my own decisions."

125

"Everyone here is a recipient of orders, Sepp! God, even von Manstein is merely a recipient of orders," Münster muttered.

"Lord in heaven! Be glad that you have the lieutenant as commander," Nitz suddenly intervened in the conflict. "We should all be happy. We could do a lot worse!"

"Thank you." Engelmann nodded to his radio operator, then he made a long face: "... if that's a compliment."

Nitz grinned. Münster, on the other hand, mumbled something else, but nobody understood him. Maybe it was better that way.

Franzi II, and Stollwerk's Panzer IV whose turret and hull looked like a lunar landscape due to the dozens of hits it had taken, rolled gently down the main street. In front of them, isolated gunfire flared up, otherwise it was relatively quiet. Russian artillery continued to slam into the northern outskirt of the village, but there were hardly any German forces there. Von Burgsdorff had already left Nikolskoye to oversee the regiment's flanking maneuver. 12th Company was to ward off the assault forces of the Russians as long as possible, but nobody knew exactly when the counter-attack of the regiment could be expected. Von Burgsdorff had failed to consult sufficiently with the pioneers, and could therefore not say with certainty how long the construction of the floating bridge would take. But now radio silence was in place for both the 12th and the regiment, so the Germans had to laager in the village and wait for the surprise.

Creaking, Stollwerk's panzer came to a standstill alongside a Ratsch Bumm with German crew. Engelmann, who protruded from his commander's hatch and perceived the surroundings in the shimmer of the camouflage light as dull surfaces in different shades of grey, instantly recognized the large Soviet gun with its extra-long barrel. The Wehrmacht gave it the designation 7.6-cm-Feldkanone 269(r). The r in brackets hinted at its origin as a Russian weapon.

Stollwerk clambered out of his cupola, then jumped down from the tank hull onto the paved road. Immediately he scurried over to the AT-gun, which apparently had a crew of only two men. Engelmann also got out of his tank and sprinted towards the gun, where he and the others were protected by the big metal shield of the Ratsch Bumm. In the twilight of the moon and the camouflage lights, Engelmann thought he could identify the gun crew as a sergeant and a private.

"Give me a sitrep," Stollwerk demanded. The one Engelmann thought he had identified as a sergeant started babbling immediately, with a pronounced Upper Silesian accent: "The road down at the entrance to the village – about at the Iltis perimeter's line – there's a immobilized T-34. Place is teeming with Russians."

"Immobilized?" Stollwerk asked. "Did you zap it?"

"No. We suspect transmission damage. That tank failed without taking fire," explained the gunner. The two officers nodded, then Stollwerk took a quick look over the shield. Apart from darkness and the outlines of the buildings as well as a shot-up Russian tank, its barrel pointing like the bony paw of death in the direction of the German positions, nothing could be seen out there.

"Distance," the captain demanded to know.

"About 350."

The two officers displayed surprise.

"Eureka!" Stollwerk exclaimed. "Only 350?"

"Yes, sir." The sergeant showed no great response, and his voice remained unaffected by the news.

"Will be fun when the sun rises," he remarked dryly.

"Do the Russians know there's an AT-gun here?" Engelmann asked.

"Think so. They just don't know exactly where."

The lieutenant let his gaze wander over the scenery with a queasy feeling. The Ratsch Bumm was not particularly hidden; on the contrary – it lay in wait in the middle of the street, scantily barricaded with sandbags and junk.

"The Russians don't dare to come up with tanks anymore, Herr Hauptmann," the sergeant continued. "They've tried infantry twice, but we've got a whole platoon and several machine guns in the buildings."

"Aha," Stollwerk said and crossed his arms.

"How many enemy forces are ahead of us?" Engelmann intervened once again.

"We sent out a reconnaissance party in the evening that scouted about 25 medium battle tanks and four infantry companies."

Engelmann shook his head in disbelief. 25 tanks? Four companies? And on our side, just a cannon and one platoon? Now the lieutenant realized why the gunner had not yet illuminated the forefield to destroy

128

the tank. One would be wise to leave the Russians in the dark about how many forces the German side really had in defense. Engelmann nodded as he followed his train of thought ... but now there were German tanks here. Now it could be illuminated!

Engelmann and Stollwerk looked at each other, and the captain seemed to suspect that his officer comrade was up to something.

"Idea, Josef?"

"Idea, Arno!"

*

Tank driver Vassili Timofej looked through the open hatch of his T-34 into the darkness. The Mladschi Serschant – a sergeant – pushed his black tanker cap into place and stretched a little.

His seat was incredibly uncomfortable. The Russian tank driver with the royal blue eyes and the dimpled mouth sucked on his lower lip and placed his head at an angle. He couldn't see what was happening, but he could hear his comrades working despite the artillery fire coming down to the north of the village. Ilyich, the eight ball, had gotten another defective tank – it had suffered a gearbox breakdown right at the village entrance.

Timofej clearly heard his comrades cursing about the defective tank. Tools clashed against each other; the metallic clanking fought through the noise of the gun thunder. Of course this was a dangerous undertaking, because nobody knew where the fascists really were now, after that outpost of them had been neutralized.

129

Only three men had been found there. Their corpses were still where the sergeant from that rifle company had mercifully shot them. As if the Germans were asleep on the meadow, their resting bodies were emerging from the ground as dark outlines. Meanwhile, Soviet artillery hammered ceaselessly at the village. If all went well, they'd soften the enemy really good.

Timofej impatiently let his fingers dance over the levers of the steering brake. He hoped they would soon advance into that village. The German outpost had already proved that the fascists here in Nikolskoye were not as strong as they had thought. Timofej also had 70 other battle tanks and assault guns behind him, but the brigade commander had stopped the attack after poor Ilyich had suffered his gearbox failure.

Timofej could only shake his head at such an order. It was true that Ilyich commanded one of only three of the improved T-34s the brigade had received. The so-called T-34/85 was a prototype given to the brigade for front testing purposes. It mounted a more effective cannon, offered space for a fifth crew member, and had a radio on board as standard. Externally, the tank was noticeable above all for its larger turret. But Timofej believed they could do without this one improved tank when taking Nikolskoye. The brigade commander, however, was terribly afraid of German Tiger panzers, and it had increasingly influenced his decisions since the beginning of the year. Timofej shook his head again. If only the Tigers would come! Timofey was not afraid. Even a normal T-34 could be dangerous for this steel monster of the fascists. All you had to do was be brave and get close.

Suddenly a light-ball rose in front of Ilyich's tank, then became a bright star in the sky and slowly floated over the Russian troops. The steel of Ilyich's T-34 sparkled in the glare, and Timofey and his comrades were lit up like it was daylight.

The men who were working on the defective gearbox immediately stopped and shut their eyes really tight. Timofej blinked and peeked into the village, then he got frightened.

Although the Russian forces were fully illuminated in front of Nikolskoye, the glow of the flare also made visible at least the rough contours of one Soviet AT-gun obviously captured by the fascists. And it was in the middle of the road! Just 350 meters away!

Timofej and his comrades had no time to react. The Germans had coordinated the lighting too well with the crew of the gun. The cannon fired – and its shell shattered a track on Ilyich's tank. But the fascists followed that up immediately, firing a second time within a few moments. The petrol tank of the precious T-34/85 burst with a loud bang. Flames flared from the hatches, while the hull was ripped open and the men working on the tank were whirled away. At the same moment, the artificial light ball in the sky went out. Total darkness returned and hid the scene from view. Only the blaze of fire that had ignited in Ilyich's tank remained, illuminating a small area around it. It flickered.

131

Timofej had not yet understood what had happened. He only saw the shapes of his twisting comrades crying in pain, scattered all around the shot-up tank.

Then the cannons of the remaining T-34s spoke, and several HE shells flew into the gloom where that AT-gun was. Timofej could not see the impacts, but he could hear the explosives tearing open the street and the walls of the surrounding buildings. Rock chunks were tossed around by the set free energy. For a moment, the soundscape was dominated by the crash of larger lumps of debris hitting the earth, and by the fine trickle of the small and minute rock particles thrown into the air by the explosions. Timofej's tank had not participated in the short but violent firestorm. His commander wasn't in the vehicle, and nothing was allowed to be done without him ordering it.

After a few seconds, the other tanks stopped firing.

Timofej listened for any sound, but apart from the artillery strikes in the distance, he could not make out anything – no hectic calls in a foreign language, no screams, nothing. Suddenly, however, a call in German rang through the night: "Brennt!"

Timofej didn't know what that meant, and didn't think much about it. But the next moment, something blew up in front of the fascists. A ball of blazes rose exactly where the AT-gun had been, illuminating the surroundings for fractions of a second. Timofej even thought he had recognized the contour of a German steel helmet in one of the windows on the first floor.

But as quickly as the eruption of fire had appeared, it disappeared just as fast. All that remained was a deliberately set fire that enveloped the buildings in the surrounding area and the street in a gruesome yellow-red glisten. Like gravestones, shadows manifested on the walls of the buildings.

Suddenly Timofej recognized the dented shield of the cannon in the middle of the flames. No question about it, that fascist anti-tank gun was going up in flames. Probably a Soviet artillery shell had landed short – or the tank bombardment had delay-ignited some ammunition. Either way, the gun was down and the road was clear. Now was the time to go in!

As ordered, his commander finally returned and swung himself into the tank via the only turret hatch of the T-34. Immediately he sat down behind the main weapon, because in a T-34 the commander served as the gunner at the same time.

"Daweite! Teperj mi ßachwatim eitch fashistich!" he shouted to his crew. *Here we go! We'll get the fascists!*

Already, everywhere on the plain, Russian tank engines were starting up. The commander explained to Timofej in brief sentences that he should move towards the main road. This would bring the tanks into the village, while the infantry to the left and right would occupy the periphery. Comrade Dimitri's T-34/85 was to take the lead for the tanks. Then Timofej would come.

With a strong sense of determination in his chest that gave Timofej the confidence to recapture Nikolskoye that night, he grabbed the handle of his driver's hatch and dogged it shut. Now there was only a narrow eye slit that gave him a glimpse into the flickering darkness out there. In the weak white light of the moon, he could just see the outlines of the tank of his buddy

133

Dimitri, who was passing Timofej's tank at that very moment with humming pistons and squeaking tracks as it toiled itself down the street. Timofej immediately recognized the new tank by its mighty rounded turret. He also got his engine started, engaged the clutch, and accelerated. With a jolt, his tank started to move.

Timofej stayed directly behind Dimitri as both pushed past the blazing tank of Ilyich towards the main road. A paramedic had taken care of the wounded comrades there. Timofej saw white gauze bandages shining in the dimness. But Ilyich was certainly dead, because he had been in his tank the whole time.

"Ilyukha, yes ßa tjeba otamshu!" Timofej cried out as he clasped his levers with all his might. *I will avenge you, my friend!*

Ilyich had been a fine man – another fine man who had fallen victim to the barbarians. Timofej made a mental note to himself – this would be the third fallen comrade, where he planned to visit his family after the war and to tell them about the heroic deeds of their son, their husband, their father. Truly, that was little solace for the bereaved, but the thought that their loved one had helped in achieving that no Russian had to learn German may provide some comfort.

His tank finally reached the paved road. Timofej felt the change in the vibrations that kept shaking his tank. He was also not unaware of the tension that was weighing on the crew at that moment, and he was glad that he was not sitting in the platoon leader's tank. He not only had to operate the cannon of his combat vehicle and command it at the same time, but also had

134

to keep an eye on the other tanks and give them orders – it was an almost impossible task.

In front of Timofej – and also in front of the leading tank of Comrade Dimitri – the first houses of the village appeared as gloomy sketches. The Russian infantry could neither be seen nor heard, but Timofej knew that it too was penetrating Nikolskoye at this very moment. The background noise was dominated by the engine rumble and squeaking of the tanks, underneath the distant thunder of Russian artillery still firing into the northern outskirt of the village. Timofey did not see a single fascist. Slowly his tank rolled along the road – passing buildings, often ruins. He did not suspect that he had just passed German tank muzzles lying in ambush only a few meters from the road, hidden between the buildings.

The Russian tank unit had by now worked their way through a good part of the main road. Twelve tanks had entered Nikolskoye. Suddenly, small-arms fire flashed in the buildings, but it was aimed at the comrades on foot, not the tanks. The Russian infantry then returned the German greeting. Soon after, close combat broke out. Houses were stormed and evacuated. Fascists made counter-attacks. All of a sudden, another flare rose in the sky. In an instant, the Russian tanks were lit up as in sunlight – but not only that. Also the German tanks, which were lurking everywhere between the ruins and buildings, and whose main gun muzzles – only meters away from the main road – pointed directly at the flanks of the Russian tanks passing by, became visible in the artificial glare. Timofej and his comrades had no chance. With a simultaneous fire attack, the Germans opened up on the Soviet T-34 column on the village's main road. Eleven Russian tanks immediately burst into flames and were shattered into a thousand pieces, but Timofej didn't notice anything anymore.

*

"Press the accelerator and get out of here," Engelmann panted into his throat microphone, while Münster threw himself at the steering levers. Franzi II reared up. Her tank treads ate their way into the ground. The panzer accelerated and pushed out between two buildings onto the main road, where burning Russian T-34s were lined up like a row of ducks until they reached the end of the village. Everywhere now the panzers of 12th Company rolled out of their ambush positions, pushing blazing Russian tank wrecks aside. Bullets from rifles and MGs struck their armored skin, giving off colorful sparks. All around, the infantry of both sides decimated each other in bloody hand-to-hand combat on the outskirts of the town. Engelmann ducked back into his cupola as far as he could in order not to offer a target for an enemy sniper, but at the same time wanted to have eyes and ears outside, because the darkness offered the German tankers a clear advantage: A Russian T-34 commander who was unable to drive protruded from his hatch and could therefore only see his surroundings through a narrow vision block. This was already a problem during the day, but at night it turned every trip in the T-34 into a blind flight. German panzer commanders

136

however made excessive use of observing the action through their open hatch. This provided them with a superior overview over the battleground, and since information was nearly everything in modern warfare, this ostensible small difference between German and Soviet conceptions of tank warfighting was crucial. It explained why German tankers were so much more successful than their Russian counterparts.

Münster raced Franzi II down the street towards the open plain before Nikolskoye. The task now was to get out of the urban area as quickly as possible, where every tank was an easy target for enemy foot soldiers.

A frenzy of orders came in over the radio. Stollwerk coordinated his tanks, skillfully leading them out of the village. Meanwhile more T-34s showed up at the end of the road. The two tank formations clashed at the edge of Nikolskoye and shot at each other from close range, but because of the German commanders' much-better visibility, it was a preponderance of Soviet tank wrecks that lined the battlefield after each exchange of armor-piercing shells.

"I hope that was the last one," Engelmann groaned as he rubbed his exhausted eyes. He alone counted about twenty enemy tanks shot to pieces. Meanwhile, the panzers of 12th Company were flying out of the village everywhere and scrambling away over the open plain. One wave of enemy tanks after the other confronted them and was shot up by the Germans.

A T-34 suddenly broke out of the darkness directly in front of Franzi II. It rolled past the Panzer III as a large dark surface only five meters away.

Ivan just can't see us! Engelmann rejoiced inwardly before he gave the order to destroy that tank and then ducked into the turret for his own protection.

Ludwig aimed the cannon at the target and fired the main gun. The shell impacted and hurled the turret of the enemy tank up out of the hull. Engelmann could be truly glad that they were acting under cover of the night. His Panzer III would not have had a chance against a T-34 in daylight and at the usual distance. Now, however, the Russians tank forces were achieving complete annihilation at the hands of a small German battle tank company because they just could not see them.

"25 tanks? They must be kidding us!" Engelmann complained, as the stream of enemy tanks did not fade away.

Finally Stollwerk gasped out the *halt* command via radio. 12th Company's panzers came to a stop. The captain then instructed his men not to disperse, but to form a closed line of attack. Engelmann dutifully lined up while a few hundred meters to his left, another T-34 was sent packing.

Again a flare raced into the sky – this time from the Russian side. Suddenly it was the tanks of the 12th that were spotlighted in the battle. Engelmann clapped his hands over his face. The brightness hurt his eyes. But then he blinked and peered under his fingers at the battlefront. He was so frightened that he was afraid for a moment that his heart would stop. At a distance of about 500 meters, he recognized the outlines of dozens of T-34s – hard to spot among all the wrecks of past battles. Immediately the Russians began to shoot. The

German panzers also opened fire. But Panzer IIIs and IVs with their short gun-barrels did not have much hope at this distance. Shell explosions roared on both sides of the steel front. Panzer Bär of 12th Company got lit up by a hit. Its ammunition load went up, then its fuel tank. For the crew, any help came too late. Another Panzer IV took a hit in the right crawler track. The massive wheels broke off, and the tank tread ripped itself apart.

As fast as the brightness had fallen on the German tanks, just as quickly darkness returned. Stollwerk gave the order to advance at top speed. Now all that could save them was a close combat encounter with the enemy who was now blind again. As the panzers rushed towards their T-34 duelists, the next artificial light-ball was already rising. It shone in the sky like a gigantic star and once again bathed the land in glaring light. The threatening silhouettes of the enemy tanks became visible once more. Engelmann swore he could count over 40 tanks just at first glance. This was madness!

The Russians fired at the approaching Germans. The first tanks burst under shellfire – but no German panzer got destroyed. It was the Russian tanks that were suddenly exploding one by one. Just as the light of the flare died in the sky, Engelmann realized what was going on: the regiment's panzers, which had made their way across the Toplinka River, were stabbing the enemy T-34 formation in the back. The Russians at Nikolskoye did not stand a chance.

North of Bern, Switzerland, June 6th, 1943

There wasn't a soul to be seen far and wide. Taylor looked around stealthily in all directions. He was in the middle of the forest, miles away from any civilization. He had cycled for half the day to reach this point. There was no road through this forest, nor were there any hiking trails. The trees stood sky-high and close together. The dense leaf canopy prevented the light rain that was currently pouring over central Switzerland from penetrating to the forest floor. The firmament was covered with grey clouds, which on this day were as dense as a wall. Although the afternoon had just begun, an unpleasant twilight had the forest firmly under control. The leaves rustled quietly in the light breeze that was blowing through the woods. The trees bent in the wind, cracked, and let individual leaves sail to the ground.

Taylor pulled his coat a little tighter around his neck as the icy fingers of the wind grabbed his limbs. He shivered and jumped from one leg to the other. He carried a woven basket half filled with brown-headed porcini mushrooms. He had bought them on the market, because in the end he didn't have a clue about mushrooms, but he also didn't want to attract attention by collecting all kinds of poisonous fungi. Nevertheless, sometimes Taylor wondered why he bothered himself with all these camouflage measures every time. Out here, he was the only soul within a mile radius – almost.

Slowly a stranger approached from the east. Taylor knew by the way he walked and by his stature that it was a man. He wore a hat pulled down over his face and also carried a basket with him. He trudged ostensibly randomly through the undergrowth, coming closer to Taylor by the minute. The German spy felt his pistol that he had tucked in his pants.

When the stranger had approached to 70 meters, Taylor finally decided that he was his rendezvous. Both nodded in greeting, then the man joined Thomas Taylor and pointed to his own basket, which was also filled with light brown mushrooms.

Taylor's opposite was a man in his late 30s with deep furrows on his face and a wide, bulging mouth. The man straightened his scarf and smiled gently, then he said: "Let's see if we can get enough mushrooms for one pan." Taylor gestured his assent before both of them headed north.

They walked silently next to each other as their eyes inconspicuously searched the area. After several minutes of hush, the stranger, an agent from Stuttgart, took the floor: "One of the two Lucerne policemen succumbed to his gunshot wounds. The other one will probably make it."

Taylor nodded. "Collateral damage ... "

"Of course. But you should be aware of what you're threatened with if the Swiss authorities catch you."

"Yes, they'll be delighted, I know ... but I don't think we met about the condition of those two cops?"

Taylor's counterpart needed a moment, then he got to the point: "The landing in Italy is a feint."

141

Taylor briefly pondered before he signaled to his interlocutor to continue.

"We have information that the Allies are instead planning to land in the Balkans this summer, in Yugoslavia to be precise."

"So Roth slipped me false information? Is that what Stuttgart believes?"

"Unlikely. Fräulein Roth and her superior seem to be badly informed."

"Now what? Are you pulling me?"

"No. I want you to stay with her for a while. The agency wants to see what else comes up. Her father is interesting."

Taylor nodded, his expression serious. The thing with Yugoslavia was bad news.

"So Balkan, huh?" he asked without expecting an answer. His eyes narrowed as he pressed his lips together. In his mind, a map of southern Europe manifested itself. Because of his photographic memory, he was able to reproduce maps in his mind with incredible accuracy, including hundreds of cities that other Germans certainly didn't even know existed. The coastal towns of Pula, Zadar, and Dubrovnik were marked on his mental map, as were the large cities in the hinterland: Belgrade, Zagreb, and others.

"With that, they can attack our eastern front from behind," Taylor reasoned out. His opposite agreed glumly. "They would cut off our troops in Greece and be right on the doorstep of Bulgaria, Romania, and Hungary," he continued.

"They take three of our allies out of play in one fell swoop. And in the worst case, they roll up the rear

142

echelon of our front right up to the Baltic Sea, and cut off millions of German soldiers from their homeland," the agent from Stuttgart finished the thought.

"That would be the end."

"But that's not gonna happen." Taylor's interlocutor confidently tapped his forehead and grinned. "Because the British have become careless, we have been able to secure important documents. We still have time to react. Von Witzleben is already moving troops from Italy and France to the Balkans. Rommel has handed off his army group and will arrive in Zagreb tomorrow. We'll give them a reception that's really heavy."

"We have to," Taylor interjected. "If the Allies gain a foothold anywhere in Europe, we'll lose the war."

We'll lose the war, his own words echoed in his head.

East of Kamenka, Soviet Union, June 10th, 1943

The Soviet offensives in the Oryol and Kharkov areas were repelled for the time being, but the peace was deceptive. Now Ivan dug himself in wherever he had been able to achieve small gains in terrain. While the German military leadership could rejoice at such defensive successes, the Russians were already horrified by the scenario of a positional war, like the Western Front of the Great War, for now what von Manstein had been preaching since the beginning of the year had happened: Because of intelligent use of his backhand blow tactics to strike against the enemy wherever and whenever they didn't expect it, because of well-thought-out retreats to advantageous terrain, and because of fighting from defensive positions, the Russian forces had been bled to death on the German defenses-in-depth. The losses, the Wehrmacht estimated, after two weeks of fierce fighting, were at the staggering ratio of eight to one in favor of the Germans. While the Soviet Union remained far superior to the Reich in terms of numbers and materials, still, the Red Army was unable to absorb such losses just like that. Von Manstein was optimistic that he had robbed the enemy of his ability to go on the offensive for at least three-quarters of a year. The possible threat of a positional war would also give the Wehrmacht time to refresh its units and finally create reserves, which von Manstein had tried to do for a long time now without results so far. One just cannot create reserves when every regiment and every single soldier is desperately needed to close all the holes in the front line.

At Stalino Ivan had, however, been able to achieve his biggest gain in terrain. Here the Red Army had even kicked the troops of the Wehrmacht out of the city and now were setting up new front lines from Mariupol on the Sea of Azov via Stalino to the banks of the Donets. At Izium these days there was still fighting; but after the Soviets had temporarily been able to build some bridgeheads over the river, they did not manage to fortify them and had to retreat again behind the northeast bank of the river.

The situation at Kharkov remained tense. Kampfgruppe Sieckenius, and other reserve units thrown into battle, had been able to avert the worst, but the city was still encircled by Russian forces from the north, east and south. A narrow land corridor in the west of the city formed the last remaining link to the Wehrmacht units in the rear area. The Russian breaches between Kharkov and Belgorod now protruded into the Wehrmacht front like pimples.

The mobile reconnaissance battalion of Special Regiment 2, Combat Formation Becker, took position east of Kamenka in a dense and hilly forest area. The Russians had been quiet here for days. Bomb craters, downed trees, and shiny brass casings lying around in the sunshine shimmering through the canopy proved that this forest had already been fought over ferociously. But now, in a volatile phase of peace, the digging had begun.

Berning's squad was situated in improvised, defensible positions to secure the platoon's camp for

145

the next few hours, while the rest of the aforementioned platoon was busy digging trench systems, earth bunkers, and MG nests several hundred meters farther west. Once the forward defense line would be sufficiently fortified, the improvised positions Berning's men sat in could be surrendered. Of course, the trench system was not ready yet. Master Sergeant Pappendorf acted according to the motto, "An emplacement is never finished," so he had his countrymen digging at every opportunity. Once they had dug trenches that could be crossed crouching, Pappendorf demanded that they be deep enough to walk upright in. If the trenches were deep enough for that at some point, Pappendorf wanted to see them sheltered. So the game went on forever. Berning was sure; if they stayed here long enough in defense, Pappendorf would let them dig connecting tunnels through the earth's core directly to Japan.

Pappendorf! Berning boiled inside. *FELDWEBEL Pappendorf!* A few days ago, the master sergeant had even received the Tank Destruction Badge from the battalion commander. Berning could have puked.

That's the way it is in this fucking army! Ugly thoughts overwhelmed him. *The little guys are holding their heads, and the superiors are getting the tinsel!*

It was a quiet and sunny day. Birds were singing their songs, and the forest was shining in green. Sunbeams fought their way through the dense canopy of leaves and shone their way to earth like silk veils.

Berning was lying in a crater looking at his watch. Another hour and a half and they'd finally be relieved. Insects buzzed around his head, surrounding him.

146

They chased past his ears again and again. Everywhere along his hairline, the pests had already stung him. It was terribly itchy, but Berning was completely at the mercy of the parasites who, to top it all off, often transmitted typhoid fever. He was also plagued by lice. No matter how often he cooked his clothes, and no matter how often the kameraden searched each other and crushed the black bloodsuckers under their thumbs, after one day at the most new ones settled in. Berning's body was littered with scabby hives. In addition, he had to struggle with a deep exhaustion that had been paralyzing his limbs for weeks and was weighing on his shoulders like a huge rock. Several times his eyes had closed; his prone position, of course, encouraged the tiredness further.

Rudi Bongartz, a comrade whom Berning had even been allowed to call a friend at times, manifested himself in the NCO's mental eye. Rudi stared at him with a blue face and a reproachful look. Berning was not able to avoid the gaze, could only bear it with trouble, as it were. The guilt that the non-commissioned officer had brought upon himself weighed heavily on him; he could not deny that – and Pappendorf also used this to blackmail him!

Berning's fingers cramped when he thought of his platoon commander. Pure hate flooded his thoughts and also flooded the face of Bongartz, washing away the lance corporal. The irrepressible hatred that blazed in Berning's chest, that heated his body and made him tremble, suppressed the feelings of guilt – for the moment.

147

Suddenly, shots were fired to his front. Berning was startled. He looked to the left and to the right, where soldiers of his platoon had taken position in other bomb craters and behind fallen trees. Again, small arms were barking somewhere ahead of them. The sounds came from far away, but they were getting closer. Then a machine gun stuttered. Berning recognized, by the dull sound and the slow firing sequence, that this had to be a Russian Maxim, sending its deadly messengers on their journey towards them.

Minutes went by. With his rifle firmly clasped and a look of concentration on his face, Berning stared into the outer perimeter. But the trees there remained completely still. Leaves rustled quietly in the wind. Shots echoed abruptly, then an explosion. This time, it was very close! Berning pressed himself against the ground as he pushed his abdomen down into the bomb crater as far as possible. He was about to reach for his binoculars when one of his soldiers to the right drew attention to himself: "Psst! Herr Unteroffizier!"

Berning looked up, "Yes?"

"Movement right before us." The soldier, a private first class, pointed with an inconspicuous hand motion into the forest. Berning's look followed the index of his finger, then he just saw it as a person in uniform disappeared behind a tree.

"Prepare to fire!" Berning ordered, whispering to the right and left. His comrades there passed the command on to their respective neighbors, and they brought their weapons into position. The carbines clacked and clattered quietly.

"Fire at will!" In the distance, the Maxim began to speak again. Small arms joined in the concert.

All of a sudden, the person spurted from cover in front of the positions of Berning's squad. The sergeant raised his rifle.

Not that easy, my dear! he swore to himself, then aimed and fired. Rifle shots also rang out from the positions of his men on the right. The person had the presence of mind to throw itself into cover behind a tree. The projectiles pelted against the trunk and shredded the bark.

Berning focused all his attention on that tree trunk. Seconds passed. Nothing happened. The sergeant looked around at his men, but they just shook their heads. Berning could not see Hege from his position, but he could now hear the jingling of the ammunition belts and the sliding of the cocking handle as it shot forward. Hege's light machine gun was combat ready.

"MG fire on enemy position at my command." Berning had the order passed to Hege, then he looked over to the other side of his squad. Senior Lance Corporal Weiss was in position there with some others, for Hege was experienced enough that he no longer needed a leader at his side.

"Weiss, take two men, grab some stick grenades, and advance at throwing range," Berning ordered them, then: "MG and grenades only on my command." His orders were passed in whispers from foxhole to foxhole. Suddenly something unexpected happened. From where the stranger had jumped into cover, a call carried over to Berning's squad – in German: "I'm on your side, you morons!"

149

Tension lay like a blanket over Berning and his men. Everyone stared spellbound into the forefield, their hands on their rifles, their fingers hovering near the trigger. Berning's eyes searched the area. Still firearms were knocking in the distance like a fist on a wooden door. Slowly the racket came closer.

"This must be a trick," Berning heard one of his soldiers say. The sergeant clutched the wooden stock of his rifle tighter. He stared over the iron sights at the bullet-spoilt tree trunk, behind which the mysterious person still lay hidden. Berning held his breath. In front of the tree slowly – very slowly – a steel helmet made its way into his field of vision. With raised hands and a submachine gun dangling from a carrying strap, the stranger finally stepped out behind the trunk. He moved very carefully towards the German positions. Berning did not lower his rifle when the person advanced; not even when he realized that that person was wearing a Wehrmacht uniform. Judging by the epaulets, he was a master sergeant.

Finally, after moments of inner struggle over whether the man was a spy or really a comrade, Berning ordered his men to lower their weapons and rose from his crater to reveal himself. He simply wanted to believe that he had a friend there in front of him instead of an enemy seeking to kill him.

The strange master sergeant approached quickly and joined Berning. He immediately pulled a pack of JUNO cigarettes out of his field blouse and offered Berning a smoke. The Austrian sergeant waved his arms in disgust. The stranger shrugged his shoulders and supplied himself with a cigarette. While small arms fire

150

was still blustering in a shrinking distance, Berning drew sharp tobacco-breath into his nose. He subjected his opposite to a brief inspection: a head of black, curly hair that was actually much too long for a German soldier, growing higgledy-piggledy; a friendly, oval face hiding under his mop of hair. The master sergeant blew out smoke with relish, then turned to Berning and asked: "You the ringmaster of this circus here?"

Berning stared at the master sergeant and didn't know what to say. Somehow this guy seemed strange to him.

"Sergeant Berning. Reconnaissance squadron, Special … " he began to report properly, but the black-haired comrade contorted his face and waved it off: "Good for you. Listen, brother. My men will be here in three minutes, and they could use some fire support. Careful, some of them are wearing half camouflage, meaning Russian uniforms. Can we do that?"

Berning stared at the master sergeant in astonishment and blinked his eyes. *What the hell is he talking about?*

"What unit are you with?" he asked. The sergeant rolled his eyes. He replied, "Special assignment. That's all you need to know. Just let my people through and stop the Ruskies. Comprendez?"

"Compren … what?"

"We've got two rifle companies on our heels, so hurry up giving your orders to your men and prepare for a fight." The noise of battle came closer and closer.

"TWO COMPANIES?" With his eyes widened, Berning looked at the master sergeant. "We're just a platoon!" he complained. Now the stranger grinned and put a hand on Berning's shoulder. "But you are a German platoon. And those guys coming up are just peasants who had rifles put in their hands by the Red Army. Here goes nothing!"

"Aren't you going to help us?"

The master sergeant shrugged his shoulders. "Oh, I would if I could. I'd really like to. But we can't fight side by side with you, kameraden. Commander's orders. Besides, it's not our job. But as I said, here goes nothing."

Berning stared at the master sergeant as if someone had slapped him with a plank. He scratched his chin with a questioning expression and absolutely did not know what to do now. Then suddenly Hege shouted from the right: "Friendlies! 200 in front of us!"

"Well, then, happy hunting!" the master sergeant proclaimed, and set off for the rear echelon. Berning threw himself back into his bomb crater. Already the beforementioned persons appeared right before his position. The sergeant counted ten men. Shots whistled after them. Some of the men wore German uniforms, while others wore Russian ones, as Berning clearly recognized. Roaring, the sergeant explained the situation to his men in short sentences and instructed everyone to be extremely careful not to shoot their own comrades. The orders were confirmed back to him from everyone, then the motley-uniformed men reached the positions of Berning's squad. This was an eye-catching bunch running through the improvised front line of 2nd Platoon just now. Some of the men had unusually long hair and looked strangely lax for German soldiers. The helmet straps of some were open,

152

dangling loosely down. One soldier was very small and slender, carrying a Russian rifle with a telescope. Another seemed wounded. He held his right arm where the uniform was ripped open and saturated with blood. These men almost looked like the soldiers of the Wehrmacht generally imagined American GIs to be: Slovenly and not caring about it at all.

One of the strange men running in the middle of the group also carried someone slung over his shoulders. Berning took a closer look and suddenly got frightened. The strange soldier carrying the other man was dark-skinned, but not like an Italian or Spaniard; the man's skin was pitch-black! Berning had never seen anyone like him in a Wehrmacht uniform. He even thought he'd never seen anyone like him before. The dark-skinned guy, however, was huge, a true giant. He carried the man on his shoulders as casually as others would carry a briefcase and sprinted almost faster than his comrades despite the load. Only then did Berning realize that the man on his shoulders was a Russian officer – a senior Russian officer! Meanwhile the rearguard of that special assignment squad passed through the improvised German defensive positions.

"Bonjour, Mademoiselles!" one of them yelled at a stunned-looking Berning. The strange group of men were heading for the hinterland.

Dazzled, the sergeant from Austria forced himself to observe the forefield. Shots still rang out loudly there. Raised voices in Russian pervaded the forest. Suddenly, however, the sergeant was overcome by a sinking feeling in his stomach like a bad bout of flu. Shocked, he stuck his head up and gave one last

153

serious scrutiny to those odd-looking strangers, who were almost out of sight.

What if they are enemy commandos? This thought had taken hold of Berning's mind and wouldn't let go of it. Had he just let an enemy special ops unit through his lines, just like that? But then he was no longer able to take counsel of his fears. On the right, one of his men yelled, "Enemy ahead, 300!" Hege's machine gun started rattling.

Berning saw dozens of soldiers in earth-brown uniforms running towards his position. Skillfully they were leaping from cover to cover, but Hege nailed some of them behind trees with targeted bursts of fire. The other German soldiers also joined in the concert of death. Gunshots rang out, and bullets hissed through the woods. But the Russians attacked in huge numbers. The red infantry worked its way up, unstoppably, under the German fire. Somewhere in the woods, a Maxim started chattering. Fire fountains sprang up in front of the bomb craters where Berning's men had entrenched themselves. Then the sergeant came up with an idea that just shot through his head like a bullet: *Concentrate fire on the enemy and pin them down until reinforcements could arrive!*

He yelled his commands at Hege, but the hard-of-hearing senior lance corporal did not react. So Berning jumped up and stormed forward towards the MG nest, which was located about 100 meters farther to the right on a slight elevation. Meanwhile the firefight became more intense. Berning gasped and snorted, his gaze narrowed. He had only one goal in mind: Hege's position. He would then send a messenger to the rear,

154

if Pappendorf hadn't already thought to come up with the rest of the platoon to reinforce his squad anyway.

Pah! Pappendorf! I'm sure he's too busy polishing his epaulettes, Berning assumed. The hatred inspired by this line of thought gave him wings and made him sprint a little faster. And he had a plan. He would grab Hege, flank the enemy, and pin him down until the reserve would arrive.

Berning knew what to do! He kept running. Suddenly his legs were knocked out from under him, and he landed hard in the dirt. He screamed, then the pain struck. It felt like a shiv stabbing him in the back of his shoulder and neck. Berning blinked his eyes. His right arm was suddenly limp. He grabbed his neck with his left hand. In claret shimmered the lifeblood that suddenly stuck to his fingers. His sight lost color, and his field of vision got smaller and smaller. Seconds seemed to stretch to eternity. Then he could see the senior lance corporal, Weiss, bending over him, shouting, but there was no sound, and Berning began to drag himself across the foliage that covered the forest ground. Then everything went dark. Had he got his million-dollar wound? With this question in his head, he lost consciousness.

Bryansk, Soviet Union, June 12th, 1943

Von Manstein and his chief of staff, Hermann Hoth, looked at each other for a moment. The Commander-in-Chief East tried to read the face of his opposite, and he realized that Hoth was doing the same thing. The two field marshals, who were alone in the railcar that von Manstein used as his mobile command post, had just put a heated debate behind them. The argument had been a loud one throughout, but conducted without either of the two attacking the other ad hominem. Now all the arguments had been made; everything had been said. And Hoth, the sly one, had actually made von Manstein ponder if his original position was the best way forward.

The clock hanging on the wood-paneled wall ticked quietly. Von Manstein looked at the situation map that lay spread out on the table in the middle of the room. It displayed the entire Eastern Front. Hoth was on the other side of the table. He also looked at the map with pressed lips and sunken eyes with dark circles under them. The general field marshal with the close-cropped hair, the high forehead, and the sharply-drawn face seemed to wait tensely for a decision from von Manstein, but the Commander-in-Chief was still in a fight with himself. Finally he breathed out long and loudly and tapped his index finger against his chin. He realized that he missed his old comrade and former chief of staff Colonel Theodor Busse, who had sometimes worked with him better than Hoth did. The later was not yet so used to life as chief of staff.

Nevertheless, Hoth was a brilliant strategist who didn't keep his opinions to himself.

Von Manstein sighed. Busse had been killed in action near Stalingrad in mid-November 1942, shortly before von Manstein had taken over supreme command of the Eastern theater.

"If we fail, Hermann," von Manstein said with a scratchy voice, "we have burned all our painstakingly scraped-together reserve forces for nothing. Then we're standing there with our pants down, and the Russians are in the key position once again."

Hoth nodded slowly. Von Manstein knew that his old comrade was aware of the dangers of the plan. But Hoth was someone who would take the risk when he sensed an opportunity. Von Manstein, on the other hand, preferred to play it safe with his very limited resources.

"A failed offensive – a single offensive," von Manstein continued, "could end up costing us the entire war. Launching a major attack is always a risk." Slowly he looked up, looking deep into Hoth's eyes. "A wrong decision at this point could cost the Reich its head."

"I appreciate that about you, my old friend," Hoth replied, "that you don't make that decision easy for yourself. But all you ever talk about is the military stalemate we have to achieve in order to make the Russians willing to negotiate. But I think we can do more. Look what's happened since the beginning of the year. Ivan has lost 2,000 tanks at Kursk; and we captured 700,000 Red Army soldiers. Then their summer offensive failed, clear across the board. At

157

least 7,000 tanks destroyed, 420,000 men killed. Our losses are an eighth of theirs.

An eighth, Erich!

Also, Russia is not an endless maw from which new tanks and men are spewed every second. We've dealt the Soviets a blow from which they won't recover so quickly. More importantly, their forces are now beaten into the ground. Now the enemy is confused and disorganized. In short: Now is its weakest moment. And we have the forces on the ground, right there: the 15th African's panzers, which we add to the Kampfgruppe Sieckenius; plus Grossdeutschland and Panzer Corps Hausser. Our starting position is also solid enough for a front of this size, now that 6th Army has pushed the enemy back behind Livny and is about to reach the banks of the Don River. We can get back to Tula, Erich! Barely 170 kilometers from Moscow! And this only by committing minimal input. Even failure – and we will not fail – would not mean the collapse of the Eastern Front."

"I don't see it that way. You're asking me to take a tremendous risk," von Manstein said in an acid tone. Once again his gaze wandered over the situation map.

If only the Chancellor had followed my memorandum, then we would have the necessary divisions right here! In a letter to the Chancellor at the end of last year, von Manstein had demanded that the Wehrmacht withdraw from Norway and Denmark in order to free up the formations stationed there, for the war against the Soviet Union. The Commander-in-Chief East knew that this proposal had been intensively discussed in von Witzleben's inner circle, but eventually the Chancellor

158

had rejected it. A mistake, von Manstein believed. The Poles had failed to realize that one cannot fight everywhere, especially when faced with a superior enemy. They had had to pay a high price for their military misjudgments, but von Witzleben's argument also had its point: every European country that the Wehrmacht evacuated would, out of hatred, immediately turn into an enemy of Germany because of the period of occupation – and thus become, as it were, a deployment area for the Allies. Whether the occupation of half of Europe was to the liking of von Witzleben or not, things were as they were.

"I demand that you *win* this war. Fight on the defensive, make them commit frontal attacks, and then conduct backhand blows against their flanks or rear. That's what you're always talking about. This operation would meet this very tactic par excellence. Erich, I'm telling you, we can win this fight! But we have to take risks. Let's take these risks now while we don't have the Americans on our back, because relying on static warfare could prolong this war another ten years in the worst case. The Western powers will not wait that long."

"My God!" groaned von Manstein. "Hitler, the fool, should never have attacked the Soviets."

"Hitler first freed us from the shame of Versailles. He solved the question of Poland, which was so dear to our hearts in Germany. He fulfilled the self-determination of the peoples in the Sudetenland and Austria, brought the German tribes home to the Reich. Never in my life have I met a more brilliant statesman."

159

Von Manstein nodded. "Yes, I was also enthusiastic about the successes. But back then, there was no talk of Russia at all. And now we have this mess ... " The field marshal knew precisely what the advantages were of von Witzleben as Chancellor over Hitler. Von Witzleben had returned military command to the High Command of the German Army, and had appointed Gerd von Rundstedt as Commander-in-Chief of the Army. Thus the political and military authority were at last separated again, as it should have been always the case – and the military had regained its freedom from politically-based decisions and meddling. This was supremely important in von Manstein's eyes.

The Commander-in-Chief East once again looked at the situation map. He bent over the table and perched his reading glasses on his nose before his finger searched and found the area of Oryol. The field marshal was still fighting with himself.

Karachev, Soviet Union, June 15th, 1943

A tall man with dark hair and tanned skin lay on the ground before Sergeant Berning. Hard and straight as a wooden plank he was. His mouth was closed and the lids shut firmly over the eyes. The man who wore a Wehrmacht uniform and the rank insignia of a lance corporal made a very peaceful impression. His face shimmered bluish, and his chest did not move.

The man was dead.

Rudi Bongartz was his name. Berning stood in front of the body and was doomed to stare at him. He couldn't move, he couldn't turn away. His body didn't listen to his orders. He stared at Bongartz – Berning could not even close his eyes. He had to stare at his dead comrade. Every night, every restless minute of sleep, Berning was accompanied by this dream – the face of the dead Bongartz burned in his mind like a glowing splinter.

*

Sergeant Berning had had a real odyssey through the various levels of German medical care before landing in the field hospital of the 72nd Infantry Division. Due to the hectic events of the past weeks, the combat group did not have its own hospital of this size.

Still, the accompanying document with the red stripe was adhered to the frame of Berning's hospital bed. The non-commissioned officer, along with about twenty other wounded, lay in a large room with arched windows and a high ceiling.

The division had had an outbuilding of the town hall cleared in order to set up the field hospital. Red Cross nurses, paramedics, and doctors in white coats ran hurriedly through the room into the adjoining rooms, which were also crammed with wounded and sick people. Groaning soldiers, sometimes screaming in pain, were pushed through the room in their beds. Next to Berning, a man who had been shot in the belly whimpered every now and then; he had been unconscious most of the time since Berning's arrival. On the quiet, the nurses blew out that the chief physician, Dr. Medical Lieutenant Colonel Krüger, could not explain why this man was still alive. Somewhere in one of the adjoining rooms, the song Erika was playing quietly from the loudspeakers of a radio.

Berning still felt a stabbing pain in his shoulder and another in his right thigh. The paramedics had put his arm in plaster, vertically protruding from his body, so that he looked like he had a wing. That's why the soldiers called this kind of plastering "Stuka." Berning hardly had any desire to move.

The hospital stank of sweat, human sebum, and urine, but all the poor mutts around Berning added their own stench as well. Added to this miasma of human evaporation was the pungent smell of alcohol, which triggered a sharp pain in Berning's dry nose. In addition, there was the stench of wound rot, pus, and gauze bandages. From time to time, the strong smell of perfume penetrated Berning's nose. Then there was usually one of the nurses with their Red Cross cap

162

nearby. The nurses seemed to be bathing in perfume to better survive the day in this hell for olfactory organs.

Berning had been almost exclusively out of it in the last few days. The strong painkillers pushed him straight into bed, to which was added exhaustion. On the very day of his wounding, he had undergone a makeshift operation at the main dressing station before that Stuka was put on him, and then he was sent back with the column of a medical company to the field hospital. Since then he had laid here in this room, and when he was intermittently conscious, a nurse helped him to take a few bites or to do his must-do; or Berning watched all the others around him dying, healing, conversing, and flirting with the girls of the hospital personnel. He himself felt completely bushed and could not stir up the energy for any activity.

Even going to the bathroom, or eating daily, was a hell of an effort that he would have preferred to avoid. His limbs trembled constantly, he was one moment cold, then the next hot. His throat was completely dehydrated and his tongue swollen with thirst, but every sip of water burned like fire in his throat.

Berning felt as if he was nothing but a rack of bones; as if all his muscles had left him. He didn't know what was going on with him, either. The nurses could not give him any information, and a doctor had not yet been to see him, at least in his waking hours.

The trembling fingers of Berning's unplastered hand grabbed the edge of the brown wool blanket. His knuckles were white under the thin skin. Slowly he pulled the stiff cover up to his Adam's apple. A steel cold, which only he could feel, reached for him with

163

icy fingers. A strong, cramping flickering of his muscles seized him. When the chill was over, Berning made a suffocated sound and finally contorted his mouth to utter a strangled laugh. His neck hurt from lying there for days. But all his sniveling sorrows seemed to him merely a dull inkling of a sensation in contrast to the throbbing and biting pain in his shoulder, where a thumb-sized projectile had torn flesh and bones from him. In addition, his skin burned and itched under the plaster – Berning feared that lice had settled there again. The war had shown him life's cruelest sides, and Berning condemned himself and all the military these days more than ever before. He held Pappendorf personally responsible for his situation. After all, it had been the master sergeant who had sent Berning all too often to do perimeter security – just as Pappendorf had, since Kursk, given almost every assignment that promised contact with the enemy to Berning.

Hadn't the sergeant by now sufficiently proven that he was capable of fighting? Of killing? What else did Pappendorf want with him?

A man in his late 50s in a white smock pushed himself into Berning's field of vision. The man's hair was tousled, his face narrow and worn out. Red, sore veins shimmered through the skin next to his nostrils. The nose itself was tuberous, his facial skin was infiltrated with irregularities. Behind the doctor came a young nurse with nut-brown hair. Berning already knew her. Her name was Renate.

164

"Well, what have we here, Fräulein Micgy?" the doctor asked, and grasped the document hanging from Berning's bed.

"Franz Berning, Unteroffizier," the sister replied obediently, "posted to us on the 12th, Doktor Krüger. Has already been operated on by the MDS. Projectile removed, shot fracture to right clavicle, penetrating gunshot wound at right thigh."

"Mmm," the doctor made a noise and turned up his nose thoughtfully. "Let's see."

The white coat stepped next to Berning's bed and pulled the blanket aside. He rudely pulled Berning's gown up, then plucked the bandage. Berning made a sorrowful noise.

"Now pull yourself together, will ya, Herr Unteroffizier?" hissed the doctor, while he pulled out a pair of scissors, cut open the gauze bandages, and removed the plaster. Finally, he uncovered the bullet's entry wound. Berning's whole shoulder had turned into a single, dark-blue-to-purple hematoma. The place where the bullet had penetrated the body was only visible as a tiny, dark red dot.

"Note: First observation reveals no signs of infection, wound canal inconspicuous, visible tissue bleeding in left chest to shoulder area. Slight lice infestation." The doctor stroked the reddened hives that had formed everywhere under the plaster, then he made a demanding gesture with his right hand. Immediately, Nurse Micgy pressed an X-ray into his fist.

"Mhmm, gunshot fracture. Splintering recognizable," the doctor muttered, studying the X-ray. Nurse Micgy nodded and jotted down more notes. The graze on the

165

neck, on the other hand, was merely of superficial nature, and Krüger paid no attention to it. Instead, he threw the blanket all the way back and removed the bandages wrapped around Berning's right thigh. The bullet through there had miraculously injured neither the bone nor the artery.

"Well, boy, I have some bad news for you," Krüger said afterwards in an apathetic voice. Berning's eyes widened. "The wound will take you out for two months, at least. And you're gonna have to stay in bed for quite some time. Be glad the bone just cracked, otherwise you might have been out for half a year."

A broad smile trembled on Berning's lips. Million-dollar wound!

"Apply lice powder and put on a new cast. I want to keep him here for another week, Fräulein Micgy. Then sick leave," Krüger dictated to the nurse, who nodded vigorously and wrote some more.

"Did I ... " Berning suddenly snuffled, " ... Did I get my million-dollar wound?"

"Million-dollar wound?" The doctor suspiciously pulled an eyebrow up.

"Am I going home ... *home*, I mean?"

"Home?"

"I would so love to see my family again ... and Gretel. I have a girl at home, you know?"

The doctor's face had hardened within milliseconds. Berning had no idea what was going on with Krüger.

"Million-dollar wound? Oh, it's like *that*, is it?" the doctor said with a bitterly angry voice. Now it was Berning whose face froze.

166

"Fräulein Micgy, prepare the man immediately and bring him to examination room 2. I want to take a closer look at the injuries." The nurse left. She hurried through the room and called a second woman in white. Krüger bent down to Berning. Old, pulsating eyes drilled into the sergeant. "If I find out that you inflicted the wounds on yourself ... You'll see what they have in store for quitters," spat Krüger as pure hatred threatened to burst from his face.

Mtsensk, Soviet Union, June 16th, 1943

Eventually Field Marshal von Manstein had decided to conduct another operation in the Eastern theater; a hastily scheduled counteroffensive of the Wehrmacht was intended to win both banks of the Oka River off the town of Tula, using two wedge-shaped attack columns, one out of the Oryol area and one out of the Smolensk area. Tula itself had to be taken too. Von Manstein had decided on a limited, small-scale offensive. His troops were no longer capable of a big push anyway. But the defensive successes of the past weeks had torn gaps in the Russian lines, which the enemy was currently hardly able to fill. Von Manstein wanted to push right into these gaps. If the offensive was successful, the German-occupied territory would be significantly expanded, but without creating a new salient that would just need more forces to defend than a straightened front line. In addition, this would push the Germans way up to within 180 kilometers of Moscow, thus positioning Reich forces dangerously close to the enemy's capital again. Finally Moscow seemed to be in reach once more.

In the north, Panzer Corps engaged the enemy from Smolensk. In the south, Kampfgruppe Hoth, created from the combat formations Sieckenius and Becker as well as the 15th Panzer Division, would strike.

Von Manstein's Chief of Staff, after struggling with the Commander-in-Chief East for quite some time, had finally received another active command when taking over his own combat formation – albeit for a limited time. Of course, the forces involved in this assault were

168

much smaller than at Operation Citadel, although the area of operations was approximately the same size. There were two reasons for the minimal-manpower approach: First of all, the Wehrmacht could hardly spare any more troops for an attack. On the other hand, this time they did not have to chew their way through a 30-kilometer-deep defensive network of the enemy, which had been installed during six months of painstaking work. The positions of Ivans in front of and around Tula were no more than a chain of hurriedly dug-out foxholes. In addition, the enemy units in the AO were weakened and demoralized. Von Manstein therefore planned a quick raid with two panzer spearheads. They were intended to smash the enemy before he realized what was happening. After that the march to Tula would actually *be* just a march, and not a series of battles.

The plan also provided for panzergrenadier units to follow the spearheads, securing the flanks before regular infantry took over the land and began digging themselves in. Once again, von Manstein was able to bring in considerable air forces for this approximately last German offensive of 1943. The blow against Tula offered him the opportunity to regain territories that the Reich had once won, and then lost back to the Soviets as the war tilted.

"At last our side is doing something again. It was high time," Münster was pleased to say.

"Not if you don't finally step on the gas," Engelmann countered, and caught an irritated look from his driver.

"I'm just saying. If all we get now is something to chew on, I'll be the happiest man in the world."

"Drive, man!"

"Yes, sir."

With a jolt Franzi II set herself in motion and rolled out of the large barn, which had been her home for the last few days, and squeakily headed for the road leading from Mtsensk via Chern and Plavsk directly to Tula. The city was 110 kilometers away from Kampfgruppe Hoth's staging area.

The attack was preceded by a 24-hour bombardment by German artillery and the Luftwaffe. Numerous kolkhozes in enemy hands along the front line had been virtually leveled by the shelling and bombing. This was reported by reconnaissance patrols, which had tested the enemy lines all night long. Heavy, hours-long rainfall had made the terrain difficult, but also facilitated it for the scouts to advance unnoticed. If their reports were correct, then the Russians were on the run.

Slowly the tanks of 12th Company drove along the main road. Engelmann's Franzi II guarded the rear; left of them, 11th Company pushed forward across wide plains. To the right, the area of responsibility of the regiment ended and that of the 15th Panzer Division began. This very formation sent forward a mixture of Panzer IVs, Tigers, and light infantry fighting vehicles, closely followed by panzergrenadiers.

Engelmann looked out of his commander's cupola. On both sides of the road, a wide-open space reigned over the land, reaching as far as the horizon. It had stopped raining, but the high humidity, which hung over the terrain like an invisible spider's web, was dragged along by the wind and blew around Engelmann's head in a pleasant way.

Already the sun fought its way through the clouds and transformed the climate into the well-known heat of the last weeks. The grass sizzled in the hellish sunshine, while the puddles collected at the roadside began to dry up.

Engelmann looked around. Perfect tank terrain. Individual kolkhozes broke up the otherwise flat land, which also lacked any obstacles. Narrow lanes mostly led off from the main road to the collective farms. But there were no farmers to be seen.

Engelmann spotted an old tractor at a large barn, its blue paint corroded by rust. The farmhouse next door, a wooden building with a weathered thatched roof, had been beaten up badly by past fighting. Fist-sized bullet holes pierced the facade, all the windows blown out. A few hundred meters farther to the northeast, 12th Company passed the lonely wreck of a T-34 that stood on the roadside. Miserable figures there witnessed the advance of the Germans as they set off in the opposite direction: A small column consisting of old men staggering under bundles, and women in headscarves carrying baskets.

*

Without encountering resistance, the regiment finally reached Mtsensk. Engelman recognized at the same time the thick smoke trails, which hung like a threatening sword over the place. Only then did the lieutenant see the first buildings devastated by the war.

171

Flames blazed unhindered in the town center. Houses looked like a giant hole puncher had raped them. Roofs had collapsed, and whole buildings had been razed to the ground. Streets and alleys were plowed to pieces by German shells.

The regiment and the left flank of the "Africans" advanced on the broad front. Three armored reconnaissance vehicles, called Special Purpose Vehicle 222, were narrow, four-wheeled armored cars with a swivel-type turret and a two-centimeter cannon, broke out of the formation and revved their engines to a howl. They bravely advanced, formed the attack column's spearhead for now, and stormed into the village over the wide stone bridge leading over the Zusha River. Not a single shot was fired. A little later, the radio started to broadcast the voice of the leader of those vehicles.

"Southern foothills of Mtsensk are free of hostiles." Stollwerk passed on the report. "12th and 11th shall pass directly through the village, the rest of the regiment should bypass left. Assemble on the other side. We're keeping formation, everyone follow me!" Stollwerk's commands rang through the ether with stoic composure.

The man can lead, Engelmann thought blissfully.

Minutes later, the panzers of 12th Company occupied the village. In the run-up to the event, a reconnaissance party of pioneers had checked the capacity of the bridges over the river, which was a slender branch of the Oka River. They had come to the conclusion that the old stone bridge could carry tanks without any problems.

172

When Franzi II plunged into the village, Engelmann's fingers instinctively cramped around the two turret lid flaps while he concentrated ferociously, trying to keep an eye on all the windows, all the breaches and all the ruins that passed by left and right – an impossible undertaking. Ludwig's foot also moved automatically onto the pedal which operated the coaxial machine gun. Urban terrain always made tank men nervous.

But in this case, the fear of enemy tank killer parties hiding in the rubble of the ruins proved to be unfounded. Apparently the Russians had left the village in a hurry when hell had broken over them. Shell craters that were meters-deep lined the roadsides. They were filled to the brim with dark, dirty water. Every now and then the tank gunners had to turn their panzer's cannon away from one side of the road as the combat vehicle dipped into a crater to avoid digging the muzzle into the ground.

Farther ahead, the street turned to the right and disappeared behind a corner house, whose perforated and unroofed gabled attic rose into the sky like a skeleton. It denied Engelmann a view of the rest of the street. Stollwerk gave the halt order. Lieutenant Engelmann leaned forward in his cupola as far as he could, but he couldn't see the reason for the stop.

Smoke impregnated the air, and fires flickered out of control in the ruins.

Engelmann finally observed Captain Stollwerk climbing out of his panzer and disappearing around the bend. After 30 seconds, he turned to Engelmann's field of vision and gesticulated wildly with his arms. Apparently he gave further commands to his crew,

173

because just at that moment Stollwerk's tank began pulling back, while its turret was turning, clattering, until the main gun's muzzle was pointing full backwards. Stollwerk now held both hands in front of his chest and showed the palms of them to his driver, then he climbed up the hull. Finally the captain disappeared into the turret, closing the lid. By radio message moments later, Stollwerk explained the problem: "The road behind that bend is not passable due to weapons effect. Wait while we explore an alternative route."

With these words, Stollwerk unleashed his panzer. The driver pushed the gas pedal as far as it would go. The engine howled and propelled the monster rapidly forward, the main gun barrel facing back at the other German tanks. The panzer accelerated towards the corner house. With a violent crash, the tank dug itself into the building and tore away half the brickwork from the ground floor. Immediately the rest of it gave way. The whole building leaned to the left, then it paused for a moment, as if it was taking another last breath inside itself. A fraction of a second later, it collapsed like a house of cards. With a loud roar, which echoed far beyond the village and the plains, the building turned into a big mountain of rubble within a blink of an eye.

"Splendid!" rejoiced Münster, and clapped his hands approvingly. Ludwig grinned.

"That's actually not allowed," Nitz remarked with a suppressed voice.

"So what if it wasn't?" Münster retorted as he grasped his control levers. Stollwerk's voice cracked

174

out of the headphones at the same time: "Alternative route found. Move it!"

Immediately the other panzers of the company woke from their sleep, swung slightly to the right, and torturously climbed their way up the debris mountain that was a house just seconds ago. Tank after tank rolled over the former building and pressed the broken stones and wooden beams deeper and deeper into the ground. Finally the tracks of Franzi II reached the former corner house and began to dig themselves into its corpse. Creaking, the tank ate its way up the mountain of rubble. When Engelmann could finally see over the apex of it, he experienced another level of devastation caused by the German bombardment: beyond the bend, the road was lined with shot-up carts and automobiles. Dead horses whose fur were matted and covered with blood were lying on the roadside with their carcasses torn open. Their intestines poured out like fat, bright red worms onto the road, where they were now flattened by the crawler tracks of Stollwerk's panzer. The thrust pressed all the blood and tissue into the part of the organs not caught by the tanks treads, which burst like squashed pimples. Bright blood sullied the side-skirts of the German panzers as they worked their way relentlessly up this road of death. The wood of the broken carts burst like matches under the weight of the tracks. The bodies of people and other animals full of splinters lay unnoticed in this part of the town. With ashen faces, the men, women, and children who covered the earth in grotesque poses looked as if they were asleep. And they did sleep, they slept forever.

175

"Serves them right," remarked Münster, who was closely observing the scenery through his eye slit.

Engelmann recognized a Red Army scout tank thrown to the side farther ahead. Two dead soldiers were lying in front of it. Their uniforms had turned to black ash threads, their skin to brittle coal. These men were burned to death.

The smell of fire went up Engelmann's nose. It became more intense, biting with every meter Franzi II drove on. Other scents mingled with the aggressive stench. Engelmann felt himself seized by a sweet, slightly decaying, stinking breath.

Immediately he let himself sink back into his chair and slammed the lid flaps shut. Pale as chalk, he struggled with his breathing.

"You all right, Sepp?" Nitz had thrown the lieutenant a worried look.

"Yes," he gasped as he collected himself. "Let's just get the hell out of this village."

Karachev, Soviet Union, June 18th, 1943

Of course, Doctor Krüger had not been able to find anything about Berning that indicated self-mutilation. So Berning continued to vegetate following the particularly rough examination by the physician, just waiting to be released for the recovery leave of several weeks. A leave that would allow him to cure himself at home before he had to report to the recovery company of his division in Münster.

So Berning would go home.

In spite of the dull pain, in spite of the numbing of the medication, in spite of the burning in his throat, the stench and the cramps in Berning's limbs, his existence was brightened. With a little less melancholy, he awaited the future. He was looking forward to seeing his father and his dear mother again. And Gretel ... he was especially looking forward to Gretel. If she had remained the same girl, he would be able to impress her as an experienced combat veteran with his wounds.

Sergeant Berning was unspeakably grateful to leave the front line. Now he had proved that he was a good soldier; he had contributed his part to the war. It was only fair that he went home for a few weeks to recover – and to be allowed to stay away from the war for a few months.

With quiet steps, Doctor Krüger moved into Berning's field of vision. This time Nurse Micgy wasn't around; Krüger's bony fingers clasped the NCO's file instead.

"Herr Unteroffizier," the doctor began with exaggerated friendliness, "how are we today?"

Cold sweat gathered on Berning's neck. He straightened up as best he could and stuttered, feeling extremely uncomfortable in the doctor's presence: "It's all right."

"Well, we're very happy then, aren't we?" Krüger grinned before letting his gaze wander over the documents in Berning's file, which he slowly flipped through.

"I've consulted your platoon leader, Herr Unteroffizier," the doctor mentioned casually, and then looked up. He stared at Berning with tiny eyes. The sergeant was holding his breath. Krüger's grin took on a bizarre aspect, then he pushed his lower jaw forward and added: "For such faithful service to your fatherland and an unconditional sense of duty, one should always be rewarded."

With a delicate hand movement, Krüger pulled a paper from the file and laid it on Berning's woolen blanket. The sergeant read its title "Villa Romana del Casale – Adolf Hitler Sanatorium for Deserved Soldiers" with a dull feeling in his body. He then looked up questioningly – questioningly, but already animated by an evil premonition, which dug out his stomach like diarrhea.

"You must have missed this one. Were you too busy fighting the enemy with doggedness?" The sarcasm was pouring out of Krüger. "In any case, our Reich Chancellor has founded a sanatorium for wounded Wehrmacht soldiers in Piazza Armerina, which opened in May: the most modern sanatorium in the world! So that you can lick your wounds in peace, I have enrolled you there."

"Piazza Armerina"?

"Sicily."

"Sicily? Si ... Sicily????"

"That's right. Feel honored. You're one of the very few who's so lucky. I personally worked for it." A threatening note flickered over Krüger's grin. "Your plane leaves on Sunday."

Berning's fingers tangled the white sheet so strongly that his ankles began to hurt.

Coast off Segi Point, Solomon Islands (GB), June 21st, 1943

Private First Class Tom Roebuck, a brown-haired man in his late 20s whose receding chin and thinning hair were his most distinctive features, clasped the bazooka with both hands and supported it propped against the floor of the amphibious tank he was in. Together with another 20 soldiers of his platoon, he stood in the loading area of an LVT-1 Alligator, which was supposed to bring them to the beach at Segi Point.

It was dark in the belly of the transport ship, which was supposed to land the battalion's Alligators within attack range of the coast. The vibrations from the craft's engines passed constantly through the aluminum plate of the Alligator. Roebuck felt the transport vessel reducing its speed. Slowly, the quiet rattling that had accompanied the Marine Raiders for so long died away.

Roebuck looked over the heads of his platoon-mates at the large metal ramp that would come down in a moment to release all the amphibious tanks the transport vessel had loaded. His fellows were in shadow in front of him. Roebuck clearly saw the distinctive contours of their circular steel helmets. Someone was coughing. Another one was constantly jingling a chain.

Two Marine Raiders whispered quietly. A Garand carbine clanged when its owner accidentally struck the muzzle against the sidewall of the Alligator.

In front, the amphibious tanks had a small superstructure with a weapon station each to the left

180

and right. There was one soldier perched behind each Browning. Only their upper bodies protruded above the hatch.

Roebuck was nervous. This wouldn't be his first combat mission, certainly not. That's why he was nervous. He now knew what it meant to be under fire and to fear for his life. Above all, however, the fight against the Japanese was more merciless and cruel than his imagination had been able to show him beforehand. The fucking Nips fought fanatically, surrender didn't seem to know them. Rather, they would storm American positions with drawn swords and let automatic weapons mow them down than surrender when fighting a lost cause. Even the wounded often fought on, attempting to sweep American paramedics with hidden grenades to their deaths. Every single battle, every skirmish was a cold-blooded slaughter – every Japanese soldier had to be pulled out of his foxhole and put down individually. The Japs were different from the Krauts – the Gunny had told them. The Germans at least understood when they were beaten.

Slowly it dawned on the soldiers of Company L of the 4th Marine Raider Battalion that this war would not end as quickly as they had hoped. When things would keep going that way, they had to storm every goddamn island between New Georgia and the Japanese mainland before Tōjō would finally fly the white flag. But the next step had to be the isolation of the Japanese fortress near Rabaul. If the Japs were no longer able to operate their aircraft and ships from there, it would mean a major blow for their campaigns in the Pacific.

The batteries of two light cruisers, which were trying to level the coastal entrenchments of the Japanese, banged dully behind the vessel's thick ramp. Latest intel mentioned that the enemy had apparently realized at the last moment the importance of the Segi Point region to the Allies, and had moved some special regiment to the southeast corner of New Georgia.

With a soft squeak, the big ramp lowered. The glistening light of the Pacific sun flooded the cargo bay. Roebuck closed his eyes and held his arms in front of his face. The engine of the Alligator began rumbling, then the tank started rolling. With a massive jolt, its front side hit the ramp, which led directly into the water.

Saviano (everybody called him "Pizza"), a slim man of Italian origin from the big city, with a distinctive moustache adorning his face, patted Roebuck on the shoulder from behind when the Alligator entered the water and left the protective belly of the transport vessel. An almost paradisiacal sight was offered to the Marine Raiders, if it wasn't for the mighty war machine of the USA that dominated the scenery. Bright blue water surrounded an island close by, which defined the horizon as far as the eye could see. Wherever the sea touched the land, it turned into a fine sandy beach, which after a few yards transformed into lush green jungle. In the background, brightly-lit mountains soared up, surrounded by mist veils.

Roebuck looked over the edge of the open cargo compartment of the Alligator and saw how amphibious tanks were rumbling into the water from the bellies of big transport ships. Farther back, the cruiser *USS Helena* and the destroyer *USS Jenkins* rode the waves of dark blue water. Every few moments, their batteries fired off a salvo that went crashing down in the hinterland of the beach. Small impact mushrooms rose where the giant shells struck. Columns of smoke stood like exclamation marks over the beach. Palms caught fire and overturned. In the firmament, the planes of a fighter squadron buzzed around. The blue paint and the white stars on the hull flashed in the sun.

Right at the front of the Alligator, Gunny, a tall man over the age of 40 whose gray hair was only a few millimeters long, turned to the men and shouted over the roar of the tank and the thunder of the ship's cannons. "Listen! You know our mission! We storm the beach, occupy the hinterland, and create a beach head for the pioneers. Two things! First, never travel to New Georgia without condoms!" The gunny grinned mockingly and with a gesture of his hand pointed to the condoms that the soldiers had put over the muzzles of their weapons. These would keep the coarsest dirt and moisture away from the barrels.

"Second, recon says the coast is defended by some special Jap regiment. I don't care what kind of guys they are – battle-hardened specialists or kids with guns. We'll go out there and slaughter those slant-eyed yellow monkeys! No mercy! No prisoners! Kill 'em all!"

The gunny got approval. Some raised their fists, others nodded silently.

The swimming tanks were eating their way through the water inexorably. They carried an entire battalion to the beach. In the background, the big guns of the Navy ships were still thundering. Their shells tore open the jungle of New Georgia. One sheaf after the other was thrown into the dense green, where huge detonations devoured the flora and fauna.

Roebuck cleared his throat. He knew what he was doing this for. In his head, his wife Marie's last letter was still present. A few hours ago, he had read her lines out loud to his comrades Pizza, D'Amico, and Juergens, who earned the nickname "Batman" for excessively reading a certain comic book series. It had become a ritual for the four Marine Raiders to keep incoming letters until the beginning of a new operation. Shortly before they moved out to fight the enemy once more, they opened the envelopes together and read each other the lines from their loved ones. Roebuck had been quite embarrassed sometimes, because his wife wrote very frivolous things. But at least he knew what he was doing this shit for. He had to protect his homeland – and Marie - from these yellow bastards, even though he would have preferred to have been with her in San Diego.

Finally the first phalanx of swimming tanks reached the beach. Immediately the battleships moved their fire farther into the hinterland of the island, but so far the enemy had not shown up at all.

"Remember," Gunny yelled at his men. "We gonna bail out and immediately head for the jungle, otherwise we put our tanks in the way of those that are gonna land with the second wave. The captain is in the LVT on the right. We'll stick to him. Load and lock!"

The men cocked their weapons and turned the safety devices on.

"Semper Fi, boys!" Gunny bellowed.

"Semper Fi!" the soldiers repeated, barrel-chested and with tense faces.

A crack was heard and vibrations went through the Alligator as the crawler tracks of the amphibious tank dug into the sand before the steely monster pushed itself out of the water with a mechanical groan.

"Go, out, out, out!" Gunny commanded and made a gesture to bail out over the edges of the cargo compartment. The GIs started to move. They jumped up at the side walls of the Alligator and pulled themselves over the edges. Pizza paused on top of the wall and indicated Roebuck to hand him the bazooka. Together with the anti-tank weapon, he let himself fall over the edge into the knee-deep water, where he immediately struggled to his feet. Roebuck followed as he overcame the edge of the cargo compartment with a smooth move and also jumped down into the water.

The sun burned relentlessly down on Segi Point. The cool water that penetrated Roebuck's boots, sleeves, and pants felt pleasant. But he knew he'd curse his wet feet at some point. Immediately he reached for the bazooka, which Pizza handed to him, and waded through the shallow water, following his comrades.

There was still no trace of the enemy. The men of Company L stormed up the beach. They finally reached the jungle border where Gunny met the company commander, Captain Morgan. Both

185

discussed the sitrep before Gunny gave new orders: "We move 50 into the forest and take defensive positions. Then wait for the tanks! Machine Gun Squad to me!"

Juergens, D'Amico, and a few others hurried over to Gunny with their heavy M2 machine guns, the tripods they needed for emplacing them, and lots of ammunition boxes, while the Bazooka Squad commander assigned Roebuck and Pizza a Navy bomb funnel with overthrown palm trees at its edges. Everywhere, weapons clattered and breeches clicked as the Marine Raiders took up positions.

While Pizza checked his carbine, Roebuck subjected the perimeter to an examining look. Once again, they were in the middle of the jungle. Palm after palm, the trees stood close together, and the ground was overgrown with ferns of all sizes. Sometimes the visibility was barely more than a few twenty yards due to the dense vegetation. The Japs could lurk everywhere, and Roebuck did not yet believe that they had retreated without a fight. He stared into an aisle that led deeper into the jungle. The Sherman tanks would take this path, while the Marine Raiders were assigned to fight their way through the coppice to the right and left of it. The Alligators had meanwhile taken up position at the edge of the forest. From there, with their machine guns, they could guard the infantry's advance for quite some time.

Minutes later, the first wave of Shermans went ashore as they rolled out of the bellies of larger landing vessels. The armored battle tanks proximately formed a column formation on the beach and shortly afterwards pushed into the aisle. At walking pace, the steely comrades drove into the jungle, tracks squeaking. Roebuck's Company L received its marching orders.

"Form a skirmish line!" It resounded from everywhere. The battalion's riflemen advanced side by side like the poles of a fence. Slowly, they pushed deeper into the jungle. The Bazooka Squad stayed close to the Rifle Platoons, ready to fight enemy tanks or fortified shelters. Ever since the Japanese relied more heavily on their tank weapon, the Marine Raiders had encountered enemy tanks on every goddamn battlefield. Morgan had decided to combine his bazookas to always have the concentrated firepower of all his anti-tank weapons in one place. Intel did not expect enemy tanks at Segi Point – but one could never know.

The battalion marched a long way inland together with the Shermans. The terrain was difficult, the ground partly swampy. Several times a tank got stuck and had to be pushed out of the mud by the Sherman behind it. Mosquitoes, flies, and other beasts the Marine Raiders didn't even want to think about buzzed around the heads of the soldiers. Fighting in the jungle proved again and again that it always increased the pace of the already-inhuman warfare. Here, it wasn't just the Japanese who were the enemy. Here, every damn creature was hostile – as was the climate, the mud, the dryness, the wetness. Diseases were inflicted on the Marine Raiders. One could have gone through the ranks and asked, and wouldn't find anyone who had never had diarrhea, headaches, fever, pus pustules, or other niceties during his time in the Pacific theater. In the humid air, every wound ignited rapidly. Over and over the Navy Corpsmen prophylactically distributed tablets, and the men had stopped asking why they were eating them like candy.

The brooding afternoon sun stood over the dense forests of Segi Point. Birds sang their strange songs. Meter-high ferns got in the way of the Marine Raiders. Razor-sharp grasses slit their hands open. Sweat was pouring out of every man's pores. The skin was moist and reddened, and everything was sticky. The soldiers groaned, they cursed, but they marched on. Under the roof of gigantic palm leaves, the heat accumulated. The Marines stewed in their own juice.

Suddenly, a thunderclap was heard on the left, and the next moment the first Sherman of the armored column got hit by an AP shell. The tank – still in motion – turned half to the side under the force of the impact. Tank men bailed out screaming as flames tried to catch them.

The Marine Raider Infantrymen threw themselves to the ground. Roebuck had clearly seen the gun smoke from that enemy cannon. Dense trails of fume rose to the left of his position about 400 yards away. He recognized two earth bunkers overgrown with fern. Muzzle flashes from handguns flashed in embrasures.

The US soldiers yelled orders at each other while Japanese shouts sounded over to them. An enemy machine gun opened fire. It vomited bullets at lightning speed; so fast that the banging of the individual shots merged into one another and turned into a constant rattling frequency. Shortly the enemy machine gun delivered some harassing fire, then it became silent again while the Sherman's drivers engaged reverse gear to get out of the AT-gun's range.

Roebuck delved into Juergens' mien with a questioning face. "What is that," he asked, when the enemy machine gun again started shooting with a seemingly unusually high rate of fire. The projectiles of a brief burst of fire chased over the skulls of the two Americans. They ducked behind a trunk.

"No fuckin' idea, buddy," Juergens replied and shook his head. "Maybe a Type 92?"

"No, Batman. Listen!"

As ordered, the enemy MG sent out just another firing burst, while the Marine Raiders shook off the shock about the Japanese surprise attack and began to move into gear. NCOs made arrangements and gave instructions.

"That piece shoots way too fast. Must be 15, 20 rounds per second! Type 92 and all the others are slower. They sound more like a typewriter."

Juergens nodded. "Whatever," he finally realized. "We'll kill it either way!"

The Bazooka Squad commander reached the position of the Bazooka and MG teams and shoved himself down. "Skipper wants us to blow up the earth bunkers and give covering fire! 2nd and 3rd Platoon attack from the right flank. Pizza, Tommy, get your bazooka ready to fire on my command.

"Batman, your fire team is with me now! Take firing position right here, engage on my command!"

The Marine Raiders confirmed the order, then Pizza jumped behind Roebuck, who lifted the bazooka on his right shoulder while grabbing its handle piece. Pizza took the first rocket from an ammunition bag and stuffed it into the rocket launcher tube from behind. Then he knocked Roebuck on the helmet, the sign for "loaded." To the left of them, D'Amico swung the tripod of the heavy MG from his shoulders and pressed its feet into the soft ground. Seconds later, Batman had locked the air-cooled Browning machine gun on it and was ready to fire.

"Bazooka fire!" the squad commander yelled. At that distance it was not easy to hit anything with the rocket launcher, but the target was an immobile one, and Roebuck was a skilled shooter. He pressed the buttstock against his shoulder, aimed through the iron sights, found his target, and finally pulled the trigger. With a boisterous sound, the rocket shot out of the tube, while a boiling hot jet of fire escaped on the back and scorched the flora behind Roebuck. He plainly felt the heat that got set free from the ignition. Within a blink of an eye, the rocket's solid fuel propulsion ignited, and the warhead dashed off with tongues of flame in its luggage. It hit the closest bunker in the middle right above the embrasure. A millisecond later, the wooden shelter was swallowed by a gigantic explosion. Desperate cries of the Japanese were heard.

"Every moment now the monkeys will run right into my biscuit," Batman gloated, and pressed his MG to his shoulder. In fact, Japanese tactics often seemed to be to just attack in vain against American positions until the GIs ran out of ammunition. Losses at a ratio of 100 to one were not uncommon in the Pacific War. Often Japanese soldiers attacked with drawn swords. But not today.

Roebuck watched the men of the other platoons move forward. With long leaps, they hurried from cover to cover and fought their way through the thicket. Finally their vanguards reached the earth bunkers. The first Marine Raiders invaded the enemy entrenchments. But there were no shots heard, no screams. Finally, 2nd Platoon reported that the area was free of enemies.

"What's wrong with the friggin' Japs?" whispered D'Amico, then the squad commander gave new orders: Bazooka teams and Juergens' MG were supposed to catch up with the platoons at the earth bunkers. Swearing in a way one should not recite, Batman eased his Browning off its tripod anchorage and lifted the weapon onto his shoulders. Then he and the others chased after the squad commander. Shortly after, they reached the earth bunkers. Their fellow soldiers from the other platoons had already taken up positions all around. D'Amico, Batman, Pizza, and Roebuck stumbled into the shelter that had been ruptured by the rocket. Four dead Japanese lay there in their own blood, their faces caked with dirt. They were half-buried by fallen wooden beams. There was no trace of the Japanese machine gun or the rest of the bunker crew. The NCOs assembled to discuss further action, while the Shermans lined up farther back in the aisle and the wounded tankers were taken care of.

Pizza and Juergens immediately tackled the Japanese corpses, searching them for valuable objects. D'Amico sat down wheezing on a beam and moistened his chapped lips with water from his canteen. Then he picked up a can of peaches from his field pack and pried it open with the shiv of his knife. Immediately he poured the juice down his throat. Right and left, the sweet stuff ran out of the corners of his mouth. Roebuck, however, examined the destroyed bunker. He found something metallic under collapsed wooden planks and now, moaning, pushed the beams aside. Lastly, he reached into the gap and grabbed the flashing metal. Immediately he felt that he had touched a big firearm with his fingers.

The barrel was still warm. With some effort – Roebuck snorted like a bull in the eyes of a rival – he pulled out the weapon under the rubble and looked at it with big eyes.

"What's that?" he asked. That weapon was long and mostly made of metal. The buttstock and parts of the grip were wooden. Under the muzzle there was a bipod, while the barrel was stored in a housing with large cooling openings. Roebuck had never seen this weapon before, but he immediately realized that it had to be a machine gun. All of a sudden, Batman and Pizza looked over his shoulders, curious to see if Roebuck had found anything interesting.

"Anybody got any idea what that fucking gun is?" Roebuck wanted to know. Juergens made a sour face. "Well, if I didn't know any better, I'd say it's an MG 42."

"MG 42?" repeated Pizza disbelievingly.

"Yes, from the Krauts."

"Can't be. Look, there's Japanese characters engraved on the side." Pizza pointed to the metal body below the top cover.

"Oh, yeah, fuckface? Then look here!" Juergens handed his comrades a crumpled photo.

"Where'd you get that from?" asked Roebuck.

"From that dead Jap over there."

Suddenly the enemy AT-gun started firing again from a new position. Outside, another Sherman flew apart. Handgun fire thundered south of Roebuck's position. Immediately the Marine Raiders kissed the ground while bursts of fire hit the ruptured earth bunker they were in.

"The fuckin' Japs are flanking us," Juergens shouted as he and D'Amico set up their Browning with nimble fingers.

Again an AT-gun bang echoed through the jungle. Immediately, another Sherman burst in two with a bouquet of sparks spreading like a volcanic eruption. The remaining tanks began in the narrow aisle with desperate turning maneuvers, while they randomly fired in the direction they assumed the enemy to be. In the dense vegetation, they hardly could detect any Japanese soldiers waiting for them.

The 2nd Platoon started to move at the same time, pushing north. Batman gave covering fire. Because of the thick undergrowth, hardly anything was to be recognized; his fire bursts simply disappeared in the green and tore up shrubs and branches. The squad commander was in radio contact with 2nd Platoon, and was therefore able to direct the MG fire accordingly. 3rd Platoon, on the other hand, dashed back to the aisle to be able to take the enemy into crossfire from there.

Suddenly Japanese yelling sounded from everywhere. 2nd Platoon had run directly into an ambush. Japanese climbed out of holes in the ground and jumped down from the treetops. With pulled

193

Guntō swords and bayonets, they involved the Americans in bloody close combat. Roebuck saw only a mixture of men in front of him running into each other. American and Japanese uniforms meshed; blades sank into flesh and rifle stocks smashed faces. A knot of screaming people rolled through the brushwood.

More and more Japanese came from everywhere. Further Shermans went down the drain, and also 3rd Platoon was under heavy fire. Once again an enemy MG 42 hammered in staccato into the Marine Raiders, killing several GIs within seconds. The Bazooka Squad commander ordered Roebuck and his fellows to fall back to the aisle. The Marine Raiders ran for their lives.

"What kind of shit is this?" D'Amico shrieked. Roebuck, however, did not react. His thoughts focused on the photo Batman had shown him just a minute ago. That picture was stuck in his mind's eye. It showed about 30 Japanese soldiers, who had gathered for one of these typical group photos. At the edge, however, stood three men of clearly Western descent. They wore the uniforms of German generals.

Southwest of Piazza Armerina, Italy, June 21st, 1943

The accommodation blockhouses were two-story wooden buildings located south of the excavation site of Villa Romana del Casale, about five kilometers southwest of Piazza Armerina, between the former thermal baths and a wide olive field. Four of these rectangular blockhouses with black pointed roofs stood next to each other. Von Witzleben had had this complex raised in a hurry, because he wanted to provide the troops with a very special health resort in addition to the usual recreation homes. 300 seats in the Adolf Hitler Sanatorium in Sicily were of course a joke, in view of millions of men under arms, but it was intended above all to fulfill the symbolic character, to show that the Chancellor was doing something for his soldiers. The waiting lists were already infinitely long, but strong contacts could also work wonders in this case. Was it a coincidence that Berning was now here, while Doctor Krüger and the head of the sanatorium, Medical Brigadier General Link, had known each other well since their student days?

Chancellor von Witzleben had already begun searching for a suitable location in November 1942 because he wanted to open his sanatorium as soon as possible. He casually mentioned his plans in the presence of Mussolini, who was immediately taken with the idea. The "Duce" was determined to build the sanatorium on Italian soil. Von Witzleben liked that, because where could you recover better than in Mediterranean Italy?

So everything went his way. Before Christmas, Mussolini and von Witzleben together determined the location: Villa Romana del Casale in Sicily. Construction works began a few days before New Year's Eve. Both heads of state pulled out all the stops; hundreds of specialists and pioneers were shipped to the island located just in front of the Italian boot tip. Thus on May 1st, 1943, the sanatorium could be opened and baptized by von Witzleben on the name Adolf Hitler. The Führer's aircraft had officially been shot down by enemy fighter planes; consequently Hitler had died an honorable soldier's death – so it had been sold to the people. Outwardly, von Witzleben's government did everything in its power to ensure that the German Reich would continue in Hitler's spirit; the Chancellor did not want to force major political changes on the already-shaken people. Therefore Hitler's name had to serve for all sorts of things these days in order to add symbolic power. Those who did not look behind the scenes of the state's work hardly noticed anything of the subtle changes that von Witzleben and his companions had initiated since November 1942; changes, which were gradually implemented – often without much attention. The Waffen SS did not exist anymore since March 1st, and the NSDAP had to surrender almost all charges of importance and influence. Although the party was still involved at the grassroots of society, spreading its ideology there and retaining its patronage over youth organizations, among other things, it also continued to represent the delegates of the Reichstag, a parliament that was in fact powerless.

Nurse Sieglinde, a brunette, cheerful, full-bodied woman of less than 25 years, pushed Sergeant Berning in his wheelchair into the small parlor that was to serve him as lodging for the next few weeks. The metallic clanging of the work done outside on the construction sites quietly penetrated the room. Berning had the feeling that this sanatorium had been opened too hastily.

The parlor was furnished according to the latest standards. The bed looked very inviting, with two bulging cushions and a blanket in bright white. There was also a dresser and a desk with a table lamp. Through a small window, the sun shone brightly into the room. Next to the bed was a small cupboard, and on the opposite side was a locker for Berning's uniform, which he had been wearing since he was dismissed from the field hospital. The wounded badge in black decorated his left breast pocket since he had not registered the one wound he got in the battle of Kursk.

Sieglinde gently pushed the wounded sergeant next to the bed and then lifted his knapsack and pannier onto the desk. Berning's arm and shoulder were still wrapped in plaster. When he arrived at the sanatorium, he had already seen other comrades wearing a Stuka.

Sieglinde smiled softly and said, "Once again, welcome to the Adolf Hitler Sanatorium at the Villa Romana del Casale in Sicily." She said this as if she had memorized the very sentence. "For meals, please come to the dining tent over by the villa complex. The path is signposted. Please excuse the fact that there are still

197

some things taking place in tents. Not all the buildings have been completed yet." Sieglinde beamed cheerfully. "In good weather like today, by the way, we dine outside in the large portico of the villa. The meal times are in the morning from 7 to 10 o'clock, at noon from 11:30 o'clock to 13:30 o'clock and in the evening from 17 o'clock to 19 o'clock. If you need help – no matter what ..." Sieglinde leaned forward and looked at him mischievously. He noticed that her breasts were tight under her dress, "... then just ring." She pointed to an electric switch that could be reached from the bed and meanwhile took the opportunity to move one step closer to Berning. Her knee touched his calf. Sieglinde smelled like violets.

"The switch is directly connected to the nurses' station on this floor. Most of the time I'm here. So, just ring when the shoe pinches, all right?" She straightened up and smiled at him as her hands stroked a crease out of her skirt. "Please remember that the head of our sanatorium, Dr. Medical Brigadier General Link, will be briefing all new arrivals in the ground floor classroom tomorrow morning. It is scheduled at 09:30. Everything else, such as use of the library or other leisure facilities as well as your individual therapy plan, you will receive tomorrow after the briefing. Otherwise, I wish you a pleasant stay with us. By the way, if you want something cool to drink, you'll find water at four degrees in your refrigerator." Sieglinde pointed with her filigree fingers to the small cupboard next to the dresser.

Berning raised an eyebrow. "A refrigerator?" he asked puzzledly.

"Yeah, right. " Once again a broad smile conjured itself into her soft face. She seemed proud to be able to offer patients such a luxury.

"A safety note on the refrigerator, though," she added meekly. "Should you ever notice that there is an unpleasant smell in your room or that liquid is leaking out of the cupboard, please leave the room immediately and inform the staff. Now I don't want to get on your nerves, Herr Unteroffizier." She had pronounced his rank very softly and sweetly. Respect and esteem resonated in her voice. Berning didn't know how to handle it.

"By the way, in the locker you'll find something comfortable to wear for yourself. Fold your uniform and simply hand it over to me, then you will receive everything freshly washed and patched back tomorrow. Now I give it a bone with the teachings. I'll let you arrive first," she laughed embarrassedly and looked at him, but she received no reaction from Berning.

"I'm Sieglinde, by the way."

"Mhm."

For a moment, she silently examined him with her big beady eyes. A brown strand fell in her face. She seemed to be waiting for another reaction from Berning, but it didn't come. Sieglinde finally smiled again – a little pinched this time – then opened the window and disappeared from the room. The noise of the construction works now reached Berning's ear unattenuated. Italian and German voices blended in each other.

Berning sighed.

Slowly, he got up from his wheelchair and hobbled to the window with a pain-distorted face.

Outside, the excavation site with its ruins of the old thermal bath ruled the view. Only flat, demolished stone walls and the hints of stone stoves were left of the former bathing complex.

Behind it was the actual Villa Romana del Casale, in the glimmering light of the burning midday sun, and in places excellently preserved site from ancient Rome. Sandstone walls rose there. Some buildings even had a stone roof. The smell of dust and diesel was in the air. Berning wondered how to recover with all the racket from the ongoing construction works. Once again he sighed deeply and leaned against the windowsill with a downcast look.

What am I supposed to do here in Sicily? crossed his mind. *What am I supposed to do anywhere other than at home in Burgenland? All I want is to go home!*

South of Tula, Soviet Union, June 22nd, 1943

From the Wehrmacht's point of view, the offensive progressed extremely satisfactory.

Already in the first days of the attack, German units broke through the Russian defensive fire in all sites of attack. In some places, the enemy had not offered resistance at all. The Luftwaffe had also landed an absolute stroke of luck when Stuka dive bombers accidentally wiped out General Reyter and his entire staff during an air raid on the second day of the offensive. Reyter was the commander-in-chief of the Bryansk Front. The severely-battered Soviet armies in the area, which had had a tough time trying to breach into German lines just a few weeks ago, had nothing left to oppose the Wehrmacht's attack. The 27th Soviet Army had practically ceased to exist. The leftovers of the Russian 3rd Army showed signs of disintegration and fled every which way. Some had absconded behind the River Don, while 122 Red Army soldiers had been shot as a measure of preserving discipline on behalf of the army command just outside of Tula. As a result of all of these events, the Bryansk Front was close to collapse.

Kampfgruppe Hoth had breached deep into the enemy front, and the Russians could not stuff the breach with forces from the north either, because there they were overrun by Hausser's panzers at the same time – and the latter also had the Panzer Corps Grossdeutschland in reserve. From the south, a relief attack by Soviet forces was likewise impossible. There the 6th German Army pressed against the Russian entrenchments at the River Don to bind the enemy. The decisive battle of Tula was imminent. Hoth's combat formation had advanced up to the southern foothills off the city. Hausser's troops had reached the River Oka. German pioneers were currently working on transitions across the water, after the Russians had blown up all bridges during their retreat. Tula itself was stuck between the gripping jaws of this German pincer movement.

Madness, Engelmann pondered, who had moved away from the rest of the company for a moment of silence and privacy. *Von Manstein, that daredevil, has truly tracked down a gap in the enemy front line and is now pushing into it by every trick in the book.*

It was night. The crickets chirped their happy songs. In the distance, a soldier sneezed.

A sense of deep satisfaction overcame Engelmann. Within weeks, Ivan had bled to death at the central Eastern Front. And now the Wehrmacht had come dangerously close to Moscow again. Engelmann suddenly had the feeling that this war could have a good ending after all – a good end for the Reich, for his family, for him. There was a spirit of optimism in him again. He therefore decided to write a letter to Elly at the next opportunity. How he wanted to share his mood with her! But he also knew about the volatility of his inner feelings. A local defeat, an unsuccessful attack, or other baleful news, and Engelmann would immediately believe again that the war was already lost. On the other hand, he could not switch off his emotions and was therefore again and again alternatingly animated by anxiety and confidence.

The lieutenant was among some tall beeches on the edge of the company's area of responsibility. The panzers were congregated under tree canopies and the men tried to get a snatch of sleep. Tomorrow morning, the regiment would continue its attack. They just could not allow the attack momentum to dry up. Engelmann felt the crushing tiredness that weighed on his head like a concrete block.

He sighed, then urinated. His urine stank and was a dark yellow – he did not drink enough, but when was a soldier supposed to drink during action? Also the Wehrmacht struggled to provide its front troops with enough water. But Engelmann had not only secluded himself from the others to pee; he also wanted to address a short word to the Lord. As long as enemy bombers flew into the Reich, he felt more comfortable in all his powerlessness when he at least asked for protection for his family. In his mind, he set forth his intercessions when suddenly a branch cracked behind him. Engelmann swung around, scared. Captain Stollwerk revealed himself, the tall officer standing in a shadowy position in the darkness. A glowing cigarette hung in the corner of his mouth, while somewhere far away Münster's voice asked a comrade how much more he would earn as a staff sergeant.

"Well, Josef?" Stollwerk said in a low voice. "Will you have a quick talk with your god before you hit the hay?"

Engelmann nodded. He felt the mockery in Stollwerk's voice, and he did not give himself false hopes of what his fellow officer might think of believers like him – even though the two officers got along splendidly in all other respects.

"I ask for protection for my family," Engelmann explained in a thin voice. Stollwerk stepped into the glinting moonlight and offered the lieutenant a cigarette. He refused without a word. Both stared into the darkness for a moment, while muffled gunfire filled the background noise for a short moment.

"What do you believe in, Arno?" Engelmann resumed the dialogue after minutes of silence.

"I believe in the superiority of our people. I believe in the final victory."

Engelmann nodded mutely and looked down.

"And I believe that the weakness revealed by our current government will be fatal one day," Stollwerk continued.

"What weakness?"

"Did you know that von Witzleben has held secret peace negotiations with the enemy by this Preussen boy?" Stollwerk said. His eyes seemed sharp and polished, like a predator ready to strike down its prey.

"No."

"That means our own Chancellor no longer believes in final victory. What a message to the men!" The captain scornfully threw his cigarette to the ground and stepped on out.

"Or he just wants to end the suffering."

"Pah! Josef! Did you know that von Witzleben allowed Jews to do military service again?"

"What difference does it make? What's the big deal?"

"What's the big deal, you ask? You want those sneaky, fake people to fight for us? I can only hope for your sake that you never get one of these Jewish rats by your side when things get dicey. Before you know it, the Jew has rammed his knife into your back and then defects."

Engelmann grunted. He didn't know what to say about it.

"The Jew is like a tumor in the German racial corpus," he was told by Stollwerk, "as long as we do not remove it, it will impair the development possibilities of our race. Such supposedly humanistic decisions could ultimately cost us the final victory! I fear von Witzleben inevitably drives our beloved Germany into ruin."

"That's some gross nonsense, Arno."

But Stollwerk gave Engelmann a look that gave the lieutenant clarity about his attitude.

"Are you satisfied with the government of von Witzleben?" Stollwerk asked.

Engelmann thought for a moment. Was he satisfied? Prisoners of war, Jews, purges ... some things were no longer as they used to be. But what could he know about it, he was just a tiny man in a gigantic system. Engelmann had to think of gruesome rumors that he otherwise preferred to put to one side; he had to think of gruesome tales about things the SS may have done in those camps. He could hardly have imagined it. Yes, the Wehrmacht waged a war here in the East – had already waged it before von Witzleben's Chancellorship. Engelmann had also witnessed cruelties since 1940, carried out by German soldiers.

But even if such acts violated martial law, were they really war crimes? Or is it just an expression of the spiral of violence that continues forever, turning ordinary men into murderous animals? Just because wise men had set up laws of humanity thousands of miles away from the battlefield did not mean that such laws could last in a fight for life and death. Certainly, Engelmann in his area of authority would prevent any unsoldierly and dishonorable action, but many things happened in the heat of the moment.

"I can't complain," he finally replied. Dozens of trains of thought were spinning in his head.

Stollwerk just nodded and looked down. The following minutes were marked by the silence of both men and the quiet rumbling of guns and artillery in the distance. Lastly Stollwerk tapped his forehead, wished him a good night, and took his leave. He disappeared into the darkness he came from just minutes ago. Engelmann reflected for a moment about what his comrade had tried to achieve with this conversation, but then he shrugged his shoulders and made his way back to his crew.

Southwest of Piazza Armerina, Italy, June 24th, 1943

Berning sat on a provisional wooden stand by the provisionally furnished sports field, after having had a meal provisionally cobbled together in the provisional mess hall's kitchen. He leaned on a crutch, wearing the comfortable, light-blue sportswear of the sanatorium. Admittedly, this so-called refrigerator had impressed him at first, but since then his mood had gone steeply downhill. Everything in this place was of a provisional nature. The whole sanatorium was one vast makeshift building. The construction machines were rattling all the time, and the builders worked late into the night at the sports facility, the sauna area, the swimming bath, and the future mess hall. In the evening, Berning lay in his bed and couldn't sleep, because the din from the construction sites and his thoughts kept him from it. When he fell asleep at last, he dreamt again and again of that one dolorous crime he had committed against his comrade – his friend – Rudi. He would carry that guilt around with him for the rest of his life.

And during the day? During the day he was bored to death and threatened to die in the stuffy and dusty heat of Sicily. What was expected of him? That he ran a big lap around Piazza Armerina with the running group? That he listened day in, day out to the archaeologist's boring lectures on the villa? That he should play football with his wounds like all halfway-healthy patients did? Or maybe he should read? Twelve hours a day? Berning already got scabies when he thought about grabbing a book. He hated those things.

He just wanted to go home. There was nothing for him here in Sicily. No family, no Gretel. Here there was only the eternal heat, the boredom, the superfluous movement therapy seminars and the "Avantis," who annoyed Berning with their much too-fast macaroni language. Italian workers were roaming the entire site – and just at that moment, a handful of Germans were playing football against an equal number of Italians on the provisional sports field before his eyes, where stakes rammed into the ground served as provisional goals. The Italian army was also entitled to some places in this sanatorium.

Berning turned a letter between his fingers he had received this morning. It was from his mother. Berning rarely received mail, but from time to time Gretel wrote. His mother's letter only reinforced the homesickness in his heart. She had written him exuberantly how proud she was of him, and that she would like to see him again.

Somehow it was funny – otherwise she never wrote; and if she did, she bestowed him just a few lines in which she expounded the gossip from his home village. But this very letter he just had received literally dripped with declarations of love. His mother's lines had an undertone begging him to make himself strong once again for home leave. She seemed to miss her son – her boys, as she always said – very much indeed. All the mother's pain, caused by sons who had been snatched from home by the war, became clear in her letter. His mother's lines made Berning's lips tremble.

208

How dare the Wehrmacht, how dare Pappendorf and Krüger to make a lovable, friendly woman so unhappy? How did all the old men in the governments presumed they would have the right to take away the children of this time? Grief and rage were increasingly blending in Berning's chest.

Meanwhile, he watched the hustle and bustle on the sports field with a tired gaze. The sweating men shouted at each other when they wanted to have the ball, or shot clumsily in the direction of the opposing goal. Some were limping; most were clearly not at the peak of their performance curve. Somewhat offside, at the other end of the stand, German soldiers squatted together. One played quite mediocre on his harmonica the song "Lili Marleen" while the others, puffing cigarettes and pipes, exchanged rumors.

Berning did not even notice that Sieglinde, coming from the canteen tent, was approaching the stand. It wasn't until she sat next to him that he became aware of her. Yet he made no effort to turn to her. He disliked any movement that wasn't absolutely necessary for survival.

"Guten Tag, Herr Unteroffizier," she greeted him in a sonorous voice.

"Grüss Gott," he replied listlessly.

"Did you like the food today?"

"So medium."

She slipped a little closer to him and was visibly embarrassed. Finally she bit her lower lip and said: "You know, when you need something, you can always come to me. Anytime. All right?"

"I know." Berning nipped every conversation in the bud. Long moments passed in which Sieglinde fought perceptibly with herself, whether she should venture a new advance or not. Finally she dared, but her now slightly-brittle voice already revealed that she could no longer bear many rejections. "May I ask you a question?

"Mhm."

"Where exactly are you from? I find your dialect very beautiful to listen to."

"German Reich."

"Aha."

Minutes went by. In front of Berning's eyes, the footballers dribbled the ball back and forth. They roared and groaned with exertion or pain – and the mood of the German players worsened every second. No wonder: they were far behind. Suddenly Berning noticed that Sieglinde was crying softly.

Oh no, he thought. As it were, he cursed all women. *Oh God no.* Against the inner desire to simply get up and go back to his room, he forced himself to ask her why she was in such a gloomy mood. Sieglinde looked up with reddened eyes: "I'm simply afraid of the future," she admitted after a moment of irritation.

"Why?" Berning asked, like out of a pistol. *No! Why can't I just shut the fuck up?* he damned his rash mouth.

"American ships are said to be sailing off the coast of the island. Rumor has it they're coming. Why else would the Americans have occupied all these small Italian islands? But the Chancellor says they want to go to the Balkans and gather all the troops there. Even this General Rommel is there, and only two weeks ago they

210

withdrew the unit in which an acquaintance of one of our nurses serves from Sicily and moved it to Yugoslavia."

"Mhm."

"What will become of us when the Americans come?"

Berning shrugged his shoulders. The Wehrmacht will work it out somehow, he thought. He wouldn't participate in it, not with his injuries. That was clear for him.

Finally, an elderly man in a wheelchair, who had to pay for his war service with his left foot, blew the final whistle. Immediately riots broke out among the players. The Italians had beaten the Germans 11 to 2. The two teams came at each other. They shouted, they laughed, they provoked. Men pushed others, yelled at each other, or were in each other's arms. Although the general mood among the players was still emotionally charged, it did not spill over into aggression. That could change quickly. In the end the Germans and the Italians went their separate ways, celebrating and shouting, whispering to each other like little girls and reproaching each other for individual situations in the previous game. Others congratulated themselves on good moves.

"Hey there, Tonti," one of the German players suddenly yelled to an Italian officer, who spoke German pretty well.

"What's the matter?" he replied with a weak accent.

"Do you know how many gears an Italian tank has?"

Tonti stared bitterly at the German, who raised his arms in a challenging manner, before the questioner revealed the solution: "Five reverse gears! And one forward gear for parades!"

The German crowd fell into a roaring laughter, while the Italians grumbled angrily.

"You!" Tonti suddenly huffed and pointed to the joke teller. "Shut your mouth!"

"What did you say?" another of the German players joined in and stormed at Tonti with his head held high. Threateningly, he pointed his index finger at the Italian. "You don't forbid a German to speak, you spaghetti-eater!"

"What did you call me, eh?"

Other Italians joined in the wild exchange of words and threw all kinds of Italian slurs at the Germans. The two teams approached each other with verbally-supported threatening gestures.

"I called you spaghetti-eater, spaghetti-eater!" the one with the red skull went on, mocking. But Tonti did not put up with such insults. He struck so fast that his opponent lay on the ground with his lip popped open before he understood what had happened. Just milliseconds later, the two teams roared at each other. A wild tussle developed before Berning's eyes.

Cursing quietly, Sieglinde stood up and stomped towards the men bandying blows, while people rushed in from all sides to bring the brawlers apart.

Tula, Soviet Union, June 25th, 1943

After two days of fierce and bitter fighting for the city, the forces of the Red Army, who were entrenched in the city center, were encircled from the north, west, and south. In the east, there was still a narrow land corridor leading to the rear echelon of the Soviets, but it was under constant fire from German batteries.

The soldiers of the Wehrmacht had advanced street by street, house by house, room by room in bloody, close-quarter combat. In man-to-man fighting, the soldiers of both sides had killed each other at close range, executing each other with bullets, rifle butts, bare hands, and teeth. But the advance of the Germans seemed to be unstoppable these days. The Red Army soldiers were pushed farther and farther into the inner city, where they were crammed together like cattle, trapped under a fire bell made of a thousand German barrels of all calibers. There were no more houses in Tula. Ruins was the appropriate term. Stones stacked on top of each other, walls blown out, and roofs shattered were all that the war had left of the once thriving city.

This afternoon, the Wehrmacht sounded the charge to storm the last Russian emplacements in this stony, leaden hell, covered in dust and blood. On the Soviet side, a wild mixture of tanks, AT-guns, infantry, cavalry, even pilots, doctors, partisans, and wounded clung to everything that could be used to extinguish lives. They awaited the German attack with fierce determination.

Engelmann and his men had not experienced the worst abominations of this struggle for Tula firsthand. Shielded behind centimeter-thick armor, they shot at buildings from a distance. Nevertheless, the nerves of the German tankers were also raw. Day and night the battle had raged; no rest, no sleep, no food had been granted to the soldiers. With faces encrusted with dried oil and dirt, chapped lips and swollen mucous membranes, the crew of Franzi II ignored all the sacrifices they made these days and concentrated as best they could on the one last fight ahead of them. The tiredness and exhaustion were written in their faces. With milky eyes and pale, expressionless – almost dead – visages, the tank men looked through their vision blocks at the debris that had once been Tula.

The sun stood glistening over the city and heated the grey walls to an unbearable temperature. The panzers of 12th Company plowed across a wide road onto the last bastion of the Tula defenders: the Cathedral of the Assumption on the grounds of the Tula Kremlin, a 16th century stronghold. Since the beginning of the battle of Tula, the German artillery had been busy shooting the Kremlin, ready to storm it. While Hausser's men pushed forward to the residential district east of the Kremlin, from which Russian weapons were still sounding after several days of drumfire, Panzer Regiment 2 had received orders to support the infantry's advance into the Kremlin.

Engelmann's panzer drove across a main road following Stollwerk's tank, who had once again taken the lead. Behind Engelmann, the remains of the 12th Company pushed through the narrow street canyons

214

of Tula. The other panzer companies approached the enemy emplacements from parallel roads in order to engage on a broad front.

Engelmann looked through his vision block. He had closed the lids of his hatch. The ruins of row houses flew past on the right and left, but the street canyon ended straight ahead. There a huge square emerged where the cathedral was located. The walls of the Kremlin no longer existed. Also the large, red brick five-dome building, which had been used as an archive since the advent of Bolshevism in the Soviet Union, was perforated like a coarse sponge. The towers, clad in black, rose into the sky like torn branches. But no matter how many explosive shells were pounding the building, no matter how often the old walls shook under the detonations of the impacts, it resisted destruction. The site around the cathedral had once been a beautiful city park now had turned into a Great War Western Front-like no-man's land. Bomb craters, some wide enough to swallow a truck, had broken up the soil. Where once old trees stood, only burst stumps protruded from the earth. A cloud of dust was spreading around the battlefield and made visibility worse; it was fed by every shell raining onto the battleground. The ubiquitous dust burned in the eyes of the soldiers and infiltrated their lungs, causing a ghastly cough.

Suddenly the German artillery fell silent. The last shells hailed down on the city center, tearing buildings apart. The drumming of the guns perfectly tuned into the advancement of the panzers and the infantry. Stollwerk's tank was the first to storm out of the street canyon into the open square. Franzi II turned slightly to the right and accelerated to close up on Stollwerk. The panzers dashed forward together, while the other tanks of 12th Company joined the push to the right and left of their leader. They formed a steely front that threatened to overrun the enemy.

Everywhere, infantrymen swarmed. NCOs shooed their men out of the sheltering buildings into the open square, where they took cover behind the tanks platoon-wise, advancing in their slipstream. Far to the right, the Tigers of the Africans accessed the battlefield. The armored monsters pushed their way over the shattered earth, and even behind them further infantrymen were scurrying around like blowflies.

"Not so fast, Hans," Engelmann warned, "the boys behind us must still be able to come with us."

"Why? Can't the dogfaces make 20 an hour?" Münster grinned doggedly and didn't even seem to notice that his commander rolled his eyes. The behavior of the driver really started to annoy him. He ignored it for now, though.

Instead he pressed his eyes against the narrow vision block. He clearly recognized the Russian fire that was pelting toward them from all the holes and breaches of the cathedral and the smaller Epiphany Cathedral standing beside it. Tracer projectiles cut through the dusty fog, collided with the tanks, and were hurled away like glowing cigarette butts. Ludwig's coaxial machine gun fired in between. With short bursts of fire, he stroked the lowest, squared windows of the cathedral. The Germans forces shot at the Russian positions from all directions while storming the site. It

216

was an incredible firestorm that hit the Red Army soldiers like an atrocious blizzard.

At that moment, the water-blue sky was overshadowed by an all-encompassing steely might. Huge wings and fuselages filled with thousands of kilos of bomb load blocked the view of the sun. Once again the metal birds of Air Fleet 6 did their best to level the residential district in the east, and to plow all Russian emplacements there that already had been hammered into the ground like nails by past air raids and artillery fire; the defenders squatting in the debris and dirt were buried alive once more. Soiled and dusted Red Army soldiers, each and every one of them at least slightly wounded, emerged from the rubble. The attack of German ground forces would follow on its heels.

An incredible crash came out of one of the big broken windows of the cathedral. An explosive shell exploded between two German panzers advancing fast. Splinters and sparks were spraying the tanks and the infantry behind them. A foot soldier shrieked and held his shoulder before going down.

"AT-gun!" Engelmann exclaimed and clung to his seat. "Second arch window from the right!"

"God!" moaned Nitz, clutching his machine gun. "Poor dogs don't stand a chance!"

But all Russian resistance seemed futile. Even before the regiment's panzers could have reacted, a full platoon from the Tiger battalion stopped and punched a salvo of explosive shells into the large arched windows. After that, the enemy AT-gun remained silent.

"We approach the cathedral up to two hundred, then the riflemen do their part," Stollwerk's voice resounded from the radio devices. "We then turn left and circuit those group of buildings up ahead. Watch out for enemy tanks! Air reconnaissance reports four T-34s behind the cathedral!"

Engelmann confirmed, then he ordered Nitz to switch to their internal board frequency.

"Hans, stay on Stollwerk!" he gasped into his throat microphone.

"As you wish, Reverend."

"And don't you fucking say that!" Apparently the message had hit home, because this time Münster refrained from any further comment. Instead, he threw himself into his steering levers and let Franzi II turn slightly to the left, just as Stollwerk's tank had done seconds before. The infantrymen, who had reached up to 200 meters to the cathedral by the tanks, raced now as if stung by an adder into the dying enemy fire and threw themselves into the foremost bomb craters. Meanwhile a whole company of Tiger panzers had taken up position on the square. After taking out two more hostile AT-guns, they pointed their muzzles at the two cathedrals. With a shattering roar, they sent the first explosive shells on their journey, thunderously digging their way into the walls and tearing large pieces out of the buildings.

A huge wall of dust arose, enveloping the enemy emplacements. But the Tigers needed no more targets – they just fired at the shadow of the cathedrals that could be seen through the dust. The next salvo of high-explosive shells swished into the wall of dust, triggering a hell of a noise behind it. Man-sized boulders of stone were thrown out of the dusty mist onto the square. In the meantime, the enemy fire nearly died. Occasionally, MG fire bursts still hit German infantrymen positions or panzers, but it got obvious that the Russians defenders were defeated here. Engelmann stretched his head against the lids of his cupola's hatch and glanced through the vision block. Between dust and sparks, he just recognized how the bombers in the sky were dropping tiny pencils that glided into the city. Once again, every single stone in the neighboring residential district would be turned over.

You gotta give up now, Engelmann implored; not without recognition for the Russians who had held their positions in this hellfire for so long. But for the defenders of the two cathedrals, the last hour had come. Engelmann observed how platoon by platoon, the infantry disappeared into the dust. At the same time, the Tigers stopped firing. Communication between the different military branches was the trump card!

"Now these dogs get what they deserve," Münster cheered while accelerating his panzer further until he drove directly on Stollwerk's side. "Finally they get what they deserve!"

The tanks of 11th and 12th Company surrounded the fogged cathedral buildings, in which the Russian defenders now fought in a last twitch against German superiority.

In their push across the huge square, the panzers had to evade large bomb craters and shot vehicles several times. Everything else – fallen trees, rubble, corpses – was chopped up by the crawler tracks and punched into the ground. At some distance, the two advancing panzer companies were followed by the pitiful remains of the regiment. They secured the edges of the square to shield the battlefield.

11th and 12th Company had almost reached the backside of the cathedrals. Desperate Russian drivers in military trucks of US-American design tried to escape the German attack there by setting off in a northerly direction. Did they know that Hausser's men were already lurking there?

The two German panzer companies sent them iron greetings. An explosive shell tore a hole in the ground next to a truck speeding away. The energy set free by the explosion overthrew the vehicle. It slid through the dirt on its side for some meters before it finally came to a halt. Another truck driver seemed to lose his nerve. He spun the steering wheel hastily and ended up straight in a bomb crater, where the truck's foreside dug into the ground, while the rear axle hung in the air and the wheels still rotated.

"HE, Siggi!" Engelmann yelled. "Theo, we'll get that jalopy in the crater too. Who knows what he's loaded with!"

Jahnke loaded the main gun while Ludwig aligned the barrel. But one of 11th Company's panzers was faster, turning the stuck car into tiny pieces of scrap that whirled around.

"Damn soldiers of fortune," Engelmann grinned, but then things suddenly got serious. The outlines of three enemy tanks pealed out of the wall of dust.

220

"Nitz, radio to all! Three T-34s at three o'clock! We'll take the left one."

"I'm already on it," Ludwig exclaimed with clenched teeth. He aimed and fired. The projectile hit right between the hull and the turret, where it burst and morphed into a fabric of flame whose tongues of fire played around the tank like strands of hair on a pretty girl's face. After a few seconds the fire was gone, but the tank was still there – fully functional.

"Heh?" Engelmann groaned in wonder, because the T-34 was less than 400 meters away.

"Lieutenant!" Jahnke creaked. "We were still loaded with HE." But the tank loader already pushed an AP shell into the loading device and let the breech snap shut.

"Loaded!" he reported. At the same time, the T-34s and the many German tanks fired at each other. After the short exchange of blows, two German panzers were on fire, while a Russian tank's turret flew out of the rotating assembly. Another T-34 had been hit by three projectiles at once, which cracked its right track. Metal fragments whirled in all directions. Franzi II also shot another shell, but missed. The projectile disappeared somewhere in the still-growing dust wall.

Suddenly the breath of the German tankers faltered, for more and more shadows of T-34s became visible in the dust wall before breaking out of it into the open. Engelmann counted over twenty enemy tanks at once ... and more kept coming. One by one, they were digging their way out of the dust.

"They didn't mean four tanks... they meant four companies," Engelmann remarked bitterly.

221

"Close in! We're getting Ivan involved in close combat," Stollwerk commanded via radio. Engelmann was aware that the captain demanded an outrageous sacrifice from his company by that, but the alternative would have been to retreat. Then probably just as many German tanks would have been destroyed without inflicting losses on the enemy. The two tank fronts clashed into each other. Barrels cracked, steel burst, tanks were torn apart. At short distance, even the German Panzer IIIs landed some effective hits, but from the overpowering T-34, every shot was deadly. German tanks dropped like flies. Tankers bailed out of their devastated vehicles, floundering across the battlefield.

And there were still more Russian tanks coming out of the dusty curtain. And more. While a detonation to the left of Franzi II threw cobble stone fragments and humus into the air, the panzer was shaken by the plain blast. Engelmann started to believe that his regiment stood no chance in this encounter. They were mercilessly outnumbered by Russian tanks, and 11th and 12th Company had already taken quite a beating.

"Our comrades took the residential district," Nitz shouted between the racket of the tank battle. The message had come in via radio. Lots of prisoners were captured during the assault. The Russians had fought bravely, but in the end had not been up to German superiority. Also the tank battle behind the cathedral would not change anything about the outcome of the battle for Tula – nothing at least from the point of view of the overall situation.

For Engelmann and his fellow tankers, it could still be the last battle of their lives, because the Russians fought as hard as ever.

The remains of the regiment now entered the site behind the cathedrals in the backs of 11th and 12th Company, but unlike Stollwerk, bold leaders seemed to be missing there, because the Panzer IVs took positions at a distance of almost 1,000 meters; from there they tried to do what they were just able to do. That wasn't much in view of the thick T-34 armor. The Russians swallowed the bombardment from a distance, as if they were pelted with muddy tomatoes. Buzzing ricochets rattled away from the tanks and went somewhere to explode.

"They smoke us! That's for sure," groaned Nitz, who pressed the radio receiver to his ear.

"Burgsdorff must make his panzers engage in close combat, dammit!" Münster said as he wiped the sweat off his forehead.

"Stay calm," Engelmann coaxed his tank men. His fingers clawed so violently into his seat shell that his ankles shimmered whitish under his skin. Now there was no more tactics, no more tricks. The two enemy tank fronts faced each other and fired with everything they had. Machine guns rattled, big main guns banged.

Those who shot faster, hit better, and had more tanks would finally win the fight – and this time it seemed to be the Russians who settled the race. One German tank after the other fell apart under heavy hits. Screams and wild orders reigned all frequencies. Engelmann saw through his vision block how Stollwerk's panzer rammed a T-34 at full speed. The lieutenant caught himself thinking about ordering his crew to flee – just bail out and scram. Suddenly a shout of joy came out of the loudspeakers of his headset.

The Tigers of the Africans had followed the regiment behind the cathedrals. 20 Tigers against just over 40 T-34 – poor Russians.

More and more Soviet tanks accelerated and drove into the formation of 11t[h] and 12th Company to stop the Tigers from firing at them. But they underestimated the capabilities of a well-trained gunner. The Tigers mercilessly let their main armament do the talking. 8.8-centimeters tank guns turned eight enemy tanks into glowing garbage in an instant. The enemy was still resisting total destruction, but the battle was already decided.

Southwest of Piazza Armerina, Italy, July 3rd, 1943

The 299 patients had been awakened this morning at the crack of dawn by the staff and gathered in the large classroom, where Medical Brigadier General Link, a broad-shouldered man with a high forehead and steel-grey eyes, appeared on stage together with an Italian officer called Tonti. The staff of the sanatorium were also present without exception. For Berning, it was the first time he saw Link in uniform. After all, Berning hadn't had to wear the plaster since the day before and was finally able to move his arm a little again.

"I had you come together today to tell you a few important things," the medical officer began straight away. After each sentence, he took a short break to give Tonti the opportunity to translate what he had just said.

"Last night, enemy paratroopers landed at Gela and Sycarus." A murmur and rustling went through the ranks of those present.

Link continued: "As we speak, German and Italian forces are defending themselves against enemy invasion troops along the entire south coast from Licata to Augusta. Ladies and gentlemen, the battle for Sicily has begun."

Link let these words have an effect on the auditorium for a moment.

"I already spoke to General Hube, who in turn spoke to Feldmarschall Kesselring. It is the unconditional will of both our Chancellor and the Italian leadership to hold Sicily at all costs! They have started to transfer additional troops from the mainland to us in order to face the enemy with all due determination." Link's gaze wandered from one attendant to the next. It finally touched Berning, who was on his way from simply shocked to being paralyzed because of the news.

With a firm voice, Medical Brigadier General Link declared, "There is therefore no reason to abandon this institution."

The murmuring and whispering in the hall intensified.

When a physician tries to assess a military situation ... Berning thought without knowing whether Link was right or wrong in his assessment. He further considered that Chancellor von Witzleben certainly wanted to prevent his "lighthouse project" from having to be evacuated.

"So if you hear the distant thunder of the guns from the coast in the next few days, please don't worry," Link continued when the noise in the hall had subsided again, "that's just our artillery blowing the enemy back into the sea."

"Well, hopefully they won't get their wind back," a young guy remarked next to Berning, who chewed his fingernails all the time.

"Only one thing will change for us," Link's voice fought its way through the muttering in the room, "we will have to vacate Block 2. General Hube will set up his command post there. He is going to arrive with an anti-aircraft unit this afternoon. For camouflage, we will affix big Red Cross flags on the roofs of all buildings.

226

I'm afraid the luxury of a single room is no longer granted to some of you, but at least you can continue to sleep comfortably, because the Anglo-American bombers won't dare to attack a Red Cross facility. Sieg Heil, comrades."

While Tonti translated the last part of the speech, Link smiled contentedly and looked into the faces of those present. Many visages were darkened and grimly serious, but the doctor seemed to believe confidently in a victory for the Axis powers here in Sicily.

Berning wasn't so sure. The Americans were considered strong, but so far in this war there had not been an open fight with them on land. On the other hand, the Wehrmacht – and above all the Italians – would do everything in their power to defend this island, for now it was no longer about any areas in the East; it was about their very own soil.

Berning felt safe enough here in this sanitarium. As a wounded man, he was first of all fine – and if necessary, American captivity would not be the worst lot either. Better than being a POW in Soviet Russia... or even a soldier on the Eastern front. Berning nodded at the thought, shaking off his shock. After all, things could work out just fine for him.

Southwest of Tula, Soviet Union, July 4th, 1943

After two months of toughest fighting, two offensives, and even more sturdy defense, Panzer Regiment 2 was now completely bled out despite some makeshift refreshments from replacement units. The formation was no longer able to participate in any significant action. So it became common knowledge that the regiment would soon be posted to the rear echelon. Everything was waiting for the marching orders. Until then, the tank men spent their time with training, maintenance work, but above all with smoking, drinking, eating, and lazing around. After all, the battle for Tula had been won; the whole offensive had worked exactly as von Manstein had planned, although a military strategy never actually survived the first contact with the enemy.

Right now everything was quiet on the Eastern Front. 2,500 kilometers of front line had fallen into complete silence, while both sides licked their wounds and began digging themselves in again. The Red Army was broken up, but also the Wehrmacht was no longer in a position to undertake any more ventures. In the worst case, this was the beginning of trench warfare.

The sun was setting. Engelmann stood in the door frame of an abandoned farmhouse, which served the survivors of 12th Company as a dwelling. The lieutenant leaned against the door frame, stared out at the wide plain, and sighed. During phases of no combat action, he found it particularly difficult to bear

228

the fact that he was out here – thousands of kilometers away from his family.

In his hands, Engelmann held Corporal Born's "The World Set Free." Since he had been in possession of the book, he wanted to read it, but to this day he hadn't gotten beyond the page with the copyright information. Sergeant Münster walked out of the narrow forest where Franzi II was hidden from curious eyes in the sky and moved across the open space between the woods and the farmhouse. Torn fences indicated that animals had once been kept here.

Münster reached the farmhouse, nodded to Engelmann, and squeezed past him into the kitchen. Jahnke, Nitz, and some other tank men occupied that room, putting away black bread with a wafer-thin spread.

"Unteroffizier Münster?" Engelmann's voice was sharp and reflected how angry he was about the recent behavior of his driver. Münster turned around with his shoulders hanging.

"Yep, Herr Leutnant?"

"You know very well that you shouldn't traipse out of the forest exactly where our tank is located, but have to move within the forest to another place in order to leave it somewhere else. If a low-flying aircraft recons you, he'll know where our tin can is right away."

Münster shrugged his shoulders. "I don't see any low-flying aircrafts."

In Engelmann's chest, something was boiling. Rarely had he felt such rage as he did at this moment. The comrades in the kitchen seemed to understand what writing was on the wall. They stopped chewing and became very attentive. Only Münster looked lethargically at nothing special.

"Herr Unteroffizier, come outside with me. I need to talk to you in private."

Münster did not respond verbally, but with all his facial features, he showed Engelmann how annoying and superfluous he thought this conversation was. Like a stammering dog, he followed his commander.

When both had won some distance to the farmhouse, Engelmann began with a calm voice: "You are the best tank driver I know. But, Jesus, what's the matter with you?"

Münster shrugged his shoulders again. "I don't know what you mean."

"I think you know very well what I mean."

Both stared at each other for a moment, then the sergeant opened his mouth: "I am just done with all this coffee crap, Lieutenant."

"How come?"

"Well, first of all, because there's no more coffee. Those wind eggs from supplies can drink their spare shit themselves ... and second, because I'm worried that we have a totally incompetent leadership that's too stupid to die to make the right decisions."

"What do you mean by that?"

"I beg you, Herr Leutnant! It's so obvious."

"No, it is not to me. Enlighten me."

"Ever since our Führer has died, things are pointing south! Von Witzleben and his lackeys are the absolute losers who have no idea of war. I mean, they disbanded our most competent and powerful military organization. What a load of bullshit! Ask any soldier

230

of the Wehrmacht. Everyone can tell at least one story where he was happy when suddenly the boys from the SS showed up. That was our elite! And these eggheads in Berlin disband it, smash their battle-hardened units, and distribute the SS men throughout the Wehrmacht, so that their military clout is destroyed forever."

"...the SS was anything but powerful..."

"No!" Münster had the audacity to interrupt his lieutenant. "The Wehrmacht is simply unable to make the right decisions. Von Manstein is such a security fanatic that he delays final victory by years! All this shit could be over by now, if only the gentlemen had some guts!"

"Oh? Is that so?"

"Of course! Stalingrad!" Münster underpinned the name of the city by raising his hands in an evocative manner. "We had the city in our hands, Herr Leutnant! THE industrial center on the Volga – and Stalin's name on it. The loss of Stalingrad would have broken Ivan's spine. Stalin would have surrendered – or at least he would have been chased out of office by his infuriated generals.

"Stalingrad, Herr Leutnant! We had almost taken the city; and what do the wimps decide in Berlin after our Führer is dead? Fall back! RETREAT! We could have ended the war before Christmas if only these do-gooders had followed Adolf Hitler's plan of conquering this damned city. Instead they now order such mini offensives as Kursk or Tula. Here one hundred meters of land gain, there three kilometers. How long is this shit gonna last? I don't intend to celebrate my 35th birthday at the front, but it seems to

231

be more important for von Witzleben that we give the poor, poor prisoners of war enough to eat and caress everyone's head once a day – those filthy bastards!"

"I think you're misjudging the situation."

"Maybe you're misjudging the situation, too. Talk to Hauptmann Stollwerk for a minute. With all due respect, the man is a veteran of the Great War and of the SS. I think he understands best what's going on. Now the Americans have landed in Sicily! They'll finish us off from all sides if we don't change tack real quick."

"Did Stollwerk say that too?"

"Mhm."

"In any case, I expect you to behave according to your rank, Herr Unteroffizier."

The two men stared at each other for a moment like rival bulls after a fight that had ended with a draw. Finally Münster slammed his heels together.

"Understood! Heil Witzleben, Herr Leutnant!"

Southwest of Piazza Armerina, Italy, July 5th, 1943

Berning grumbled into himself while pressing his head into the pillow. There was a sergeant snoring piercingly whose bed had been placed at the other end of the tiny room. It sounded as if he would saw up an entire forest. But it wasn't just the sleeping noises of his new, overweight roommate, whose right hand had been smashed by a splinter of a grenade, it was above all the Allied bombers who flew day and night into the interior of Sicily since the beginning of the invasion to bomb airfields and troop gatherings. They kept Berning from sleeping, and now the enemy bombers were roaring high up in the sky again.

He closed his eyes and wished he could do the same with his ears. He had not perceived any German airplanes or at least Italian ones so far, and those who now flew over the Adolf Hitler Sanatorium certainly were no friendlies, for they came from the southwest and headed to the northeast. At least the AA-guns stayed silent; they would add a whole new level of racket to the already-vociferous background noise. Apparently they didn't want to draw the enemy's attention to this facility, and had only set up the guns for emergencies.

Berning's eyes were reddened, and heavy tiredness dazed him. But he couldn't sleep with all that noise drilling into his skull like a cutter head. The roar of the engines became louder and louder as the bombers made their way across the sanatorium.

"Can't you make your war somewhere else?" Berning whispered pleadingly. Nevertheless, he had to think of what Link had said: Throw the enemy back into the sea.

"Pah!" Berning spat out. *Morons, morons, morons, morons! Throw them back in the sea my ass!*

The Americans, who had landed at Licata, Gela, and Vittoria, had advanced everywhere up to twenty kilometers inland. The British and Canadians, who had landed at Augusta, Syracuse, and Avola, had already joined forces with the Americans to form a united front line that cut through Sicily like a knife. Piazza Armerina was only nineteen kilometers away from the vanguard of the US forces.

"Damn Avantis! They can't even defend their own fucking country," Berning groaned and slowly tried to get used to the fact that he probably wouldn't sleep that night anymore. Two o'clock was already over. At least the pain of his wounds had degenerated into a dull and numb feeling.

The only thing that kept him from going mad was the prospect of getting out of here soon. Now that the enemy had gained land so quickly, Berning counted on an hourly evacuation order for the sanatorium. Perhaps the sitrep even played into his hands, and he would still get into a hospital close to home.

A siren went off. Evenly howling, the sound bored itself into Berning's head. First he sighed, with rage filling his chest like water fizzing into a bowl. Then he paused. Never before had the siren sounded. In the next moment, the AA-guns started firing. The light anti-aircraft guns consisted of four 2-centimeter autocannons each, producing a continuous thunder that threatened to destroy what was left of Berning's hearing. The guns were located directly next to the block he was in. Clattering, the AA-guns sent glowing projectiles into the sky. The blast waves they produced made the window panes tremble. Anti-aircraft shells glided through the night like burning eels.

Berning's roommate woke up smacking. "What now ...?" he began to speak, then the first bomb explosions rang out in the forecourt of the housing blocks.

The blast of the detonations tugged at the buildings with all its might, finally causing the glass of the windows to burst. Berning threw his blanket over his body, protecting himself, while the fine splinters rained down on him like a hail shower. His roommate fell out of bed.

Hell had broken loose out there. An entire bomb carpet hit the sports field and the excavation site. The wooden stands ruptured like glass balls. Leg-sized, torn wooden planks shred across the site, knocking against the walls of the blocks. When Berning pulled himself together and, rising above his coughing roommate, looked out of the burst window, his blood froze in his veins. Against the moonlight, white parachutes shimmered in the night sky, slowly floating down to the earth.

Paratroopers! Berning was paralyzed for the moment. Without a doubt, the enemy wanted to capture General Hube.

Berning hobbled to the locker, tore open the door leaf, and rummaged through a mountain of clothes that the obese sergeant had stuffed into it yesterday. He

235

finally found something to wear – his field grey uniform – and put on his blouse and pants.

Slowly his roommate got up, too. He spat contemptuously. His arms and face were cut by glass fragments.

"We're under attack!" Berning yelled.

"Shit," the fat one coughed.

But Berning didn't hear him anymore. While a violent stimulus of pain that felt like being stabbed flashed in his injured shoulder, he suppressed an outcry and limped out into the hallway, where now everywhere doors were ripped open and bewildered-looking people showed themselves.

"We're under attack!" Berning yelled again. "Paratroopers!" At that moment, he wondered if it had been clever to put on his uniform instead of his spa clothes.

Wild screaming broke loose. People panicked, sprinting down the aisle and running each other over. Berning made his way through the crowd.

He had only one goal: Get out of the block, into the olive grove, and then keep a low profile. Tomorrow morning, he'd see where he was. But he did not want to run into the arms of an American commando unit in total darkness, which would certainly not be here to take prisoners. Tomorrow morning, if the situation required it, he could still surrender to a regular enemy unit. Or let the Germans collect him – depending on who won.

When Berning stormed down the stairwell, he was not unaware that the bombing of the sanatorium had stopped. Instead, handgun clamor flared up outside.

The firing of rifles and submachine guns resounded through the corridors of the block. Italian and German shouts mixed to a hectic confusion. Even the AA-guns were still barking.

Berning stumbled out of the main entrance and ran towards the bombed-out sports field amidst a cluster of people. Muzzle flashes gleamed at the excavation site. Bright flashes of light danced around the grey shades of the walls lurking in darkness. One patient was pierced by a projectile and went to the ground howling. The rest pushed themselves apart and ran screaming in all directions.

Someone grazed Berning's shoulder. A violent pain whipped through his arm and made him yell. Then the slowly-healing penetrating gunshot wound in his thigh became noticeable and paralyzed him for the blink of a second. Berning grabbed the injured leg and gritted his teeth so hard that he began to feel a pain there as well. With a powerless moan, he stretched his head upwards and looked around. Fleeing wounded and nurses became shadows in the darkness. Somewhere, a woman screamed. Now the background noise was reigned by the shootout taking place all over the site. In the north and in the south, carbines fired. Suddenly a machine gun started buzzing. Berning couldn't identify the sound, but it surely wasn't a German weapon. With constant rattling, the MG sent its bullets over the sanatorium grounds.

Berning looked behind him over to the blocks. In the flickering flashlights of the bellowing AA-guns, which still weaved long filaments into the sky, as well as in the light of the lamps still burning in the rooms inside the blocks, Berning received a visual idea of what was going on. German soldiers, partly only half-dressed, stormed outside through the entrance door of the one block General Hube had seized for his staff with machine guns in their fists. Most of them immediately collapsed in a hail of bullets. A few, however, jumped into cover behind an Einheits-PKW car and returned fire.

At this very moment, the anti-aircraft gun next to the block abruptly went silent. The gunner held his chest, then tilted sideways from his seat. His comrades noticed the debacle and dragged the man over to the wall of the building, where they bent over him worriedly. Berning understood that enemy commandos who came right out of the olive grove were about to overrun every German and Italian resistance. He pulled himself together and turned to the east, where no fighting noise could be heard or muzzle flashes could be seen. One German anti-aircraft gun was still firing, it was positioned somewhat away from the buildings, but the sounds had changed. Instead of a dull, flowing staccato, the racket it made while shooting now was much higher. The clanking and clattering of impacting projectiles followed on its heels. The anti-aircraft gun had joined ground combat. But now engines were humming in the distance. Vehicles were approaching at great speed. More guns were buzzing. Small fireballs danced over the outer wall of Hube's block. Inside, the lights were wavering.

Without wondering how the Anglo-Americans deployed vehicles twenty kilometers behind the front line, Berning bit his lower lip and hurried off as fast as

238

his maltreated body would allow. He limped eastwards, quickly vanishing into darkness. While screams still reverberated through the night and the firefight in his back slowly subsided, he reached hilly terrain with thorny scrubs.

He kept limping, groping with his hands in front of his body so as not to run into any obstacles. He gasped and grunted because of the vast exertion the brief sprint meant for him. His breathing was fast, and his pulse was pounding like a sewing machine in his throat. His skull was heating. Berning finally slowed down, had to slow down. His shoulder was burning; if he was unlucky, the wound had opened again under the strain. His thigh had turned into a radiator: as hard as stone and as hot as a blast furnace. Finally the leg locked itself against any further movement. Thus Berning had to stop. Only now did he really feel how much the short hurry had consumed him. His pharynx was burning, and his mucous membranes were swollen. He felt like he had a jellyfish in his mouth. His wounds were pounding. A strong stitch on the side began, as if someone had rammed a shiv between his ribs. Slowly, very slowly, his breathing and pulse calmed down. Berning panted more quietly now.

Without a warning, something cracked right in front of him. Before Berning could have reacted, a dark figure emerged from the gloom and pressed the muzzle of a submachine gun against Berning's chest. The sergeant let out a brief scream and threw his hands in the air. His feet – he only wore wool socks – got entangled, then he stumbled and landed on his bottom. But the gun didn't let go of him. The stranger gently pressed the gun's muzzle against Berning's thorax, thus pushing Berning against the ground. He groaned in pain and begged for his life: "No, no, please, no!" He almost sobbed. Fear of death seized him, killing the last remains of his courage, made him wait petrified whether the stranger would kill him or let him live. Suddenly the pressure the cold muzzle exerted on his body eased, then the supposed assailant took the weapon back.

"Name? Rank?" a harsh voice demanded that clearly was of Holstein origin.

"B...B...Berning. Unteroffizier Berning."

"All right. I'm Lieutenant Donner. On your feet, Unteroffizier. From now on, you are under my command! We still have a bone to pick with the Americans, and I need every man for that. Follow me!"

Berning stared at his opposite in disbelief, but that Donner guy turned away and headed east. Berning hesitated, then rose and trotted after him.

*

Lieutenant Donner, who wore the blue clothes of the sanatorium and was armed with a MP40, marched straight through a field of razor-sharp, withered bushes that had thrown their dying branches like nets to all sides. They pricked Berning, scratching him bloody. Limping and mutely cursing, he kept pace.

This Donner guy, who he had gotten to know so far exclusively by his voice, seemed to be nobody to tangle with. Over the years, Berning had developed a nose in the military for identifying such people. Such pappendorfish slave-drivers and wannabe heroes.

He reluctantly let the lieutenant lead him behind a hill into a hollow. There sat three other figures, one of them all dressed in white, so that she herself shimmered in the dark.

"I found one more," Lieutenant Donner announced. "But I'm afraid the so-called Allies are now swarming all over the site, so we'll move as soon as Tonti gets back."

The figures nodded eagerly.

"Sieglinde, would you please be so kind as to surrender your weapon to the sergeant here?" Donner pointed to Berning, who only now realized who the person in white was.

"Sieglinde?" he asked into the darkness.

She seemed to recognize his voice immediately. "Herr Unteroffizier Berning?"

"Yes! It's Franz!"

"Oh, this is a joyful surprise."

She threw herself at Berning so fast that he didn't know what happened to him. He first raised his hands as if he would surrender; but then, when he realized that she was clinging more and more tightly to him, pressing her head against his chest and crying softly, he laid one hand on her back.

Uncertain of what to do, he patted her until Sieglinde slowly let go of him. She finally put the warm wood of a K98k carbine into Berning's hands.

"I only have the five bullets in my rifle," she sighed in a trembling voice.

Berning nodded.

241

"Listen!" Donner drew attention to himself. "The enemy has launched a comprehensive offensive in the night and has finally broken out of his beach heads at Gela and Licata. Armored units are already advancing on Piazza Armerina and are probably already passing us, as far as the information from our friend from the Flak goes."

A guy wearing a complete uniform of the Wehrmacht next to Sieglinde tapped the metal of his submachine gun with his fingers while he nodded.

"From the looks of it, they've picked up Hube's command post. But let's wait and see what Tonti has to say."

"Shouldn't he be back already?" asked the Flak soldier.

Donner checked his wristwatch, then he replied: "We wait another 15 minutes, then we march off."

"I don't trust the Avantis," one of the others whispered.

"Neither do I." Donner grinned. "But as my old Scharführer always said, I would even defend my homeland with sticks and stones if there were nothing else. Now it's about their homeland – and they won't give it up as easily as they did with Africa."

Berning immediately felt the admiring glances that Donner's revelation had triggered in the two comrades. The Flak soldier put his thoughts into words: "You were in the Waffen SS?"

"Correct. I'm a Untersturmführer – at least I was one up to von Witzleben's General Decree that forced a lieutenant rank on me. But don't worry, I haven't forgotten where I come from!"

242

Donner showed his teeth shining in the darkness. Then he continued with the issuing of orders. "On the situation: I assume that the enemy has already sealed the deal and that we are therefore in the mousetrap. But I am sure Kesselring will answer the enemy advance at dawn with a massive counterattack that will throw the Allies back to the beaches. We got 42 Tiger panzers on the island, and as many other tanks. So we are just fine."

Berning wondered how much was really fine – and for whom. His wounds also became more and more unpleasant again.

Probably some stitches were ripped open by the events of the night, but he did not dare to reach under his bandage and try to feel if there was blood. Instead, he listened to Donner's explanations with a queasy feeling. *I wish he'd just stayed in bed!*

"Our task must therefore be to mar the enemy wherever possible in order to contribute to the overall success of our troops here in Sicily. First, we march a wide circle around the site and pick up everyone who has escaped the enemy. We need every man; we also need weapons, ammunition, food. If, contrary to expectations, Kesselring's offensive should be delayed or get stuck somewhere, we must expect to be able to endure several days or weeks on our own.

As long as we stay behind enemy lines, we contribute to the final victory where we can. The nature and strength of the enemy must be clarified. Are we dealing with Britons? Or with Yanks? Heavy weapons? Tanks? Clarify all this whenever possible.

Otherwise we concentrate on guerilla attacks against their supply lines or scattered units. As soon as we meet our own regular troops, we get ourselves attached and help to throw the enemy off the island for good.

"So be prepared to be on your feet a lot in the near future. Holiday season is over."

"Herr Leutnant?" Berning breathed barely audibly.

"Yes?"

Berning hemmed and hawed, barely daring to speak. He had to struggle with every word: "I am badly wounded ... I can hardly move ..."

Despite the gloom, the sergeant realized that Donner didn't like this statement at all. He replied, "I have a collapsed lung. Now what?"

Both stared at each other. Berning didn't know what to say.

"Listen to me, Herr Unteroffizier!" Donner raised his voice and lived up to its name, which literally translated to thunder. "We're not in some fucking Russian dump here. This is Europe! Our home! If the enemy gets to establish himself here, we'll be in a lot of trouble. Now it's time to grit our teeth and act. The Reich expects the utmost from every single German man to decide this battle in our favor. So swallow the tears and pull yourself together! It's fighting or death! With a rifle butt, a dagger, or pure fists, if necessary. From now on, we will defend every meter of ground! We won't retreat until the last man standing! Do you understand me?"

Berning owed the lieutenant an answer. Looking for help, his gaze got stuck on Sieglinde, who just sat there and stayed quiet. Finally he begged, "I just thought..." He was aggressively interrupted by Donner. "Leave the thinking to the horses, they have a bigger head. Now let's do this, men!"

"... Yes..." Berning returned meekly.

"Well then." Donner snorted contemptuously. "Also, keep your eyes open for any civilians. We have to make sure we put the nurse somewhere."

Outraged, Sieglinde stood up.

"Well, listen! I can also fight for the Reich," she demanded, but Donner beckoned.

"Your fighting spirit is in all its glory, Fräulein, but war is not for girls. We better make sure you make it to the rear echelon. Your nursing skills soon will be needed there."

Sieglinde seemed to want to rebel further, but remained silent in the end.

Minutes went by. Suddenly a figure jumped over the crest, doing long leaps. The men in the hollow communicated wordlessly coming to the ready. But then the Flak man lowered his MP. Instead, he claimed, "That's Tonti! I can tell the Itakas from afar by their lousy way of walking."

The Germans suppressed a laugh. Like a snake, the Italian Primo Capitano slid down the slope into the hollow. He just had a pistol with him and was otherwise wrapped in sleeping clothes. Panting, he reached Donner and immediately explained the situation to him in German, revealing a strong accent: "All Americans up there. All fights over. No sign of the general. All the Germans surrendered."

"Pah!" Donner spat out disdainfully. "Fucking cowards!"

The Flak man signaled consent.

"They should all be shot!" An incredible hatred foamed out of Donner that truly frightened Berning.

Oh no, he begged inside.

Donner continued with brutish loathing pouring out of him like sweat: "Anyone who dares to surrender or run away should be shot! Shoot them all! Surrender is cowardice before the enemy and betrayal of the Reich, nothing else! Damn dogs!" He spewed his words full of abhorrence and anger. Berning heard the officer grinding his teeth after he had finished his hateful tirade – and for a moment, he was overcome by the fear that Donner was thinking about assaulting the Americans just to execute the prisoners – the cowards. But the lieutenant looked up. "Primo Capitano, I cannot give you any orders, but I would be delighted if you'd accompany us. We're going to make sure we outwit the American fools."

Tonti agreed.

"Well, then! Follow me!" Donner left the hollow to the northeast. The rest rose and followed him without exchanging a single word.

Oh no, Berning sighed again, and then he started moving too.

*

They had been on the road for about an hour, without happening across the enemy, without meeting any friendlies, without encountering anything at all.

246

Slowly the night cleared up. The first glimmer of light of the day already rose above the horizon and bathed the landscape of Sicily in whitish splendor. Bone-dry dust lay in the air and scratched Berning's lungs as he limped and tried to keep up – but his leg hurt more and more. It would fail sooner or later.

Slowly it dawned on Berning that they were entrapped. In all four directions, guns thundered as the battle for the island raged. Artificial lightning flashed across the grey sky, and fires shone blood-red in the distance. The Americans must have pushed halfway across the island in a maniacal advance, simultaneously attacking Hube's command post to chop off the head of the German troops, and now trying to hold the land they had gained.

Ducked, the colorful group approached a dusty road that roughly led from south to north in the light of dusk. It meandered in both directions across the hilly terrain like a string. Dry scrubs and dry grass dominated the landscape alongside the road.

The many plants with their light green, almost white leaves gave the island at the tip of the Italian boot its typical Mediterranean occurrence, as did the single standing cork oaks, whose meagre leaf canopies reminded one of deer antlers.

Suddenly a machine gun rattled across the street. The muzzle flash twinkled in a small grove of cork oaks. The Germans and the Italian immediately jumped into the ditch beside the road.

Berning pulled Sieglinde with him and gently pressed her into the dry grass so that nothing would happen to her. Whirring bullets chased over the heads

247

of the small group, then the fire ebbed as fast as it had come.

Silence. Seconds passed.

Tense, the men looked at each other in the ditch. They put their fingers over the triggers of their guns. As Donner seemed to evaluate their options, Berning started to be afraid of the lieutenant coming up with some sort of suicide mission.

Suddenly Donner grinned, apparently satisfied with the results of his thoughts, before he pointed to Berning and ordered: "You..." He didn't get any further, because from across the street, voices suddenly came over to them: "Ciao, siamo italiani!" That was Italian, not English.

As if by magic, the tension was taken away from the mixed fighting community. Tonti breathed out, then he smiled broadly and climbed up the ditch.

"Allora sto tranquillo!" he shouted to the men over there. Suddenly the machine gun started to fire again. Tonti stumbled, overturned, and slipped back to the bottom of the ditch. The Germans stared in shock at the gaping bullet wounds that colored the light blue suit of the Primo Capitano dark red. No pulse could be felt – Tonti was dead. On the other side of the street, a roar of laughter started.

"Fuckin' moron!" one who must have had tears in his eyes from laughing yelled.

The Germans looked at each other with ice-cold faces and eyes filled with hatred. Sieglinde's features had frozen to stone, her eyes shimmering. She couldn't take her eyes off the dead man. Berning grabbed her hand and nodded to her. "We'll be okay," he had wanted to say, but he wasn't so sure about that. Apparently, however, the wordless gesture was enough, because Sieglinde relaxed noticeably. She tried to smile at Berning, as if to say, "Yeah, we'll be fine."

But Berning's heart was beating and beating, even threatening to spin over. He didn't want to die in the pampas of Sicily!

Like the situation couldn't have gotten any worse... suddenly it got worse. Over on the other side, an engine started. Clattering crawler tracks were set in motion. The whole street and ditch vibrated as a steel monster rolled out of its position.

Donner lay flat on the ground and gently crouched up the ditch wall. When he reached the edge, he took a look. He immediately retracted and glided back down to the others.

"Two Shermans over by the trees," he said in a quiet way. "Plus a machine gun nest plus about twenty men." Donner looked at his fighting companions for a moment, then breathed out resignedly and lowered his gaze. It worked for the lieutenant. An anxious twitch scurried across his lips.

"Men," he whispered. "I think that's it. We'll never get out of here. Put down your weapons and get out of the ditch!"

The Flak man and the other soldier nodded diligently and dumped their weapons as ordered. But Berning just stared at the lieutenant.

What? was the only question that dominated his mind at that very moment. *You stunner! What about "fighting till the end," Herr Leutnant? We never give up?*

We'll kill them all! With knives and fists! And who surrenders gets shot? Ha!

So that's what it's supposed to be? Great heroic speech given, then marched for an hour, then the end? You ridiculous Piefke!

Of course he was happy about Donner's decision – it was at least better than battling tanks with knives and fists. But at that moment he simply could not get over how clearly the lieutenant violated his own principles, defended with fiery speeches. But Donner meant business. The lieutenant laid down his weapon in the grass too, then he rose with a look like a dog who had done something wrong. With his head bowed, he marched up the ditch and threw his hands into the air. Sieglinde's look for help found Berning, but he smiled appeasingly and laid a hand on her shoulder.

"It'll be all right," he whispered. "We can't do anything more anyway."

Donner reached the top of the ditch and stepped onto the road. There he stood still with his hands high up.

"So, these greaseballs give up?" an English voice cawed.

"Man, fuck it," another, indifferent voice pushed its way into the background noise. The machine gun went off again.

Berning could only just see Donner's head out of the ditch, which at that moment burst apart like a watermelon. The soldier behind him also collapsed immediately.

The Flak man poured back into the ditch. A bullet bore into his left forearm, then he slipped and bent his foot. A terrible whip sounded as his Achilles tendon

250

ruptured. In pain, the man cried out. He bent like an infant in the womb.

Berning was paralyzed with fear. Sweat flowed down his body in streams, gathering under the bandages that were already itching and chafing. Sieglinde froze too.

Once again the Americans laughed loudly. "Three wasted, two to go!" yelled one.

Sieglinde threw herself at Berning. Tears rolled down her cheeks. Berning, however, sat in the grass as if petrified, unable to stir a fiber of his body, unable to grasp a clear thought. He had not yet comprehended the full extent of their dangerous situation. The Flak man moaned quietly and contorted his face into a mask of cruel pain.

Seconds passed without the enemy making any more noises. Berning slowly released himself from Sieglinde's grip and pushed her aside. He embraced his weapon while not losing sight of the top of the ditch slope.

What are those bastards doing now? His mind was racing after a thousand of thoughts. Did they approach the trench? Or would they just wait and see? Berning, Sieglinde, and the wounded Flak soldier had become playthings of the Americans, nothing more. Their life depended on the mood and the good will of some cocky GIs. It would be easy for the Americans to simply fill the trench with grenades, but apparently they wanted to play with their victims. The Germans had become experimental rats in a cage, powerless at their own fate – at the mercy of complete strangers.

251

"Hey, dickhead!" an almost youthful voice shouted in English from over there. "We just want your girl! Wanna make bum-bum! Okay?" Apparently they had recognized the German uniform, because the Americans no longer spoke Italian.

Sieglinde, who probably understood a bit of English – or at least correctly interpreted the lurid grunt that had accompanied the youthful voice, was startled. Then she buried her face in her hands. She cried bitterly. Meanwhile, the Flak man fished for a submachine gun and a magazine, stuffed it into the gun, and loaded it. With his lips pressed together, he looked up at the slope of the trench. Slowly, the first sunbeams blinked over it.

Berning's thoughts chased each other, but no matter how hard he tried, he couldn't think of a way out. They were trapped.

Damnit! Any normal Yank would just take me prisoner, but I have to get to the one frigging butcher-mason-murderer-company of the US Army, he scolded internally. But the gallows humor pushed his fear away only for milliseconds.

"Just give up!" the youthful voice resounded in English. "We won't shoot! Promise! We just want your girl!"

Laughter accompanied the shout, but Berning did not understand English and therefore did not know what they were demanding. Instead, he feverishly sought a way out. To his right, the ditch ended after twenty meters, to his left it ran a good eighty meters beside the road, before it came out there as well. There was no getting away from here!

252

"We'll get you!" another Yank yelled exuberantly. He could hear the rattling of guns and equipment. With a bitter voice, the Flak man said that the Americans would now come for them. Berning pulled up his rifle and aimed for the edge of the trench. Only five rounds, plus repeating after each shot! What could he possibly do with it? Every GI had at least one semi-automatic weapon in his hand. And the fight that was about to begin would take place at a distance of twenty meters. The Germans didn't stand a chance. Berning briefly peered over to Donner's submachine gun, which lay a few meters beside him in the grass. But he didn't dare put his rifle away. So he was staring at the edge of the ditch slope. Something cracked at the top. Nothing was visible. Suddenly movement occurred next to him. Sieglinde had jumped up and leaped for Donner's submachine gun. She checked the weapon and magazine with great accuracy. With her eyes bloodshot, she came to the ready. Three weapons were now pointed at the edge of the ditch. The muzzles trembled. The wounded Flak man groaned faintly. There was movement up there, very clearly audible. It cracked. It rustled. But nothing was to be seen!

Berning blinked. His eyes itched. And hurt. He kept his eyelids open as long as he could. With burning eyes, he stared at the top of the ditch. Somebody whispered upstairs. Then the rattling of guns again. They were very close, but still nothing was to be seen!

Suddenly an American steel helmet looked over the edge of the trench. The Flak man, Sieglinde, and Berning fired immediately. The helmet disappeared behind the edge again. Small earth fountains tore

253

humus and grass out of the ground at the top edge of the ditch. Berning repeated his rifle. The procedure just took a second. Too long! He pulled up his weapon again and blindly shot into the whirl of dust and earth, where the American helmet had just been visible. Sieglinde shot away the entire magazine of her gun.

In the middle of the German fire, another American with a submachine gun jumped forward, roared, and gave off a long burst of fire into the ditch before disappearing from Berning's field of vision again. The Flak man screamed. Thumb-sized red holes covered his legs. A blink of an eye later, a hand grenade flew through the air in a high arc. It landed on the belly of the Flak soldier, who strained to lift his bright red head and desperately stared like a wildebeest in the face of the lion at that explosive device resting on his body. Berning threw himself to the right, and Sieglinde did the same. The Flak man turned himself, burying the grenade under his body. The explosion tore him into bloody pieces.

Further detonations sounded.

That's it! That's it! They must have thrown more grenades in the ditch! Berning pressed both hands against his head and waited for the end.

Long moments crossed the land. Hectic shouts filled the air. Among all the detonations mingled the distant banging of cannons.

Berning raised his head. There were not hand grenades! This thought came to his mind at the moment when one Sherman morphed into a big ball of flames on the street.

254

A battle broke out, but apart from the fighting noise, it passed Berning by. He pressed his face into the pricking grass and was incapable of anything. He just let things happen around him. His hand searched and found Sieglinde's. She squeezed his. She trembled all over her body, but she calmed down noticeably when Berning wrapped an arm around her. Sieglinde snuggled up to him like a cat.

The second Sherman blew up with a loud roar. The Americans retreated. Under MG fire, they set off in a southwesterly direction. But it wasn't just here on the road that the battle raged. The whole plain, littered with dry scrubs, witnessed a tank battle at that very moment. Soon US Sherman tanks were on the run, while countless of their brothers remained burning in the sun of Sicily. From northeast, beige-painted Tiger tanks appeared on the mountain ranges.

Half an hour passed in which Sieglinde and Berning lay there and waited for things to happen. She clung to him with all her might, and the physical contact was also a blessing for Berning. Subtle red specks covered Sieglinde's nurse clothing.

More time passed by before finally a tank roared thunderously up the road, stopping at the level of the two Germans. Italian voices sounded as men audibly got out of the combat vehicle to investigate the former position of the Americans.

Berning slowly rose. Sieglinde looked at him pleadingly. He grabbed the back of her head, gently stroked her hair, and kissed her on the forehead.

"Everything's gonna be okay now," he said under his breath. "It's over." She nodded apathetically.

255

Berning took Sieglinde by the hand and climbed out of the ditch with her, leaving behind the ripped corpses of Donner and the others. On the road there was a Tiger tank without a Balkenkreuz on it – this tank was under Italian command. Berning had already heard that the Italians were now producing German weapons under license, but he hadn't seen anything of it so far.

The tank commander, a beardless man with black hair, looked out of his turret hatch. When he saw the sergeant and the nurse, he was frightened at first, but then he slumped down calmly. It must have taken him a moment to recognize the German uniform.

"Ciao Germans!" the man shouted in bad German, beaming with joy. "Yo, Tigre's a good Carro Armato! But engines bad! How are you?"

Berning shrugged his shoulders, and only then did he realize the strong, dull pain that was emanating from his injured shoulder. He unbuttoned his field blouse and shirt and uncovered the bandage. It was soaked in fresh blood.

"See, see," commented the Italian. With his hand, he formed a telephone receiver, then he disappeared into the turret of his tank. Berning used the moment to let his gaze wander across the plain, while Sieglinde still held his hand tightly.

Italian tanks were now driving everywhere. Berning counted four Tigers and four Panzer IVs. The rest was of Italian origin.

Sure, Berning said to himself, counting the months back to Hitler's death. *It all doesn't happen that fast.*

Suddenly the Tiger commander stretched himself out of his hatch again. In the background, two Italian soldiers searched the corpses of killed Americans.

"Wait here. Germans are coming for you."

*

One hour later, Berning was lying on a bed in a Wehrmacht ambulance. Sieglinde sat next to him and held his hand. While the truck rumbled along a winding road and moved away from the front line that split Sicily in two halves with every second, she looked him in the face with her water-blue eyes. She smiled gently and wiped a strand off Berning's face. He exhaled loudly in a mixture of relief and exhaustion. For him, the war was interrupted for another time. The wound on his shoulder was wide open again. It needed urgent treatment. The ambulance was ordered to bring Berning directly to Messina, from where all the wounded were shipped to the Italian mainland, while hourly freighters with fresh troops reached the port in the North of Sicily. Field Marshal Kesselring and Chancellor von Witzleben wanted to hold Sicily at all costs, not to mention the Duce Mussolini. Nevertheless, the Adolf Hitler Sanatorium was closed for the time being, and Sieglinde also had to see where she was headed now. The sergeant of the Medical Service, who was sitting in the driver's cabin, had promised to ask her about the whereabouts of the Spa Battalion 1 once they reached Messina. So that's where she and Berning would part company.

Sieglinde looked Berning in the eye. He looked back and smiled gently. His injuries burned like hell, but right now it was fine.

Sieglinde slowly leaned towards him. He lost himself in her eyes, which seemed as deep as infinity. Her delicate fingers felt pleasantly warm in his hands. She kept leaning forward. Her breasts, which loomed under her nursing dress, touched Berning's body. They were soft as a pillow. Sieglinde bent over even further. Their faces were only a few inches apart. She closed her eyes, puckered her lips, and let them rest on his.

In a wild rapture, Berning shot up and pushed Sieglinde away so that she almost fell from her seat.

"How dare you?" he yelled. "I got a girl at home!"

She stared at him in amazement. Her eyes became glassy. A world collapsed for her.

"I ... I ..." she stammered in a fragile voice.

"I think you're crazy," Berning hissed and wiped his mouth.

"But... I thought you liked me."

"No! How did you come up with something like that?"

A broken look struck an angry one. Berning shook his head vehemently, then turned his back on her.

"I don't believe this! Godforsaken dame!" he grumbled and closed his eyes.

Segi Point, Solomon Islands (GB), July 7th, 1943

The Japanese, who fought in such an unusual way at Segi Point, had endured up to July 5th against always newly-landing forces of the US Navy as well as the US Army. Even concentrated air raids could not break the enemy resistance. Only the high losses caused by the continuous fighting on the ground as well as the apparently desolate supply situation of the Japanese with medicines, food, and ammunition forced the enemy to give way and leave Segi Point to the Americans.

So finally the pioneers could go to work and build the airfield which was so important for all further operations in the area. Nevertheless, the Japanese had already caused a delay in American plans – and New Georgia was still partly in enemy hands. Any day that the Japanese could stay there longer would further delay the isolation of the important Rabaul Fortress and keep the Japanese in the game longer.

While the pioneers were working on the large open space with all kinds of construction machines, and the sounds of metal hitting each other echoed over the plain, Roebuck and Pizza had sought shelter in the shade of a palm tree on the adjacent edge of the forest.

Although that palm tree stretched its huge fan leaves like an umbrella around the two Marine Raiders, they sweated all over their bodies. The unbridled heat made their skin shine in the light. They had unbuttoned their field blouses; Pizza had also cut off the sleeves. But even if they would completely have exposed themselves, it would still have been too hot on their bare skin.

Both silently followed their own thoughts. Roebuck decided to write a letter to his wife in the course of the week. Her picture jumped into life in front of his mind's eye. Marie was beautiful, curvaceous, with a firm bosom. The images she sent him over and over again delighted and tormented him at the same time. How he'd love to be home with her now! How he'd love to make love to her! Or just be with her; that would be enough for him right now.

Batman finally came running with a photo in his hand. He panted.

"What's up, Batman?" Roebuck asked impassive.

"I asked around a bit about the photo," he proclaimed.

"What photo?"

"The picture with the Krauts on it."

Pizza and Roebuck looked up. Juergens enjoyed for a moment the undivided attention he now had, then he explained. "The Captain of 3rd Platoon is as well-read as a fucking teacher. I showed him the picture. He says the guy on the left is a general of the Germans. Nehring is his name."

"And who is that?"

Juergens looked at his fellow Marine Raiders. After a few seconds, he shrugged his shoulders. "I don't know."

"Great news, Batman. Really, great news." Pizza's sarcasm was swelling out of every syllable.

260

North of Polistena, Italy, July 26th, 1943

The Axis powers gathered all the wounded of the Battle of Sicily initially in gigantic military hospital cities which, like tumors, had wrapped themselves around Polistena. This army of military hospitals sucked the town at the foot of the Sila mountains dry like a vampire a body full of blood.

The battle for the island had already caused 26,000 wounded, and the majority of them were temporarily kept in Polistena before being transported to military hospitals spread all over Italy.

The wounded were grouped together and moved the moment they were ready for relocation to make room for all the freshly wounded the fierce battle for Sicily produced on a daily basis.

Berning was to be transported next week to finally arrive in his recovery company, but who knew if this would happen, now that the Axis powers had officially given up Sicily and started their retreat. The invasion of the Italian mainland was only a matter of time, which was why the German and Italian medical service units did not know what to do next. Where would the Allies land? Where should they take all those wounded? How quickly could a transfer happen?

The whole Polistena region was in chaos these days, and Berning's only consolation was that his wounds healed superbly. Still, he had to stay hundreds of kilometers from home in a tent crowded with moaning, stinking, and dying people. He prayed he wouldn't catch any infection here. He now had no chance of recovery leave, because his time in the AH Sanatorium was considered as such.

Here in Polistena, however, Berning had learned something interesting about Lieutenant Donner, namely that the old SS officer had not experienced a single battle in his soldier days, and his lung injury was caused by a car accident during a furlough. Two comrades apparently knew the guy from before, and small as the world was, they now lay in the same tent as Berning with burns and splinter wounds. The two vented their spleens quite a lot about the lieutenant. Donner didn't seem to have enjoyed a good reputation in his old SS unit anyway.

Velikiye Luki, Soviet Union, August 21st, 1943

Now Berning had passed his homeland twice, on the way to Italy and then, at the beginning of August, on his way to the heart of the German Reich, where his assigned recovery company was stationed. From there, less than two weeks later, he had already been set on march towards Russia again.

He had not been able to make a stop at home. Now it was already one year ago that he had been in Podersdorf am See for the last time; that he had seen Lake Neusiedl. It had been a year since he last had been with Gretel ... sometimes Berning also had to think of Sieglinde. He hadn't seen her since Messina. He still wondered how strange this girl had behaved.

Now then, Army Group North, he pondered while he climbed down the stairs at the train car and touched the platform of the station with his boots. In fact, he liked the Eastern Front better than Italy at the moment. In the east at least everything stood still, while in the so-called Italian boot, the Axis defenders now banked on an Allied invasion of the mainland every day.

Even at the Velikiye Luki sector, everything was quiet. At the beginning of the year, 8,000 encircled members of the Wehrmacht had threatened to perish in the city, but the then-Commander of the Army Group, Field Marshal Rommel, had reacted wisely and rescued the encircled men with a mixture of escape attempt and relief attack from outside the pocket. In February, he also had managed to push the Russians back behind

263

the city. Since then, the front line had stood still in this sector.

Together with Berning, hundreds of comrades had arrived in Velikiye Luki. Returners from vacation or sick bay, and even two complete companies of the Field Replacement Troop colored the platforms field grey. Men from the gendarmerie, thanks to the metal signs hanging on chains around their necks, also known as watch dogs, roamed the station grounds, demanding pay books, marching orders, and holiday tickets. There were enough soldiers who tried to get away illegally, and even some who decorated their breasts with medals without justification. The few civilians dressed in simple clothes remained reserved and squeezed around the German soldiers.

Many of the soldiers had arrived directly with carabiners – they were no longer taken from them as it had been done at the beginning of the war, so that they were directly able to defend themselves in case of a partisan attack on a train ride. Berning, however, was unarmed; his company had to get a weapon for him. But first he had to find his unit. A dull feeling in his stomach accompanied him as he visited the station commandant's office to ask for his company. Deep down inside, he blatantly wished that Pappendorf had fallen or at least been posted in the meantime. He really did not know how long he would endure his harassments – just now, after months without the sergeant ... pardon, master sergeant ... he carried the terrible fear in himself that he could no longer bear this man's loathing and rage at all. With anger, with fear, with hatred in his belly, he continued the search for his company.

*

Berning pushed open the door to a narrow farmhouse located in the east of the city – about three kilometers behind the main battle line. He met Master Sergeant Pappendorf in his dressed-up uniform as if he was about to go to a military parade in a small room. Hege was also present. Pappendorf fished documents out of a wooden box, browsed them briefly, and then placed them on a pile that was carried by the machine gunner who had been promoted to lance corporal lately. As Hege saw Berning, he showed his brown teeth, which looked like being covered with a thick layer of oil.

Then Pappendorf also turned to the newcomer. The master sergeant looked at Berning with the expression that almost always adorned his face: he pinched his lips into a slender line, his eyes narrowed into tiny slits.

Berning immediately felt the urge to go for his platoon commander's jugular. He gritted his teeth against each other and sensed the deep hatred that had grown inside him for some time now. It was Pappendorf's fault that he had to be bored beyond belief in Sicily instead of visiting his home, his family, and Gretel. Because of Pappendorf, Berning had been directly involved in the battle for the island, in which he almost had gone west. Pappendorf was about to

265

destroy Berning's whole life. The sergeant boiled inside.

But he didn't let his thoughts show. Instead, he went into a position of attention and reported back to the master sergeant in accordance with the regulations.

"Well," said Pappendorf and grinned gloatingly, "the vacationer has finally returned."

Bern, Switzerland, September 8th, 1943

Taylor stood at the window of his small apartment in Bern and stared out into the blue sky. The sun shone brightly and made the facades and roofs of Bern's city center gleam. Fine powder clouds were moving over the firmament, which stretched like a floating sea over the city. Laughter from young people reached Thomas' ear. Children were playing in the streets. Entangled couples enjoyed the afternoon sun, spending their money on ice cream and cool drinks. In the distance, the tram was tinkling.

But Thomas wasn't looking for exuberance today. With a stare, he lost himself in the distance. He didn't take any part in what was going on out there. Thoughts – bad thoughts – drove him around. He feared for the Reich. He wasn't sure if the war was still to be won. Inwardly he begged for a little fortune of war for his nation in these difficult times.

The Allies had already been unable to be repelled from Sicily, and now they had landed on the Italian mainland. It was heard that they had already established several beachheads there. Salerno, Taranto, Bari – all in enemy hands. Once again the Wehrmacht and the Italian troops had failed to reject the British and US landing forces at the beaches, to throw them back into the sea. But that would have been the only way to overcome the incredible material and personnel superiority of the Western powers – after all, the concentrated economies of the United States, England, and the Commonwealth stood against those of Germany and its mostly small allies. That was like half the world against more or less two and a half nations. The economic performance, the mere population numbers, and the military equipment of half the world against the Axis powers. As long as it could be managed to defend the beaches and kept the coasts free of enemies, victory was accomplishable. But not in the hinterland – not far from the coast, where man would stand against man and tank against tank. And the enemy simply had more men and more tanks.

Slowly Thomas shook his head. One would now have to withdraw formations from the East in order to strengthen the Italian theater. Then Ivan would soon breakthrough in some sector of the Eastern Front, and Axis divisions would be dragged back from west to east to plug the holes in the front line there. The Allies would finally find the next weak point and for example invade Norway or Greece. Again, formations would have to be withdrawn from the East to help out at these theaters of war. A vicious circle. Thomas believed in the qualitative superiority of the German military, but in this war, which became more and more a conflict of the whole damn world against the German Reich, every quality aspect was threatened to be washed away by the sheer mass of the enemy.

Thomas sensed a dull feeling in his stomach. He was desperately searching in his mind for a way how his country could benefit the most from his capabilities. In any case, he was no longer sure whether the best place for him was here in Switzerland. However, he did not want to leave either – not leaving her. That was another difficult conflict he had with himself.

Behind him the lock of the door clicked, and the door was pushed open the next moment. Luise stormed into the room, beaming with joy. "750 kilometers!" she moaned and fell round Thomas' neck. "750 kilometers!" She almost cried. Thomas grabbed her shoulders. Finally, Luise calmed down. Her gaze caught him. A blonde strand fell into her face, which Thomas carefully stroked behind her ear. Luise smiled broadly. Her big eyes, blue and wide as the ocean, focused on him. Her full lips, brimming with red lipstick, seemed to whisper an invitation. Luise made Thomas smile himself, although he didn't feel like it at all. A pleasant tingling sensation penetrated his stomach, and he couldn't take his eyes off her.

"750 kilometers," she whispered once more.

"What do you mean?"

"I measured it on the map. Only 750 kilometers lie between the Allied troops in Italy and the Swiss border. We can breathe a sigh of relief soon, Aaron. OUR people can breathe a sigh of relief!" Slowly she leaned forward. Thomas stared at her, unable to move. She bent further forward, the curves of her blouse bumping against Thomas' arms.

"I want you, Aaron," she whispered in his ear. "Now!"

Then she let go of him and bit her lower lip boldly. Slowly, she stepped backwards and sat down on the bed. Her big eyes did not leave Thomas. He was still standing there rooted to the ground, just staring at her. Luise spread her legs and grinned. At that moment, Thomas was struck by two thoughts: *First of all, I must undress immediately. Second: Balkan, my ass!*

Podersdorf am See, German Reich, September 16th, 1943

The old wooden door opened and Sergeant Franz Berning entered his family home in his uniform and with his rifle in his hands. He looked into the visage of his incredibly old father. Berning got scared. His old man reminded him of a mummy: the face had collapsed and was torn apart by endless wrinkles. The hair was long and grey and tousled. Age marks covered the thin old hands. Scratched, dry skin adorned the face. The over-indebted postal office clerk Gustav Berning looked like 70, but he was not yet 60.

Franz Berning had made it home after all, but he would have gladly renounced the reason for his short leave.

"Grüss Gott, my boy," a weak voice trembled from the deep, sad mouth of the father to the outside. The Burgenland dialect was unmistakable.

Franz's eyes became glassy. He could hardly bear the sight of his father.

Only last year, when they had last seen each other, he had been such a proud and strong man. That was before Mother became ill ... "I'm so sorry ..." Franz whispered and stepped into the narrow hallway. He put the rifle on the ground, then tore his field cap off his head. "I am so sorry, Father," he whispered once more and fell into his old man's arms. He was too late – one day too late. Mother's funeral was yesterday.

"It's all right, boy," breathed the father and stroked his son's pigtail. "You can't help it."

Then they both cried.

Franz could have really done it. He had received the news in time and had been granted special leave immediately. But then partisan attacks against rails delayed his journey by two days.

Franz cried loudly and intensely, the father rather quietly. He had already shed many tears, while Franz had always remained strong until now – after all, he had always been surrounded by other soldiers before whom he did not want to expose his feelings. But now he couldn't hold it back. Big tears rolled down his cheeks. He hadn't been able to say goodbye. That was the hardest thing for him to bear. The last time he left home in the direction of the Eastern Front, that was in summer '42, he hadn't known that he would never see his mother again. Of course, she had cried when they had said goodbye to each other, just as most mothers cry when their children go to war. But at that time nobody knew what was growing in her body – spreading inevitably. His parents had kept her bad condition secret until the very end. Franz had only learned about it from the news of her death. Now he looked at her last letter in a different light. Reading it again nearly destroyed him.

Both father and son were still in each other's arms for a few minutes before slowly separating from each other. The father, whose face was swollen and red, looked at his uniformed son from head to toe. "You look fine," he remarked, then invited Franz into the parlor.

*

They sat at the small dining table and drank tea, which his father had put on. While outside there was a strong breeze blowing against the windows and late summer was overwhelmingly suppressed by uncomfortable temperatures, in the small kitchen, the slightly pungent smell of black tea unfolded. Franz shared some miniscule stories from the front without going into any detail or really talking about the fighting against men, about him trying to kill them before they could kill him. But he didn't have to hide anything either. Gustav Berning had fought against the Italians in the Great War and knew what war was like. The father, on the other hand, gossiped a little about news from the village. So Franz learned that his two cousins were well. One served in Greece, the other in Norway – lucky bastards! Franz had no siblings and the family was quite small, so the father would be all alone as soon as Franz left again.

"When do you have to go again?" the old man asked at the same time.

"On Sunday."

Father nodded.

"Then don't sit here with me, boy," he suddenly said. A little life actually returned to his old face; it was flashing in his eyes. Franz looked up questioningly.

"Off to Gretel you go! She's waiting for you, you know."

"Honestly, she doesn't even know I'm here." Berning got an odd feeling he could not describe. "I am gonna stay only a few days. Farewell on Sunday would break her heart."

A touch of anger, or at least a lack of understanding, rose into his father's visage as he rose threateningly. Franz didn't even understand why.

"Boy, don't be stupid!" the old man insisted. "You should live every minute you can!"

"What do you mean?"

"There's a pretty girl waiting for you, Franz! Honestly, boy, on Sunday you're going back to the front. And we both know the war! Maybe you won't come back. You have to be so honest with yourself. So get what you can get."

Franz stared at his father with his mouth open. They had never talked so "openly" about women's stories before.

"Your mother told me to tell you something else," Gustav Berning continued.

"Yes?"

"I shall ..." now the father looked a little embarrassed to the floor, hemming and hawing, " ... have the man talk with you."

Franz had a sense of foreboding. He suddenly felt very uncomfortable and leaned back in his chair insecurely. Father, however, did not say another word, but reached into the drawer of a commode, took out two paper sachets, and threw them onto the table. "Only intended for the German Wehrmacht. To be disposed immediately after use," was written on it. Franz didn't know what to make of it. Of course he knew the contents of these sachets and of course they had already been distributed in his unit, not to mention that he himself had used some of them in summer '42. The question, however, was where Father had gotten

274

Wehrmacht material from. Gustav, though, immediately continued talking, for this conversation seemed as unpleasant to him as it was to his son. Franz would like to be somewhere else right now.

"Well, the man talk," the old man cleared his throat and sat down. "Boy, listen, do whatever you think is right, I don't give a damn. But use these," he pointed to the sachets, "or marry her. If you ever father an illegitimate child, then I swear to you by the Lord, I'll get the belt out again and beat you black and blue! I'm not too old to give you a beating yet."

Both stared at each other. Franz waited for a sign of relaxation from his father, but he seemed to mean every word he had said. After minutes of silence, Father leaned back in his chair, grabbed his cup, and drank a sip of black tea.

"Now put those things in your pocket, Franz," Father finally ordered and pointed to the condoms. Franz immediately did as he was told. For a few more seconds, they both remained silent.

"Go, boy," the father finally told his son, "for Sunday will come quicker than you like."

Franz nodded and rose.

"I'll just go change."

"No, you don't. Believe me, boy. Stay in uniform. It's better." Father grinned, then Franz nodded, turned around, and left the room. "Don't worry! You'll definitely see me again before I leave," he called back. The old man's face was flooded with grief and joy at the same time.

*

That same night, Franz and Gretel climbed the hayloft of her parents' barn, where it was bitterly cold. Only Berning's flashlight cut through the darkness with a garish glow – he didn't want to light candles in a wooden hayloft covered with straw. The low hanging roof creaked and groaned under the wind, which whistled at the barn. There were strong gusts outside. A shutter kept clapping against the house wall somewhere.

Franz and Gretel lay close together in the straw, wrapped in thick horse blankets. They stroked each other and drank Sturm, which at this time of the year was almost overripe. It tasted unbelievably sweet. All the same, the alcohol took full effect. In the glow of the lamp, Gretel looked very attractive. Light and shadow played in her soft face and with her little nose. Her blonde hair shimmered.

"You know, I am so proud that my Franz defends the Reich in Russia against these barbarians. The other girls are already red with envy, because their boyfriends are only stationed in Norway or France, where there is nothing heroic to do. I think it's great that you're part of the most important campaign in this war."

"... Yeah, great."

"You're a real man, Franz. Sometimes I get all too excited when I think about what you're going through over there. And you're so brave. You were in Russia, and even when you were wounded in Italy, you fought." She smiled softly and caressed Franz's chest.

"Yes, perhaps. But it's not that great, Gretel."

276

"Oh, don't be so modest! It's so bad when you think that these subhumans wanted to attack our fine Reich! Our squad conductress explained all this to us. How the Russians were already lurking behind the border with their soldiers and tanks. They just wanted to rob us and take over our country! Can you imagine that? And now they see what they get out of it."

The youth organizations that the NSDAP had integrated into the state after rising to power were still active these days. Even von Witzleben could get something out of the idea of a German youth united under one roof, since this granted the state access to a monopoly on education of the next generation.

Gretel looked at Franz, but he was somehow absent-minded. With an empty look, he stared past her into the glow of the flashlight, while the wind whipped the roof above them.

"What's the matter?" she asked.

"Nothing. It's nothing."

"But you look as miserable as sin."

"No, it's fine."

Suddenly her hand lay on his thighs while her face was very close to his. "Tell me, Franz," she whispered and seemed very excited. Aroused.

"What is it?"

"Tell me about your war stories."

"I don't know if this belongs here."

"Come on, don't chicken out! Tell me of your feats of valor and I'll be yours." Her hand slowly moved up his loins. Franz twitched and felt her incite him.

"Well, once ..." he began and felt uncomfortable. Then he looked into her eyes, which were already very close

- and begged for more. "Once," he repeated, "we were surrounded by Russians ... well ... I mean our squadron and some other units. The Russians were everywhere... well... so..."

"Stop beating around the bush!" she demanded and grabbed his crotch. Franz winced.

He wanted her!

"Well, we were surrounded. And they came from everywhere. Three, four times as many as we were. And they had tanks! Our own tin cans already had been smoked. I was up in a building with my machine gunner and two others. One of them was already dead and the machine gunner was wounded. So it was more or less just me." Gretel's eyes got bigger and bigger. Her hand massaged his crotch. Franz straightened up a little, and he spoke faster now: "So it was up to me. I shot like there's no tomorrow. Twenty or twenty-five Russians I eliminated. But then I realized that all this was no use as long as the enemy tanks were still driving around."

"Good-oh," Gretel breathed.

"So I took my men and ran downstairs. *Grab satchel charges!* I shouted. The men did, and then we dashed outta the building. But at the same moment our own panzers were approaching the battleground, and of course they made short shrift of the Russians, I mean, nothing can compete with German workmanship, right? So me and my men scanned the village, and we secured everything and overpowered the last resistance. Suddenly I'm all alone in an alley and a door opens. There's a Russian standing right in front of me."

278

Gretel was already half on top of Franz and became even more excited with every word.

"Franz, what happened then? Did you have to strike him dead?"

"No, no, no, no. He immediately pulled up his rifle and tried to shoot me."

"Oh, God, how terrible!"

"But I was faster, of course, and there he was lying in the dirt."

"Unbelievable."

"... Yes..." Franz stared into the darkness for a moment.

"And the Slavic bastards hit you too," she exhaled with a pretend dismay as her fingers ran over the scar on his neck.

"Yes."

"And you weren't allowed to go on home leave for that?"

"Ah no, it was nothing much. Things went straight on."

"Oh my Franz, you are so strong." She pressed her hot body against his.

"Have you never killed a Russian in close-combat melee?" she wanted to know with a deep desire pouring out of her eyes and full lips. Franz stared at her.

What's the frigging matter with this girl? he wondered for a moment.

But as her hand rubbed his crotch even swifter and the hard bulges, which were visible under her dress, pressed against his body, he hurried to tell another war story. "Once we were attacked as we lay in position.

279

The Russians broke through our lines and suddenly were everywhere." Franz paused for a moment while his heart beat strongly. He hesitated. But then he continued: "They were everywhere. Then I see a red soldier wrestling with a good comrade of mine. I run there and stand right next to them. The Russian was squeezing the air out of my comrade, was trying to choke him. He almost succeeded."

"God no, what a barbarian!"

"Yeah, you said it."

"Did you shoot him, Franz?" Gretel looked at him seductively. Berning's eyes became opaque. A lump got stuck in his throat. But Gretel gazed at him... she wanted him.

Franz said: "No. I didn't want to waste a bullet at that distance. I pulled him down from my comrade and fought with him for a second. Got him down real quick. Then I thought it wouldn't be bad to take him as prisoner, so we can squeeze some information out of him. Thus I captured him."

"And your comrade?" she whispered. Her hot breath caressed his face.

"He's all right. Thanked me for saving his life." Berning took Gretel in his arms. Their lips approached each other.

"You're my hero," she said, closing her eyes. "Now that you're on your leave, let the woman do her job." With these words, she pushed him into the straw and opened the buttons of the field blouse for him.

West of Oryol, Soviet Union, September 16th, 1943

Engelmann watched from the edge of the forest as a column of Wehrmacht vehicles, reaching to the horizon on both sides, slowly drove across the dusty road leading to Oryol. Opel Blitz trucks, horse-drawn carts, and standard passenger cars blocked the road and made any progress possible only at walking pace. Drivers greeted each other; Russian volunteers sat on panje wagons with pinched expressions. Small treks of civilians, who apparently carried all their belongings with them, trotted with lowered heads past the German military machinery, which almost had been condemned to a standstill. Also motorcycles roared, humming along the side of the road. Sometimes the motorcyclists waved provocatively at the men in the four-wheeled vehicles – and reaped wildly-gesticulated outbursts of rage in gratitude from those damned to wait.

Thanks God that we are out of reach of the Anglo-American Air Forces, Engelmann thought. *The boys over there would make a great target.*

He would smile if his family did not have to live every day with the hazard of getting battered by huge enemy bomber formations. At least he could quickly distract himself from such feelings, for in his hands he held a piece of home; a letter from Elly. While in the background his crew sat on Franzi II's hull and turret playing cards, and other fellow countrymen of the 12th Company dozed in the shades, Engelmann ripped open the envelope and pulled out the classy stationery on which Elly used to write. Just as he was about to read the first line, Münster's ringing laughter sounded across the plain mingling with the constant hum of a thousand engines. Engelmann looked north. He spotted his driver at the armored command panzer of 12th Company. Münster's head and torso stuck out of the high grass. He leaned against a tree and pulled a cigarette with relish. Captain Stollwerk gesture-richly told the sergeant some story, but Engelmann was too far away to hear exactly what it was about.

Pfft, hero tales, he said to himself in disgust. He chuckled cheerlessly as he saw Stollwerk shape his hand into a pistol and then make a movement as if he were firing at something. Or someone. Finally the captain grinned, and Münster laughed out loud again.

Once again Engelmann envied his comrades for their levity. While the overall situation had changed dramatically since Operation Citadel, and in some cases even improved, Engelmann was once again dominated by pessimism.

He briefly recapitulated the events since May of this year in his mind: after the investment of several Soviet armies in the Kursk pocket, the Wehrmacht had succeeded in fending off several Russian offensives. Not only had immense losses been inflicted on the enemy, but also an enormous breach had been achieved in the hastily set-up enemy front lines. A rapid attack carried out by armored and mechanized forces directly hitting that breach had allowed the Wehrmacht to break through as far as the banks of the Oka and Tula Rivers. Moscow was suddenly within reach again. But now the German armies in the East were finally beat-up. They were no longer capable of conducting mobile warfare. Not only tanks and trained crews were lacking, but also ammunition, food, and above all, fuel. Nevertheless, this summer the Wehrmacht had achieved everything it had been able to achieve in view of its unfavorable starting position: The red flood had been stopped, and dozens of Soviet armies crippled or destroyed for the time being. The enemy, who at the beginning of the year had had ten times more tanks than the Wehrmacht and an almost endless supply of people and raw materials, had been shot immobile. Accordingly, quiet had now returned to the Eastern front. Small skirmishes still took place, the artillery occasionally sent greetings to the other side, but the time of the great offensives was over – at least for this year. Both sides lay entrenched in their positions, digging deeper in. This could finally lead to some kind of trench warfare similar to the cruel static war of the Western Front in the Great War, which had swallowed and digested millions of soldiers.

Engelmann had to gulp in view of these prospects. Once the trenches were deep enough and the emplacements were fortified with barbed wire, mines, battle stations, and bunkers, any attempt to attack would die out in the fire of the defenders.

Then again, one final offensive next year could put an end to everything; therefore the Wehrmacht would have to assemble its armies and march against Moscow for one last time. But Engelmann was also aware that the Russians would also use the time of "rest" for reinforcing their troops. If the Wehrmacht managed to deliver 3,000 new panzers to the Eastern Front by the beginning of next year, there would be 10,000 new Russian tanks. If the German divisions could be refreshed during the period of quiet, the Russians would refresh their divisions as well and also produced thirty new ones out of thin air. Time worked against the German Reich, Engelmann was sure of that. There was also the difficult situation in the West. The enemy had stormed Fortress Europe with its invasion of Italy. Within weeks the Western powers had conquered Sicily, and now they had landed on the southern tip of the Italian boot. Because of these events, the Grand Council of Fascism had discussed Mussolini's dismissal. Due to the efforts of von Witzleben to treat Italy as an equal ally, the Duce eventually had been able to unite a scant majority behind him. Nevertheless, the vote clearly showed how unstable the most important European ally of the Reich was.

Did the Axis powers really had to offer opposition to the concentrated might of the USA and the British Empire? Or would the enemy already be in the Alps in winter? Engelmann preferred not to answer these questions. It simply was vital for the Axis powers to tack down the Western Allies in the southern part of Italy. But with the Eastern Front, English ships in the Mediterranean, American bombers over the Reich's territory and weak allies like Italy, but also Hungary or Romania in the heart of Europe, Engelmann just could hope that the German Reich would not collapse under such pressure from all sides. His eyes became glasslike when he wondered how long this war would last. It was now the fourth year – that was how long the Great

War had lasted. How much more war would Europe be able to endure? Engelmann inevitably had to think of the Seven Years' War ... of the Thirty Years' War, of the Hundred Years' War ...

Engelmann shook himself to get rid of such thoughts.

After all, for his regiment, the next stop was the rear echelon far behind the front line – the real rear echelon, not like here in Oryol, where they were only a few kilometers away from the Russians. No, Panzer Regiment 2 would be pulled completely out of the front sector. The battle-weary forces urgently needed reinforcements and the veteran comrades a rest. France it should be, rumored the moccasin radio, but Engelmann would believe that only if he would hold the marching order in his hands. In addition, 9th Company would finally be revived, and Engelmann would again be commander of a platoon.

Lastly, Lieutenant Engelmann turned to his wife's letter. For too long now he had kept it waiting and had dealt with his everlasting military thoughts.

If this is not a sin, then I don't know either, he sniggered inwardly before his eyes were focusing on his wife's peppily-written lines.

To Lieutenant Josef Engelmann, August 29th, 1943
F.P. 34444

My Sepp!

How much I hoped to get a message from you over the summer that you were in Germany and could still come visit us for a day or two. Unfortunately, nothing arrived. Did they decree a writing ban again? Did you have to stay in Russia after all and couldn't go to Germany or Italy or France? That's how you thought it might happen. At least I hope you're not right on the front line anymore. When I see what is happening these days everywhere, then I become quite anxious and sometimes I am completely at a loss. Gudrun is supposed to have a sheltered life, but that is not possible in war. The Allied bombers are now over Germany every day and every night. They hit the harbor hard, and the St. Jürgen Hospital was also completely destroyed. First the explosive bombs went down and blew the roof up, then the incendiary bombs followed and fell directly into the children's clinic. The poor little souls burned in the fire, screaming. A friend of Uncle Theo's is with the fire department. Three days after the incident, he hanged himself in his apartment because it was said that he had seen the charred little children and could not bear it. At least that's what they say! I heard it at his funeral from all kinds of people. You should have seen that! Half of Bremen was there to say goodbye to the man!

Oh, I just hope that all this suffering at least passes our little family by. We didn't do anything bad to deserve this. Especially not Gudrun. Please write soon how you are and where you are. I'll hang on till you come back, but I won't cope without a message from you for much longer!

In love,
Elly

Berlin, German Reich, September 17th, 1943

In the last third of 1943, the number of bomb attacks by Americans and British against German cities increased by the day. Hamburg had been hit severely in the summer. The bombs and the subsequent firestorm had destroyed large parts of the old town. In the sky above the German capital, hostile bomber units were no more a rarity too. The Luftwaffe, whose fighter forces were spread over the entire continent and which in the fourth year of the war could no longer compensate for the enormous losses of man and material, had to watch the bomb terror almost helplessly. Berlin was partly in ruins, but despite the increasing number of air raid alarms, daily business had to continue. So did the Chancellor's office.

With an earnest countenance, Erwin von Witzleben brooded over a letter. Next to him stood Louis Ferdinand von Preussen, a tall man with a high forehead and thick black hair. Some grew grey already. He often had a cheeky smile on his lips and was known and loved for his likeable manners, but on this day, when he looked at the document next to the Chancellor, his forehead was also wrinkled; his face revealed all the concerns he carried within him.

Von Witzleben had made Louis Ferdinand von Preussen Reich Foreign Minister, because he, as son of the crown prince of the former German Empire, had preserved so many contacts to Great Britain, France, and Russia that there could have been no better man for the post. Louis, who was still secretly dreaming of the crown in a reestablished German monarchy, was subject to an eternal inner discord as Reich Foreign Minister: on the one hand he had to face Germany's war opponents with strength and dominance, but on the other hand his interlocutors were often old friends or – worse – relatives.

And then there was the fact that it was deeply contrary to his mind to go to war with such great nations as England or Russia, even though the latter had fallen prey to the madness of communism. If it were Louis Ferdinand's way, he would rather end the war today than tomorrow, but of course he was also a fervent patriot, which was why he would certainly not turn the German Reich into a junk shop for allied interests.

Stacks of documents and letters were scattered all over the Chancellor's desk, and one of them was over eight months old. Nevertheless, it was of particular importance: it was an anonymous letter from a sender who named himself "Werther" and in which he assured the Chancellor that he would immediately cease his espionage activities now that the Nazis had been expelled from power.

But von Witzleben did not worry about this particular letter, which had already been the subject of many discussions and disputes within his cabinet, because he held a completely different note in his hands.

"All right," he said and put the document aside. "My English isn't the best, but I think I got the message." He sighed deeply. "So the Allies remain adamant on an unconditional surrender?" the Chancellor concluded.

Louis Ferdinand carefully examined von Witzleben's visage, which darkened with every second. The Chancellor seemed to have expected this answer, although he was not prepared for it. Briefly a twitch played around his mouth, then he asked: "So? After all, this is a joint declaration. What was your impression on site? From the individual parties?"

Louis Ferdinand had been in London until four hours ago to discuss possible peace negotiations with the Allies.

"Especially the English and Russians," he began with resignation in his voice, "insist on the unconditional surrender. Then again this Hull guy..."

"...the American?"

"Right. Hull makes me feel like I can talk to him. I think the Americans can basically do without war with us."

Von Witzleben nodded slowly. You could see that several trains of thought arrived at his mind station. Deep wrinkles formed on his forehead. His fingers danced around on the tabletop.

"Now they know what they are up to," the Chancellor thought out loud. "I will convene the cabinet for Sunday. We must plan our future course in light of recent developments."

The coming together of the major warring nations could certainly have brought more hopeful results, but on the positive side, it had to be noted that the warring parties – after Hitler's secret negotiations with England in 1940 – spoke to each other again for the first time.

The door to von Witzleben's office was pushed open. An angry Ludwig Beck in a suit with a tie stormed in.

Behind Beck was von Witzleben's young adjutant, whose face was a silent apology for not having been able to stop the President of the Reich. The Chancellor indicated to him that he should close the doors, while Beck already started to rage furiously: "I can no longer be made a puppet of warlords! I demand that you resume peace negotiations immediately!"

"If it were that simple," the Chancellor sighed and rose. Then he said: "Herr Reichspräsident..." He didn't get any further, because Beck interrupted him rudely. "Save your phrases. You brought me into this government last year under certain agreements..."

"And we kept them." Von Witzleben was irritated.

"You have been going on with this war for almost a year now – and apart from a few kilometers of terrain gain here and there, it has led nowhere. How long are your politics going to last?"

"As long as it's necessary."

"And then the bomb terror of the Americans and the British! Do you want to wait until the last German city has been wiped off the face of earth? How many Germans have lost their lives since last November just to push this pointless struggle forward? I don't want to start with Italy!"

"Don't worry, we won't lose Italy..."

Beck interrupted the Chancellor again: "No, we will lose THIS WAR! You must stop this madness instantly!"

Now Beck fell silent and waited for a reaction from his counterpart. Louis Ferdinand von Preussen felt as if he had been faded out of the scene.

"I would have expected more understanding of the strategic context from you in particular," von Witzleben replied calmly and licked his lips.

"Well, I'm curious," Beck responded while crossing his arms.

"We have used the year since Hitler's death solely to correct the mistakes made. The Führer had been so determined in his offensives against Stalingrad and the Caucasus that he did not want to hear how fatal his plans actually were. When we took over here, these offensives were in full swing and we had to make great efforts to prevent the total annihilation of Heeresgruppe Süd, because the enemy was already trying to block our troops' way back. Against this background, our successes in Kursk and Tula are overwhelming."

"And how many lives did that cost? I ask you, how long do young Germans have to bleed and die in foreign countries because old men here in Berlin play their war games?"

"Please do not close your eyes to what we have achieved. The Eastern Front is stable again. Feldmarschall von Manstein has given us breathing space!"

"Then please negotiate the truce already! You can't fly to London and expect that you won't have to make any concessions to our opponents..."

"The Allies still insist on unconditional surrender. So it's our turn to convince them that the German Reich is not beatable."

"Aren't we beatable?"

"There will never be any concessions under my Chancellorship! I will not stand idly by as Stalin assimilates the East of our Reich and the Saarland and Alsace fall to France. Think about the Germans who live there!" Von Witzleben and Beck stared at each other like two cats of prey claiming the same territory.

"With each month, you just delay the inevitable." Beck's words now almost had a begging character. "The Russians have a sheer endless mass of soldiers and tanks, and the Americans are already in Italy. And don't think I am stupid. It is all over town that France is the next target for Allied actions against us. Another front in the west would spell doom for our Reich. Do you want to wait until you can call out your claims to the Allies from your office window? STOP THIS MADNESS NOW!"

Von Witzleben twitched. "We will meet the enemy in France and defeat him there."

"Like we did in Italy?" For a moment, Beck had thus evoked a dead silence.

"Italy is a dead end," the Chancellor concluded eventually, "and once we have fended off an invasion in central Europe, we will have the Western powers off our backs. They won't dare a second time."

Beck's facial expression almost turned into insanity. The old general showed his teeth, then pressed his lips together as his visage filled with anger. Louis Ferdinand became scared at the sight, but Beck just shook his head.

"Pah!" he spat, "Warmongers! You're hardly any better than the Nazis! Just a bunch of warmongers!" And with these words he stomped out of the room, leaving behind him long moments of stillness. Von Witzleben and Louis Ferdinand looked at each other. Finally, the aristocrat broke the silence. "I heard about different invasion rumors: France, Norway, Denmark."

"We must assume that it will happen in France. Anything else would be unreasonable and would only bring the Allies another Italy, from where there is no way into the hearts of our Reich. If we reject the invasion in the West and let the Russians bleed to death in the East using von Manstein's backhand blow strategy, then the German Reich has a realistic chance," von Witzleben proclaimed in a thin voice. Tiredness seemed to have seized him.

"How sure are you about that?"

"We are at war, my friend. Nothing's for sure." A faint grin scurried across von Witzleben's face.

"I can only see that the Soviet Union and the USA are two far superior economies. The world war has already proved that these days final victory will be achieved by the one who has the most effective economy behind him, not the one with the best army."

"But the American is too busy with the Japanese to be able to focus all his attention on us. As you yourself said before, basically they don't want any war with us," the Chancellor interjected.

"What if Japan folds?"

"We must do everything we can to ensure that this does not happen. The Japanese are extremely important to us in two ways - not just because of the Americans. The Japanese also bind strong units of Soviet forces which otherwise would be used against

294

us. So believe me, Japan's support has been high on my agenda since the beginning of my tenure."

"With all due respect, we lack the strength to support others."

"My good Herr von Preussen, without going into detail, I can assure you that we are already doing so."

Louis Ferdinand gazed at his counterpart with a questioning expression. The Chancellor explained briefly. "The Japanese are in the same boat as we are. Surrounded by our common enemies, cut off from important resources. If one goes down, the other goes down, for one alone is not equal to the concentrated power of our enemies."

"What are you implying?"

"Technology, material, education, knowledge. This is how I handle it with all our allies, and believe me, I am aware of the risks of this procedure. But at the moment every ally counts – and every ally must be strengthened wherever possible. Only Japan is a case in itself; our strongest ally, but unfortunately almost unattainable. We didn't start pulling the submarines out of the Atlantic theater for nothing."

"We pulled our submarines out of the Atlantic?"

Von Witzleben laughed up. "Apparently so discreet that even our own ministers didn't notice it," he rejoiced.

Von Preussen, however, could not cheer, as he became aware of how much the Chancellor kept him on a short leash, how little he as Foreign Minister was actually involved in the business that Germany handled with its allies.

"But... England? We have to cut the island off from supplies."

The Chancellor shook his head firmly. "Take a look at how the figures have developed since the beginning of the year. The battle for the Atlantic has become futile, and I will not send our men on suicide missions anymore. We need our subs much more in European waters for the protection of the homeland – and for special assignments in the Pacific."

Aftermath

The year 1941 was in its final days. Private Tom Roebuck spent the evening with his wife Marie in their small flat under the pointed roof of an apartment building on the northern outskirts of San Diego, California. It would be their last night together before he had to leave. Their marriage was still fresh. They had met at the beginning of the year and got married in September. At that time the world was still in order – at least in the States. Since December 7th, however, everything was different. The USA had been surprisingly attacked by the Japanese. Immediately afterwards, Nazi Germany had declared war on America. Roebuck had received his marching orders. The Corps apparently wouldn't even allow him to celebrate New Year's Eve at home.

Drizzle sprinkled the windows. Gilded bells and colored glass balls adorned a small Christmas tree, which sat enthroned on the dining table. Marie, whose great-grandparents came from Austria, had drawn the curtains so that the neighbors of the opposite apartment could not watch her making love to her husband. Since Tom had return from his base, she seduced him at every opportunity, pampering him extensively with all the means at her disposal.

She would never admit that before him, but she was afraid that he would take an Asian woman as his lover in the Pacific, so she wanted to use the short time the Marine Corps allowed her to convince him of what he had in her.

Now both sat on the carpet in front of the sofa. Intertwined, they listened silently to faint jazz music coming from the radio. An evergreen by Benny Goodman was played. The refrain accompanied by the saxophone just filled the room with "He's not worth your tears." Minutes of silence passed. Marie got his scent up her nose, which she liked very much. She felt his deliberately-beating heart and his breathing. Very slowly, his chest rose and fell.

She had put her right hand on his thorax and let her fingers play around with the black hair Tom had there. The minute hand passed 10 pm. She sighed softly. He'd have to get on the train early in the morning. One more time she wanted to surrender herself to him that night. One more time. Her lips burned, but she was terribly afraid Tom might fall for the beguiling creature of an exotic Asian. At least that was how she imagined them. One more time she wanted to sleep with him.

"Marie," he whispered suddenly. His rough voice gave her name a special sound.

"Yes?" she breathed.

"Marie, honey." His eyes reminded her of a glass of milk. "You're the most wonderful woman a man could ever wish for." He smiled at her. Gentle and soft were the features around his mouth when he did that. Immediately, a tingling sensation set in in her belly. Marie smiled back, then sadness attacked her that deformed her facial features.

"Tomorrow you'll get on that train," she whispered in a trembling voice, "and then you'll be gone for so long. I could cry when I think about it."

She lowered her head, but Tom grabbed her chin and gently lifted her face until her eyes met. He always did that when she was sad.

She loved him.

"Next Christmas we'll be together again. The lieutenant colonel said the Japs can't stand a year against us."

"But then what? Then they'll send you to Europe!"

Tom laughed gently. "Little Marie." He pressed her head against his chest and kissed her temple. "Little Marie, you have no idea of the military, I find. You're overestimating the Germans. Look at the Great War. As soon as our boys landed in Europe, we crushed their ridiculous army."

She looked at him with wide eyes – expectant. Her lips shivered.

"Believe me, Hitler will go to hell before Tōjō," he assured her.

Acknowledgement

I would like to thank my father, who is my most productive supporter. My wife also deserves a special mention because she is the one who inspires me every day and makes me happy.

Once again I would like to thank my publisher Hansjoachim Bernt, whose commitment and constant criticism of my concepts and texts have made the Panzers series what it is.

In telephone conversations lasting hours, we played through all situations, discussed the advantages and disadvantages of a concept, and sometimes came to different conclusions. Often these conversations have drawn my attention to weaknesses in my ideas.

Of course, I would also like to thank Richard Moncure for his work on this text.

Note from Tom Zola

Dear readers,

while the book itself was edited by some true English experts, I wrote this small note myself. Since English is not my mother tongue, this note contains some weird Germanized grammar and sentences for sure. I suggest you read it in a strong German accent ☺

I would like to take the chance to thank you for buying our book. The EK-2 Publishing Team put a lot of effort into the PANZERS series, especially was the translation one hell of a job. As said, we are glad to have real English experts on board (at this point I would like to gratefully thank Richard Moncure and Wendy Chan for their marvelous efforts and commitment!!!) Even for native speakers it is one heck of a task to work on a text that is full of technical terms and detailed military descriptions.

On the one hand you have ranks, German trivia and other national or regional specialties. Should we translate German nicknames like *Stuka* for the Junkers Ju 87 or should we leave it in its German form in the text? Almost from line to line we struggled with this very question and had to find a new answer to it each time.

When it comes to ranks, we did translate them to obtain a better reading experience, although in direct speech we sometimes kept original German or Russian ranks – that depends on the overall paragraph and how it would influence readability.

On the other hand, in the original text there are a lot of references to typical German trivia, which gave all of us a hard time translating them. Things like the military function of a "Kompanietruppführer" only exists in the German Army. There is no translation, no comparable function in other armed forces, and it even is very difficult to explain its meaning without a deep understanding of the functioning of the German military. So, what should we do with such things? How should we translate the text in a way that its originality does not get lost, but that it is at the same time fully understandable in English? Believe me, finding that balance is no easy task! I hope we have gotten most things right!

Our overall goal was to provide a very unique reading experience for English readers. This text is written by a former German soldier (me), it focuses on a German perspective and is very technical in its details. I often find posts and articles on the Internet that are about Germany or the German Army, written by foreigners in English, hilariously mistaking our very special little German idiosyncrasies (no accusation meant, I would struggle similarly trying to understand a culture I am a total stranger to). Thus, I hope it is interesting for you to read something from Germany that really tries to translate these idiosyncrasies correctly into English. Nevertheless we tried everything to preserve a special German touch. That is why we sometimes left a German word or phrase in the text. At the same time, we tried to ensure that English readers can understand everything without using a dictionary or Wehrmacht textbook from time to time and that the whole thing stays readable.

Another thing we did in order to manage this balancing act is that we separated German words for better readability and understanding although they are not separated originally. We Germans are infamous for our very long words like Bundeswehrstrukturanpassungsgesetz or Donau-Dampfschifffahrtsgesellschaft. In English words are separated way more often to keep them short. Germans say Armeekorps, English folks say army group. So for example we made Panzer Korps out of Panzerkorps in the text hoping that this will help you to read the book without stumbling too often.

The PANZERS series consists of 12 books, and I promise in book 12 I provide a satisfying ending. No cliffhangers!

Additionally, EK-2 Publishing holds a bunch of other German military literature licenses that we really would love to introduce to English readers. So, stay tuned for more to come! And please give us feedback on what you think about this book, our project and the EK-2 Publishing idea of bringing military literature from the motherland of military to English readers. Also let us know how we can improve the reading experience for you and how we managed the thin red line between readability and originality of the text.

We love to hear from you!!

info@ek2-publishing.com

(I am connected to this email address and will personally read and answer your mails!)

In the following I provide some additional information: a glossary of all words and specialist terms you may have stumbled upon while reading, an overview of Wehrmacht ranks, German military formation sizes and abbreviations. Since I wrote those glossaries myself, too, I recommend you keep the German accent …

Glossary

76-millimeters divisional gun M1942: Soviet field gun that produced a unique sound while firing, which consisted of some kind of hissing, followed by the detonation boom. Therefore the Germans Wehrmacht soldiers called it "Ratsch Bumm".

Abwehr: German Military Intelligence Service

Acht-Acht: German infamous 8.8 centimeter Flak anti-aircraft and anti-tank gun. Acht-Acht is German meaning nothing less than eight-eight.

Afrika Korps: German expeditionary force in North Africa; it was sent to Libya to support the Italian Armed Forces in 1941, since the Italians were not able to defend what they had conquered from the British and desperately needed some backing. Hitler's favorite general Rommel was the Afrika Korps' commander. Over the years he gained some remarkable victories over the British, but after two years of fierce fighting … two years, in which the Axis' capabilities to move supplies and reinforcements over the Mediterranean Sea constantly decreased due to an allied air superiority that grew stronger by the day, Rommel no longer stood a chance against his opponents. Finally the U.S.A. entered the war and invaded North Africa in November 1942. Hitler prohibited the Afrika Korps to retreat back to Europe or even to shorten the front line by conducting tactical retreats. Because of that nearly

300 000 Axis' soldiers became POWs, with thousands of tons of important war supplies and weapons getting lost as well when the Afrika Korps surrendered in May 1943, just months after the 6th Army had surrendered in Stalingrad.

In the PANZERS series von Witzleben allows the Afrika Korps to retreat just in time. Axis' forces abandon North Africa by the end of 1942, saving hundreds of thousands of soldiers and important war material.

Arabic numerals vs. Roman numerals in German military formation names: I decided to keep Arabic as well as Roman numerals in the translation, therefore you will find a 1st Squad, but an II Abteilung. Normally all battalions and corpses have Roman numerals, the rest Arabic ones.

Armee Abteilung: More or less equivalent to an army. The Germans of WW2 really had confusing manners to organize and name their military formations.

Assault Gun: Fighting Vehicle intended to accompany and support infantry formations. Assault guns were equipped with a tank-like main gun in order to combat enemy strongholds or fortified positions to clear the way for the infantry. An assault gun had no rotatable turret, but a casemate. This made them very interesting especially for Germany, because they could be produced faster and at lower material costs than proper combat tanks.

Assistant machine gunner: In the Wehrmacht you usually had three soldiers to handle one MG: a gunner and two assistants. The first assistant carried the spare barrel as well as some small tools for cleaning and maintaining the weapon plus extra belted ammunition in boxes. The second assistant carried even more ammunition around. In German the three guys are called: MG-1, MG-2 and MG-3.

Ausführung: German word for variant. Panzer IV Ausführung F means that it is the F variant of that very tank. The Wehrmacht improved their tanks continuously, and gave each major improvement a new letter.

Avanti: German slur name for Italians.

Babushka: Russian word for "grandmother" or "elderly woman"

Balkenkreuz: Well-known black cross on white background that has been used by every all-German armed force ever since and also before the first German unification by the Prussian military.

Battle of Stalingrad: The battle of Stalingrad is often seen as the crucial turning point of the war between the Third Reich and the Soviet Union. For the first time the Wehrmacht suffered an overwhelming defeat, when the 6th Army was encircled in the city of Stalingrad and had to surrender after it had withstood numerous Soviet attacks, a bitterly cold Russian winter and a lack of supplies and food due to the encirclement. Hitler was obsessed with the desire to conquer the city with the name of his opponent on it – Stalin – and thus didn't listen to his generals, who thought of Stalingrad as a place without great strategic use.

In reality the battle took place between August 1942 and February 1943. The encirclement of the Axis' forces was completed by the end of November 1942. The Axis' powers lost around 300 000 men. After surrendering 108 000 members of the 6th Army became POWs, of which only 6 000 survivors returned to Germany after the war.

In the PANZERS series von Witzleben listens to his generals and withdraws all troops from the city of Stalingrad in time. Thus the encirclement never happens.

Beck Doctrines: A set of orders issued by President of the Reich Ludwig Beck that demands a human treatment of POWs and civilians in occupied territories. The doctrines are an invention of me, neither did they exist in reality, nor was Beck ever President of the Reich (but the main protagonists of the 20 July plot, of whom Beck was one, wanted him for that very position).

Bohemian Private: In German it is "Böhmischer Gefreiter", a mocking nickname for Hitler, which was used by German officers to highlight that Hitler never got promoted beyond the rank of private in World War I. Besides basic training Hitler never attended any kind of military education. It is said that president

Hindenburg first came up with this nickname. He did not like Hitler and wrongfully believed he was from the Braunau district in Bohemia, not Braunau am Inn in Austria.

Brandenburgers: German military special force (first assigned to Abwehr, on 1st April 1943 alleged to the Wehrmacht) that consists of many foreign soldiers in order to conduct covert operations behind enemy lines. The name "Brandenburgers" refers to their garrison in Brandenburg an der Havel (near Berlin).

Büchsenlicht: Büchse = tin can (also archaic for a rifle); Licht = light; having Büchsenlicht means that there is enough daylight for aiming and shooting.

Churchill tank: Heavy British infantry tank, with about 40 tons it was one of the heaviest allied tanks of the war. Through the Lend-Lease policy it saw action on the Russian side, too. Its full name is Tank, Infantry, Mk IV (A22) Churchill.

Clubfoot: Refers to Joseph Goebbels, a high-ranking Nazi politician, one of Hitler's most important companions and Reich Minister of Propaganda (Secretary of Propaganda). He coined names like "Vergeltungswaffe" (= weapon of revenge) for the A4 ballistic missile and glorified a total war, meaning all Germans – men, women, elderly and children alike – had to contribute to "final victory". He is one of the reasons why German children, wounded and old men had to fight at the front lines during the last years of the Third Reich. "Clubfoot" refers to the fact that Goebbels suffered from a deformed right foot.

Commissar Order: An order issued by the Wehrmacht's high command before the start of the invasion of the USSR that demanded to shoot any Soviet political commissar, who had been captured. In May 1942 the order was canceled after multiple complaints from officers, many of them pointing out that it made the enemy fight until last man standing instead of surrendering to German troops. In the Nuremberg Trials the Commissar Order was used as evidence for the barbaric nature of the German war campaign.

Comrade: This was a hard one for us. In the German military the term "Kamerad" is commonly used to address fellow soldiers, at the same time communists and social democrats call themselves "Genosse" in German. In English there only is this one word "comrade", and it often has a communistic touch. I guess an US-soldier would not call his fellow soldiers "comrade"? Since the word "Kamerad" is very, very common in the German military we decided to translate it with "comrade", but do not intend a communistic meaning in a German military context.

Comrade Lace-up: A nickname German soldiers invented for Austrian soldiers during World War 1 ("Kamerad Schnürrschuh")

Danke: Thank you in German

Eastern Front Medal: Awarded to all axis soldiers who served in the winter campaign of 1941/1942.

Edi: Eduard Born's nickname

Einheits-PKW: A family of 3 types of military vehicles (light, medium and heavy) that featured all-wheel drive and were supposed to replace civilian cars the Reichswehr had procured before. The name translates to Standard Passenger Car.

Eiserner Gustav: German nickname for Iljushin Il-2 "Shturmovik" (= iron Gustav). Gustav is a German male first name.

EK 1: See Iron Cross

Elfriede: Nickname, Engelmann gave his Panzer IV. Elfriede was a common German female given name during that time.

Endsieg: Refers to the final victory over all enemies.

Éxgüsee: Swiss German for "sorry". By the way German dialects can be very peculiar. Bavarian, Austrian, Low German or other variations of German are hard to understand even for Germans, who are not from that particular region. Especially Swiss German is one not easy to understand variation of German, so often when a Swiss is interviewed on German TV subtitles are added. For interregional communication matters most Germans stick to High German, which is understood in all German-speaking areas.

E-series tanks: Series of German tank designs, which should replace the tanks in use. Among those concepts was yet another super heavy tank (E-100) that was developed parallelly to the Maus tank.

Fat Pig: Refers to Hermann Göring, one of Nazi Germany's most influential party members. As the commander of the Luftwaffe he was responsible for a series of failures. He also was infamous for being drug-addicted and generally out of touch with reality. Moreover he coveted military decorations and therefore made sure that he was awarded with every medal available despite the fact that he did not do anything to earn it. Göring was the highest-ranking Nazi leader living long enough to testify in the Nuremberg Trials. He committed suicide to avoid being executed by the Allies.

Faustpatrone ordnance device: See Knocker

Ferdinand: Massive German tank destroyer that later was improved and renamed to "Elefant" (= Elephant, while Ferdinand is a German given name – to be precise, it is Ferdinand Porsches given name, founder of Porsche and one of the design engineers of this steely monster). Today the Porsche AG is known for building sports cars.
Like many other very progressive German weaponry developed during the war, the Ferdinand suffered

312

from Hitler personally intervening to alter design and production details. Hitler always thought to be cleverer than his engineers and experts. E.g. he forced the Aircraft constructor Messerschmitt to equip its jet-powered fighter aircraft Me 262 as a dive bomber, while it was constructed to be a fighter and while the Luftwaffe already had lost air superiority at all theaters of war (so you need fighters to regain air superiority before you can even think about bombers). Same story with the Ferdinand: Hitler desperately wanted the Ferdinand to take part in the battle of Kursk, so he demanded its mass production on the basis of prototypes that hadn't been tested at all. German soldiers had to catch up on those tests during live action! Despite its enormous fire power, the Ferdinand proofed to be full of mechanical flaws, which led to lots of total losses. Due to a lack of any secondary weapon and its nearly non-movable main gun the Ferdinand was a death trap for its crew in close combat. Another problem was the Ferdinand's weight of around 65 tons. A lot of bridges and streets were to weak or narrow to survive one of these monsters passing by, let alone a whole battalion if them.

Nevertheless the heavy tank destroyer proofed to be a proper defense weapon that could kill a T-34 frontally at a distance of more than two miles.

Its full name is Panzerjäger Tiger (P) "Ferdinand" (or "Elefant") Sd.Kfz. 184. Sd.Kfz stands for "Sonderkraftfahrzeug" meaning "special purpose vehicle".

Flak: German for AA-gun

Frau: Mrs.

Front: May refer to a Soviet military formation equal to an army group

Führer: Do I really have to lose any word about the most infamous German Austrian? (By the way, it is "Führer", not "Fuhrer". If you cannot find the "ü" on your keyboard, you can use "ue" as replacement).

Gestapo: Acronym for "Geheime Staatspolizei" (= Secret State Police), a police force that mainly pursued political enemies of the state.

Gröfaz: Mocking nickname for Adolf Hitler. It is an acronym for "greatest commander of all times" (= größter Feldherr aller Zeiten) and was involuntarily coined by Field Marshal Keitel. During the battle of France Keitel, who was known for being servile towards Hitler, hailed him by saying: "My Führer, you are the greatest commander of all times!" It quickly became a winged word among German soldiers – and finally the acronym was born.

Grüessech: Swiss salute

Grüss Gott: Salute that one often hears in southern Germany and Austria. It literally means "Greetings to the Lord".

314

Heeresgruppe: Army group. The Wehrmacht wasn't very consistent in naming their army groups. Sometime letters were used, sometimes names of locations or cardinal directions. To continue the madness high command frequently renamed their army groups. In this book "Heeresgruppe Mitte" refers to the center of the Eastern Front (= Army Group Center), "Heeresgruppe Süd" refers to the southern section (= Army Group South).

Heimat: A less patriotic, more dreamy word than Vaterland (= fatherland) to address one's home country.

Heinkel He 177 Greif: German long-range heavy bomber. "Greif" means griffin. The Germans soon coined the nickname "Fliegendes Reichsfeuerzeug" (= flying Reich lighter) due to the fact that the He 177's engines tended to catch fire while the bomber was in the air.

Henschel Hs 127: German ground-attack aircraft designed and produced mainly by Henschel. Due to its capabilities to destroy tanks German soldiers coined the nickname "can opener".

Herein: German word for "come in". Hey, by the end of this book you will be a real German expert!

Herr: Mister (German soldiers address sex AND rank, meaning they would say "Mister sergeant" instead of "sergeant")

Herr General: In the German military, it does not matter which of the general ranks a general inhabits, he is always addressed by "Herr General". It is the same in the US military I guess.

Hiwi: Abbreviation of the German word "Hilfswilliger", which literally means "someone who is willing to help". The term describes (mostly) Russian volunteers who served as auxiliary forces for the Third Reich. As many military terms from the two world wars also "Hiwi" has deeply embedded itself into the German language. A lot of Germans use this word today to describe unskilled workers without even knowing anything about its origin.

HQ platoon leader: In German "Kompanietruppführer" refers to a special NCO, who exists in every company. The HQ platoon leader is best described as being the company commander's right hand.

IIs, IIIs, IVs: In German you sometimes would say "Zweier" (= a twoer), when talking about a Panzer II for example. We tried our best to transfer this mannerism into English.

Iljushin Il-2 "Shturmovik": Very effective Russian dive bomber, high in numbers on the Eastern Front and a very dangerous tank hunter. There are reports of groups of Shturmoviks having destroyed numerous panzers within minutes. Stalin loved this very aircraft

316

and personally supervised its production. The German nickname is "Eiserner Gustav" (= iron Gustav). Gustav is a German male given name.

Iron Cross: German war decoration restored by Hitler in 1939. It had been issued by Prussia during earlier military conflicts but in WW2 it was available to all German soldiers. There were three different tiers: Iron Cross (= Eisernes Kreuz) – 2nd class and 1st class –, Knight's Cross of the Iron Cross (= Ritterkreuz des Eisernen Kreuzes) – Knight's Cross without any features, Knight's Cross with Oak Leaves, Knight's Cross with Oak Leaves and Swords, Knight's Cross with Oak Leaves, Swords and Diamond and Knight's Cross with Golden Oak Leaves, Swords and Diamond –, and Grand Cross of the Iron Cross (= Großkreuz des Eisernen Kreuzes) – one without additional features and one called Star of the Grand Cross. By the way the German abbreviation for the Iron Cross 2nd class is EK2, alright?

Island monkeys: German slur for the British (= Inselaffen)

Itaka: German slur word for Italian soldier. It is an abbreviation for "Italienischer Kamerad" meaning Italian comrade.

Ivan: As English people give us Germans nicknames like "Fritz", "Kraut" or "Jerry", we also come up with nicknames for most nationalities. Ivan (actually it is

317

"Iwan" in German) was a commonly used nickname for Russians during both World Wars.

Jawohl: A submissive substitute for "yes" (= "ja"), which is widely used in the German military, but also in daily life

K98k: Also Mauser 98k or Gewehr 98k (Gewehr = rifle). The K98k was the German standard infantry weapon during World War 2. The second k stands for "kurz", meaning it is a shorter version of the original rifle that already had been used in World War 1. Since it is a short version, it is correctly called carbine instead of rifle – the first k stands for "Karabiner", which is the German word for carbine.

Kama: Refers to the Kama tank school, a secret training facility for German tank crews in the Soviet Union. After World War 1 the German Armed Forces (then called "Reichswehr") were restricted to 100 000 men because of the treaty of Versailles. Also no tanks and other heavy weaponry was permitted. The Germans sought for other ways to build up an own tank force, so they came to an agreement with the Soviet Union over secretly training German tankers at Kama. The German-Soviet cooperation ended with the rise of the Nazis to power in Germany.

Kampfgruppe: Combat formation that often was set up temporarily. Kampfgruppen had no defined size, some were of the size of a company, others were as big as a corps.

Kaputt: German word for "broken"; at one Point in the story Pappendorf uses this word describing a dead soldier. This means that he reduces the dead man to an object, since "kaputt" is only used for objects.

Katyusha: Soviet multiple rocket launcher. The Katyushas were feared by all German soldiers for its highly destructive salvos. Because of the piercing firing sound, the Germans coined the nickname "Stalin's organ" (= Stalinorgel).

Kinon glas: Special bulletproof glass produced by German manufacturer Glas- und Spiegelmanufaktur N. Kinon that was used for German panzer's eye slits. The well-known Tiger scene in the movie Saving Private Ryan would not have happened this way in reality, because one could not just stick one's firearm into the eye slit of a German panzer in order to kill its crew.

Knight's Cross: See Iron Cross

Knocker: German nickname for the Faustpatrone ordance device, the ancestor of the well-known Panzerfaust. German soldiers coined the nickname due to the bad penetrating power of this weapon. Often it just knocked at an enemy tank instead of penetrating its armor because its warhead simply bounced off instead of exploding.

Kolkhoz: Also collective farm; alleged cooperatively organized farming firm. Kolkhozes were one important component of the Soviet farming sector. In the eyes of the Soviet ideology they were a counter-concept to private family farms as well as to feudal serfdom. In reality kolkhozes were pools of slavery and inequality.

KV-2: Specs: Armor plating of up to 110-millimeters thickness, a 152-millimeters howitzer as main gun; ate Tiger tanks for breakfast … if its crew managed to move that heavy son of a bitch into a firing position in the first place.

Lager: Short for "Konzentrationslager" = concentration camp

Landser: German slang for a grunt

Leopard: German light tank project that was abandoned in 1943. The full name is VK1602 Leopard.

Luftwaffe: German Air Force

Marder II: German tank destroyer based on a Panzer II chassis

Maus tank: Very heavy German tank that never left development phase. It weighed 188 tons and was armed with a 128-millimeter Pak canon. Maximum speed was around 20 Kilometers per hour on a street and far less in terrain. By the end of the war two prototypes were build. The correct name is

Panzerkampfwagen VIII Maus (= "tank combat vehicle VIII Mouse").

MG 34: German machine gun that was used by the infantry as well as by tankers as a secondary armament. And have you ever noticed that some stormtroopers in the original Star Wars movie from 1977 carry nearly unmodified MG 34s around?

MG 42: German machine gun that features an incredible rate of fire of up to 1 500 rounds per minute (that's 25 per second!). It is also called "Hitler's buzzsaw", because a fire burst literally could cut someone in two halves. Its successor, the MG 3, is still in use in nowadays German Armed Forces (Bundeswehr).

Millimeter/centimeter/meter/kilometer: Since Germans make use of the metric system you will find some of those measuring units within direct speeches. Within the text we mostly transferred distance information into yards, miles or feet.

Moin: Means: good morning. "Moin" or "Moin, Moin" are part of several dialects found in Northern Germany. Pay this region a visit and you will hear these greetings very often and actually at EVERY time of the day.

MP 40: German submachine gun, in service from 1938 to 1945

NCO corps: This was a hard one to translate, since we did not find any similar concept in any English armed force. The NCO corps (= Unteroffizierskorps) refers to the entity of German noncommissioned officers. It is nor organized not powerful by any means, but more of an abstract concept of thought.

Officer corps: Same thing as in NCO corps. The officer corps (= Offizierkorps) refers to the entity of German officers. It is nor organized not powerful by any means, but more of an abstract concept of thought.

Pak: German word for anti-tank gun (= abbreviation for "Panzerabwehrkanone")

Panje Wagon: Small-framed two-axle buck car, which was pulled one-piece by a horse. Typical vehicle for eastern European and Soviet agronomies.

Panther: Many experts consider the Panther to be the best German WW2 tank. Why, you may ask, when the Wehrmacht also had steel beasts like the Tiger II or the Ferdinand at hand? Well, firepower is not everything. One also should consider mobility, production costs and how difficult it is to operate the tank as well as maintain and repair it on the battlefield. While the hugest German tanks like the Tiger II suffered from technical shortcomings, the Panther was a well-balanced mix of many important variables. Also it featured a sloped armor shape that could withstand direct hits very well. Since the Panther tank development was rushed and Hitler personally demanded some nonsensical changes the tank finally also suffered from some minor shortcomings, nevertheless it proofed to be an effective combat vehicle after all.

Panzer 38(t): Or Panzerkampfwagen 38(t) was a small Czechoslovak tank adopted by the Wehrmacht after it occupied Czechoslovakia. The 38(t) was no match for Russian medium tanks like the T-34 and was only adopted, because the German Armed Forces desperately needed anything with an engine in order to increase the degree of motorization of their troops. Whenever you find a letter in brackets within the name of a German tank, it is a hint at its foreign origin. For example, French tanks were given an (f), Czechoslovak tanks an (t). Since the 38(t) was riveted instead of welded, each hit endangered the crew, even if the round did not penetrate the armor. Often the rivets sprung out because of the energy set free by the hit. They then became lethal projectiles to the tankers.

Panzer II: Although being a small and by the end of the 1930s outdated tank, the Panzer II was the backbone of the German Army during the first years of the war due to a lack of heavier tanks in sufficient numbers. With its two-Centimeter canon it only could knock at Russian tanks like the T-34, but never penetrate their armor. The full name is Panzerkampfwagen II (= tank combat vehicle II).

Panzer III: Medium German tank. Actually the correct name is Panzerkampfwagen III (= tank combat vehicle

III). Production was stopped in 1943 due to the fact that the Panzer III then was totally outdated. Even in 1941, when the invasion of Russia started, this panzer wasn't a real match for most medium Soviet tanks anymore.

Panzer IV: Very common German medium tank. Actually the correct name is Panzerkampfwagen IV (= tank combat vehicle IV). I know, I know … in video games and movies it is all about the Tiger tank, but in reality an Allied or Russian soldier rather saw a Panzer IV than a Tiger. Just compare the numbers: Germany produced around 8 500 Panzer IVs of all variants, but only 1350 Tiger tanks.

Panzergrenadier: Motorized/mechanized infantry (don't mess with these guys!)

Panzerjäger I: First German tank destroyer. It featured an 4.7-centimeters gun. The name literally translates with "Tank Hunter 1".

Papa: Daddy

Penalty area: Soccer term for that rectangular area directly in front of each soccer goal. When a rival striker enters your team's penalty area, he or she impends to score a goal against you. By the way, soccer is an enhanced, more civilized version of that weird game called "American Football" – just in case you wondered ;)

Piefke: Austrian nickname for Germans, often meant in a denigrating manner

Plan Wahlen: A plan that was developed by Swiss Federal Council Wahlen in order to ensure food supplies for the Swiss population in case of an embargo or even an attack of the Axis powers. Since Hitler had started to occupy all neighboring nations he considered to be German anyway, a German attack on Switzerland felt very real for the Swiss. Because of the war they suffered supply shortages and mobilized their army. They even suffered casualties from dogfights with misled German and Allied bombers, because Swiss fighter planes attacked each and every military aircraft that entered their airspace (later they often "overlooked" airspace violations by allied planes though). Switzerland also captured and imprisoned a good number of German and Allied pilots, who crash-landed on their soil.

Since the war raging in most parts of Europe influenced the Swiss, too, they finally came up with the Plan Wahlen in 1940 in order to increase Swiss sustenance. Therefore every piece of land was used as farmland, e.g. crops were cultivated on football fields and in public parks.

I think, the situation of Switzerland during the war is a very interesting and yet quiet unknown aspect of the war. I therefore used the Taylor episode to explore it.

Order of Michael the Brave: Highest Rumanian military decoration that was rewarded to some

German soldiers, since Rumania was one of Germany's allies until August 1944.

Ratte tank: 1 000 tons tank concept, called land cruiser or landship. Ratte should feature more than ten guns of different calibers and a crew of over 40 men. The project never saw prototype status. Ratte means rat.

Reichsbahn: German national railway (Deutsche Reichsbahn)

Reichsheini: Mocking nickname for Heinrich Himmler (refers to his function as "Reichsführer SS" (= Reich Leader SS) in combination with an alteration of his first name. At the same time "Heini" is a German offensive term used for stupid people.

Reichskanzler: Chancellor of the German Reich

SA: Short form for "Sturmabteilung" (literally: storm detachment); it had been the Nazi Party's original paramilitary organization until it was disempowered by the SS in 1934.

Scheisse: German for "Crap". Actually it is spelled "Scheiße" with an "ß", but since this letter is unknown in the English language and since it is pronounced very much like "ss", we altered it this way so that you do not mistake it for a "b".
Same thing holds true for the characters Claasen and Weiss. In the original German text both are written with an "ß".

Scho-Ka-Kola: Bitter-sweet chocolate with a lot of caffeine in it

Sd.Kfz. 234: Family of German armored cars

Sepp: Short form of Josef, nickname for Engelmann

Sherman Tank (M4): Medium US-tank that was produced in very large numbers (nearly 50 000 were built between 1942 and 1945) and was used by most allied forces. Through the Lend-Lease program the tank also saw action on the Eastern Front. Its big advantage over all German panzers was its main gun stabilizer, which allowed for precise shooting while driving. German tankers were not allowed to shoot while driving due to Wehrmacht regulations. Because of the missing stabilizers it would have been a waste of ammunition anyway. The name of this US-tank refers to American Civil War general William Tecumseh Sherman.
Let's compare the dimensions: The Third Reich's overall tank production added up to around 50 000 between the pre-war phase and 1945 (all models and their variants like the 38 (t) Hetzer together, so: Panzer Is, IIs, IIIs, IVs, Panthers, Tigers, 38(t)s, Tiger IIs and Ferdinands/Elefants combined)!

Sir: Obviously Germans do not say "Sir", but that was the closest thing we could do to substitute a polite form that exists in the German language. There is no match for that in the English language: In German parts of a sentence changes when using the polite form. If one asks for a light in German, one would say "Hast du Feuer?" to a friend, but "Haben Sie Feuer?" to a stranger or any person one have not agreed with to leave away the polite form yet. During the Second World War the German polite form was commonly spread, in very conservative families children had to use the polite form to address their parents and even some couples used it among themselves. Today the polite form slowly is vanishing. Some companies like Ikea even addresses customers informally in the first place – something that was an absolute no-go 50 years ago.

In this one scene where the Colonel argues with First Lieutenant Haus he gets upset, because Haus does not say "Sir" (once more: difficult to translate). In the Wehrmacht a superior was addressed with "Herr" plus his rank, in the Waffen SS the "Herr" was left out; a soldier was addressed only by his rank like it is common in armed forces of English-speaking countries. Also one would leave the "Herr" out when one wants to disparage the one addressed, like Papendorf often does when calling Berning "Unteroffizier" instead of "Herr Unteroffizier".

SS: Abbreviation of "Schutzstaffel" (= Protection Squadron). The SS was a paramilitary Nazi-organization, led by Heinrich Himmler. Since the SS operated the death camps, had the Gestapo under their roof as well as had their own military force (Waffen SS) that competed with the Wehrmacht it is not easy to outline their primary task during the era of the Third

328

Reich. Maybe the SS is best described as some sort of general Nazi instrument of terror against all inner and outer enemies.

Stavka: High command of the Red Army

Struwwelpeter: Infamous German bedtime kid's book that features ten very violent stories of people, who suffer under the disastrous consequences of their misbehavior. Need an Example? One story features a boy, who sucks his thumbs until a tailor appears cutting the boy's thumbs off with a huge scissor. The book definitely promises fun for the whole family! (Nowadays it is not read out to kids anymore, but even I, who grew up in the 90s, had to listen to that crap). In the U.S.A. the book is also known under the title "Slovenly Peter".

Stahlhelm: German helmet with its distinctive coal scuttle shape, as Wikipedia puts it. The literal translation would be steel helmet.

Stuka: An acronym for a dive bomber in general (= "Sturzkampfbomber"), but often refers to that one German dive bomber you may know: the Junkers Ju 87.

Sturm: Among other things Sturm is an Austrian vocabulary for a Federweisser, which is a wine-like beverage made from grape must.

Sturmgeschütz: German term for assault gun

Tank killer: Tanks specifically designed to combat enemy tanks. Often tank destroyers rely on massive firepower and capable armor (the latter is achieved by a non-rotatable turret that allows for thicker frontal armor). Also called tank hunter or tank destroyer. The German term is "Jagdpanzer", which literally means hunting tank.

T-34: Medium Russian tank that really frightened German tankers when it first showed up in 1941. First the T-34 was superior to all existing German tanks (with the exception of Panzer IV variant F that was equipped with a longer canon and thicker armor). The T-34 was also available in huge numbers really quick. During the war the Soviet Union produced more than 35 000 T-34 plus more than 29 000 of the enhanced T-34/85 model! Remember the Sherman tank? So the production of only these two tanks outnumbered the overall German combat tank production by a factor of more than two!

T-34/85: Enhanced T-34 with a better main gun (85-millimeters cannon) and better armor. It also featured a fifth crew member, thus the tank commander could concentrate on commanding his vehicle rather than have to aim and shoot at the same time.

T-70: Light Soviet tank that weighted less than 10 tons. Although it was a small tank that featured a 45-millimeters main gun, one should not underestimate the T-70. There are reports of them destroying Panthers and other medium or heavy German panzers.

Tiger tank: Heavy German combat tank, also known as Tiger I that featured a variant of the accurate and high-powered 88-millimeters anti-aircraft canon "Acht-Acht". The correct name is Panzerkampfwagen VI Tiger (= tank combat vehicle VI Tiger).

Tin can: During World War 2 some German soldiers called tanks tin can (= Büchse), so we thought it would be nice to keep that expression in the translation as well.

SU-122: Soviet assault gun that carried a 122-millimeters main gun, which was capable of destroying even heavy German tanks from a fair distance.

Vaterland: Fatherland

VK4502(P): Heavy tank project by Porsche that never got beyond drawing board status despite some turrets, which were produced by Krupp and later mounted on Tiger II tanks.

Volksempfänger: Range of radio receivers developed on the request of Propaganda Minister Goebbels to make us of the new medium in order to spread his propaganda. It literally translates with "people's receiver" and was an affordable device for most Germans.

Waffen SS: Waffen = arms; it was the armed wing of the Nazi Party's SS organization, which was a paramilitary organization itself.

Waidmannsheil: German hunters use this call to wish good luck ("Waidmann" is an antique German word for hunter, "Heil" means well-being). As many hunting terms, Waidmannsheil made its way into German military language.

Wound Badge: German decoration for wounded soldiers or those, who suffered frostbites. The wound badge was awarded in three stages: black for being wounded once or twice, silver for the third and fourth wound, gold thereafter. US equivalent: Purple Heart.

Zampolit: Political commissar; an officer responsible for political indoctrination in the Red Army

Wehrmacht ranks (Army)

All military branches have their own ranks, even the medical service.

Rank	US equivalent
Anwärter	Candidate (NCO or officer)
Soldat (or Schütze, Kanonier, Pionier, Funker, Reiter, Jäger, Grenadier … depends on the branch of service)	Private
Obersoldat (Oberschütze, Oberkanonier …)	Private First Class
Gefreiter	Lance Corporal
Obergefreiter	Senior Lance Corporal
Stabsgefreiter	Corporal
Unteroffizier	Sergeant
Fahnenjunker	Ensign
Unterfeldwebel/ Unterwachtmeister (Wachtmeister only in cavalry and artillery)	Staff Sergeant
Feldwebel/ Wachtmeister	Master Sergeant
Oberfeldwebel/ Oberwachtmeister	Master Sergeant
Oberfähnrich	Ensign First Class
Stabsfeldwebel/ Stabswachtmeister	Sergeant Major
Hauptfeldwebel	This is not a rank, but an NCO function responsible for personnel and order within a company
Leutnant	2nd Lieutenant

Oberleutnant	1st Lieutenant
Hauptmann/Rittmeister (Rittmeister only in cavalry and artillery)	Captain
Major	Major
Oberstleutnant	Lieutenant Colonel
Oberst	Colonel
Generalmajor	Major General
Generalleutnant	Lieutenant General
General der ... (depends on the branch of service: - Infanterie (Infantry) - Kavallerie (Cavalry) - Artillerie (Artillery) - Panzertruppe (Tank troops) - Pioniere (Engineers) - Gebirgstruppe (Mountain Troops) - Nachrichtentruppe (Signal Troops)	General (four-star)
Generaloberst	Colonel General
Generalfeldmarschall	Field Marshal

Check out these German military fiction books

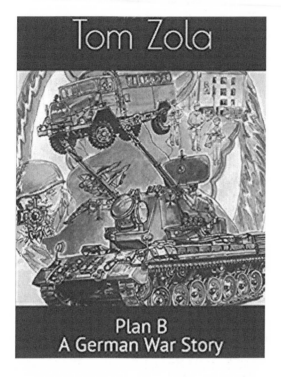

Meet Hartmut Schober, who was drafted into the Bundeswehr, the German armed forces, during the final peak of the Cold War. Learn what military training was like in those days. Find out about nasty drill instructors, brawls with Brits and Americans, huge NATO exercises and Darth Vader's storm troopers invading a suburb of Cologne.

IRON TUBE

UNRESTRICTED
U-BOAT
WARFARE

A GERMAN WAR STORY
by Peter Brendt

Early in 1917, the Imperial German U-boat U-15 is patrolling for the English merchant shipping off of Ireland. Lieutenant Commander Müller, by his man called "the old man" has received new orders: Germany has declared the unrestricted U-boat warfare in the waters around England! For the second time! Müller is a veteran of the submarine war and knows about the dangers. Armed with just a few torpedoes, single U-boats have to go against an enemy who is superior in firepower, speed and pure numbers. Soon, the outlooks spot a convoy escorted by several destroyers and the hunt is on ...Iron Tube - Unrestricted U-Boat Warfare is a breathtaking military fiction story, offering insights into the hardly known submarine war of World War I as well as German cultural and naval singularities. Peter Brendt once was a German navy sailor himself, so he knows what he is talking about.

336

Published by EK-2 Publishing GmbH
Friedensstraße 12
47228 Duisburg
Germany
Registry court: Duisburg, Germany
Registry court ID: HRB 30321
Chief Executive Officer: Monika Münstermann

E-Mail: info@ek2-publishing.com
Website: www.ek2-publishing.com

Cover art: Pete Ashford
Author: Tom Zola
Translated from German by Jill Marc Münstermann
English translation edited by Richard Moncure
Final editing: Jill Marc Münstermann
Proofreading: Wendy Chan
Cover Design: Jan Niklas Meier
German Editor: Lanz Martell
Innerbook: Jill Marc Münstermann

Paperback ISBN: 978-3-96403-031-3
Kindle ISBN: 978-3-96403-030-6
1st Edition, December 2019

Made in the USA
Monee, IL
29 April 2020